Escape

A Derrick King Novel: Book 2

The story of Miriam King

By Daniel L Copeland

"Wow! One of those, edge-of-your-seat, can't-put-it-down, feels-like-you're-there books. The characters are complex, fully developed, and real—as if you know them. Copeland is a master storyteller—one of the best that I have read."

Rod Leonard

Escape
A Derrick King Novel, Book 2
The Story of Miriam King
Published August 2020
First Edition

ISBN: 978-1-970773-03-3

IngramSpark Edition
Published by Chipping Away Publishing

In the Beginning

This is the story of Miriam King.

Miriam felt responsible for Derrick's exile to the commoner world.

She promised to help him.

Circumstances developed faster than she anticipated, forcing her to act before she was ready.

But she had a plan.

When curfew lifted on March 31, Miriam walked out the front door, putting her plan into action.

Things didn't go as she planned.

Now, she's under house arrest.

But she promised Derrick she'd come.

Escape

A Derrick King Novel: Book 2

Preface

ON MARCH 31st, MIRIAM NEARLY drowned in the sea. She had no boat. She wore no life vest. What she did have was well-advanced hypothermia when a security patrol spotted her clinging to a buoy that marked the boundary between Pacific Edge and the commoner world.

Lucky to be alive.

The security patrol ignored protocol, and one man reached down from the hovercraft and plucked her from the sea. They didn't think she would last until the shore patrol launched a boat. That part they got right.

They flew her straight to the medical center, where medical staff stripped off her wet clothes, covered her with warmed blankets, and packed warm bags of water around her.

Then, the Tribunal Chief Justice ordered her released.

She left the medical center barefoot and wrapped in a thin sheet. She was certain they would have booted her out naked if being naked were not illegal in Pacific Edge. Father carried her to the transport. A breeze whipped through the streets. On the way home, the transport blew frigid air. The stupid robot failed to respond when Father asked for heat.

The Tribunal meant her release to be a death sentence.

But they didn't understand.

She didn't have time to die.

Dying would have to wait.

It was almost noon. She wore flannel pajamas and was covered with two heavy blankets, yet she shivered uncontrollably. She had had little opportunity for contemplation since Derrick had been exiled. Now, trembling on her bed, knees to her chest, doors locked from the outside, and staring at a blank communications monitor, she pondered why they had not relocated the entire King family.

The Tribunal could have removed them from Pacific Edge because of her behavior. Too many questions, too much disruption, yet they were still here. That made little sense.

Why?

She had never thought Derrick prevented such a move. She never believed he was unique in any way. Chosen wannabes like Derrick filled the classrooms of James Carver Academy.

Plus, the Tribunal had exiled Derrick.

But now, the Tribunal wanted him back.

It is Derrick.

He is unique.

Derrick believed his problems all started on his birthday, March 12. He was wrong.

PART ONE

1

Three Months Earlier, December 17

MIRIAM HAD PARTIALLY HACKED—she liked the word hacked—the Pacific Edge computer system three months before Derrick decided to play knight in shining armor. Dumb brother's heroics resulted in an injured Marcus Carver and an exiled Derrick King. Before December 17, Miriam had never heard the term computer system. But after she got access to the computer system, she discovered information denied people in Pacific Edge. From behind the electronic curtain, she explored the material fed through New America Media. A loop, go to the end, change the name, start over.

But she already knew that.

They recycled the same crap—crap, another word she liked.

In the fifth grade, Miriam began noticing odd things about New America News. After several weeks, sometimes months, they repeated stuff, reporting it as something different each time. Miriam remembered each story's scene and location. She assumed the ability to remember things was normal, supposed everyone could but was too lazy.

She noticed some locations sounded real, and others sounded fake. Places like Canada, Mexico, and Germany sounded legit, whereas places like Gotham, Mordor, and Tatooine sounded invented.

Miriam totaled 4,712 scenes and 18,927 unique combinations before she stopped counting.

Many scenes showed savages driving odd-looking transports through a desert wasteland. Several transports were open, with people hanging all over them. Some transports had two wheels, most had four, some had more. Some were large, some were small. Some people were strapped into high-mounted seats that whipped about as the transport raced across the desert. People wore an odd variety of garments. Some wore rags, some wore metal hats, some wore protective shields, some wore shirts without sleeves, some were almost naked. New America Media blurred the nearly naked savages because Pacific Edge didn't allow nudity or near nudity in public or on the communication monitors. One woman had no hair, and the top of her head was black, as was her forehead. These people were always in the same desert, whether New America Media said the incident was in California, Arizona, Tennessee, Idaho, New York, Florida, Mordor, or some other place.

Other scenes were in jungles. Most people in jungle scenes looked like soldiers, but the media said they were commoners fighting among themselves. Another time, the same people in the same scene might be drug lords fighting in the jungles of Chicago. Some flying machines and heavily armored transports were said to be law enforcement, still a lawless bunch, according to the media. Law enforcement machines displayed the old United States of America flag on their drab green machines.

Miriam thought the jungle scenes looked real, but the desert scenes, though elaborate, looked staged. She couldn't explain why she thought that.

How she came to this knowledge was a fluke, or so she thought.

2

TO ACCESS INFORMATION USING THE MONITOR on the wall, people spoke to a digital assistant, stating what they wanted. Then, what they wanted came on the screen if it were allowed. When Miriam asked the digital assistant for information, it often replied, "Access denied."

On December 16, Miriam's digital assistant wouldn't respond. Her parents called for a technician. Technicians came during the day, so the next day, Miriam became ill. She locked herself in the bathroom and made loud barfing noises until her parents were sufficiently convinced. She wanted to watch the technician fix the malfunctioning monitor. It was only a screen on the wall, and she didn't understand how it could be repaired. Perhaps they will replace it. Either way, she wanted to see how it was done.

When the technician arrived, Miriam sat on the couch under a blanket. Father had programmed the automated home security system to allow the technician entry. The technician froze in the doorway when he saw her on the sofa.

"Oh, I am sorry. I'm here to be fixing a communication device. The home was to be empty. I am being so deeply sorry," he said, bowing and backing out of the house.

"Wait!" Miriam tossed the blanket off, bolting to her feet, one arm outstretched, palm out. "It's okay. I was sick this morning and didn't go to school. But I'm fine now. It's my communicator. I really need it for my studies. Please don't leave. It's okay. Really." Miriam forced a calm face despite the shock she experienced at the sight of the technician. He was very dark, but he didn't look like the black athletes she saw on the communication monitors when Father watched sports.

"I'm not supposed to enter if family members are home."

"It's okay. My parents know I'm home and that you were coming." Miriam motioned with her hand. "Come in. I'll show you my screen."

The technician hesitated, looked over his shoulder, and then took a step forward.

Miriam realized he was more afraid of her than she was of him. She marched to the door and stuck out her hand. "Hi, I'm Miriam King."

Slowly, gently taking her hand for a moment and a single downward shake, the technician said, "Nice to meet you, Ms. King."

"Just Miriam. And you are?"

"AJ Patel."

Miriam closed the door before AJ Patel could change his mind and bolt. Trotting up the stairs, Miriam said, "Follow me, AJ Patel." She didn't look back to see if the technician had followed, remained anchored to the floor, or fled. Miriam turned when she entered her bedroom. He was there, standing in the hallway as if an invisible barrier prevented his entrance. Miriam suspected this might be a problem.

She pointed to the wall, although the monitor was large and ominous, and said, "There it is."

"Yes, thank you. I am seeing it."

Miriam thought for a moment. "Can you fix it from there?"

Oopsy. Occasionally, her smart-aleckiness came out when she didn't want it to. Yet, to her surprise, AJ Patel smiled.

"No. I cannot be fixing it from here. However, I am seeing why you might be having problems with it."

Was it possible? Had Miriam found a kindred smartass soul? "Well, then, come in and get started."

"Yes, well, it would be most improper for me to be in a young girl's bedroom with her present. If you will wait downstairs, I'll get started promptly." AJ Patel didn't move.

"I want to watch," Miriam said. "I'm interested in how things work. I want to be an engineer or something like that when I grow up." *That sounded lame,* she thought as soon as the words left her mouth.

"That would be quite out of the ordinary," AJ Patel said.

"Do I look ordinary to you?" Miriam asked. Now, that sounded authentic.

He smiled, nodded, and stepped into the room. "Depends on which side of the wall you live on," AJ said, and then added, "I am hoping I still have a job after this."

"You'll have no complaints from me unless you're like a murderer or something." Miriam paused. "Uh, you're not a murderer right, of course, if you were a murderer, you wouldn't tell me, would you? Okay, I'll be quiet now." Miriam sat on the edge of her bed.

"I am not a violent man, Miriam King."

AJ Patel set a black plastic case on Miriam's desk, from which he pulled several items, including a white flat rectangular device that had many buttons. Miriam couldn't see it well from her vantage point. He picked up a small, strange tool with a black handle with a silver metal shank. Moving to the side of the communication screen, he stuck the tool into small indentations that she had not noticed, or maybe she had seen them, but they meant nothing to her, so she formed no lasting memory of them. Miriam would later realize that this one insight changed everything.

AJ Patel removed two small pieces of metal he called screws and then gently dislodged a small flat panel that hid several holes of various shapes and sizes. He inserted a cord that led to the flat rectangular device he had removed from his black box of items.

"What is that?" Miriam pointed to the rectangular device.

"This," AJ Patel picked it up, "is a keyboard. And this," he held up a small, odd-shaped black device, "is called a mouse. Don't ask me why it's called a mouse because I do not know the answer to that question."

"What does it do?" Miriam asked, although she thought she understood.

"It allows me to get into the OS."

Before AJ Patel continued, Miriam whispered, "Operating system."

"That is correct. But I'm surprised you know the term operating system."

"You told me," Miriam said. Noting the puzzlement on AJ Patel's face, she continued, "You said it allows you in the OS. OS—operating system." Miriam held her hands, palms up, as if the answer was obvious.

AJ Patel stared at her a moment and then said, "Okay."

AJ Patel held down a button on the side of the screen for several seconds, and then he released the button, and then pushed it once firmly but for a short duration. Then he sat at her desk and held down two keys on the keyboard until a window appeared on her communication monitor. In the window, a small rectangular box labeled PIN appeared. AJ Patel entered six numbers: 7, 23, 15, 4, 9, 77. Then the screen changed, listing the following options: Restore, Reinstall, Online Help, and Utilities.

AJ Patel moved the mouse on the desk, which moved an arrow on the screen. When the arrow was positioned over the box that said Utilities, Patel tapped the front of the mouse with his index finger, and another window opened. On the second window, AJ Patel positioned the arrow over a box that said First Aid and again tapped the mouse with his index finger. A third window appeared that had two boxes, a white one that said cancel and a blue one that said run. He quickly tapped the return key on the keyboard, which opened yet another box, and AJ Patel immediately tapped the enter key again.

AJ Patel turned to speak to Miriam, startled when he discovered she was right behind him with her head over his left shoulder. "Whoa," he said. "I was not realizing you were there."

Miriam stood straight, giving AJ Patel a little space. "Sorry," she said. "What have you done?"

"I'm running the OS first aid program. It may fix whatever caused your computer to be having a problem."

"Computer?"

"Yes, the communication device is a computer monitor, albeit one of limited capabilities. The computer is like a brain that runs things. But you didn't learn that from me. You are only supposed to think of this as a communicator, if I understand correctly."

Miriam started to ask a question, decided against it, and instead asked, "Where can I get those?" She pointed to the keyboard and mouse.

"Why would you want them? They are unnecessary for the communicator's function."

On this, AJ Patel was correct. And to be truthful, Miriam didn't know why she wanted them. The communicator only accessed information New America allowed. She could send messages to Mother, Father, and Derrick, and it showed Chosen programming and news.

"I could fix this myself next time. Save you the trouble of coming here," Miriam said.

That slight smile crept onto AJ Patel's face. "They are paying me to do this job, Miriam King. Are you wanting me to be unemployed?"

Her reason sounded lame the minute she said it, but the quickness of AJ Patel's response surprised her. Often, she would give a plethora of lame excuses to her Father and Mother, her teachers, and Derrick. Especially Derrick. Her absurdity and sarcasm flew right past them, but not AJ Patel.

"I like to learn things," Miriam said.

AJ Patel nodded. "That I do believe. Not for your own good sometimes, I suspect."

"I'm pretty smart," Miriam said too quickly, without assessing the necessity or gauging the impact of such a statement.

"I believe that too. But you know not of the OS functions, and there's no way for you to learn such things."

Miriam chewed her bottom lip, contemplating the wisdom of saying what she was thinking. "True. They only let us see what they want us to see. I doubt any of what they call news contains any truth."

A chime sounded from the communication screen. A disembodied voice said, "First Aid scan complete. You may now restart."

AJ Patel turned his attention to the keyboard. Miriam took up her place, peering over his left shoulder. Patel moved the arrow over a small box that said, "repair details." The screen immediately filled with lines of words and numbers unfamiliar to Miriam. Patel moved quickly, saving the file as a thing called PDF, and then opening an application called Mail, also something Miriam had never seen. Patel clicked on 'new message', and in the 'To' line he typed ajpatel@ITservices.com. In the subject line, he wrote—Miriam King disk repair. He used the arrow to pull the PDF he had saved into the message, and then he selected send. The message folded up and zoomed off the screen.

Miriam said nothing.

AJ Patel pressed three keys. The screen went black. After a few moments, the usual screen appeared. This time, a sunset over the ocean. Written over the sunset, the words: Blessed are you to be Chosen.

"That should fix it. I will review the details at my office to see if any additional issues might require repair. If I find anything that might cause additional problems, I'll schedule another appointment."

"What about me getting a keyboard and mouse?" Miriam asked.

AJ Patel smiled. "You are a persistent one."

"You have no idea," Miriam said.

"As we discussed earlier, you have no way to learn the OS." Patel motioned to the keyboard and mouse. "These would be of no use to you."

"I told you. I'm pretty smart."

AJ Patel's smile didn't fade as he shook his head. "I have no doubt, but …"

Miriam cut him off. "You pushed cmd and r to open the screen, and then you opened the Disk Utility and selected First Aid." Miriam continued to explain each command that AJ Patel had performed. She recited the first two lines of information on the details screen, although she could have recited them all. Finally, Miriam said, to restart the machine you pushed ctrl, cmd, and eject. She didn't tell him she also memorized ajpatel@ITservices.com.

It was AJ Patel's turn to say nothing.

Miriam stared at him.

"It's impossible to get these. Only technicians like me can possess them."

"There must be a study program I can get them from. Money isn't a problem."

"Money is never a problem for the Chosen, is it?"

"True," Miriam said.

AJ Patel said, "I'm sorry. That was unnecessary. Forgive me."

"What you said is true. You should never be sorry for speaking the truth."

AJ Patel nodded his head, eyes cast downward. He looked up slowly and said, "I would get in big trouble if I were to get them for you."

Miriam thought for a moment. "What if I found them somewhere? You couldn't get in trouble for that."

"This might be a trap. They do that sometimes to catch people. Punishment is most severe to ensure we stay in line."

"That doesn't surprise me. I understand there's no reason for you to take such a risk. There's no reason for you to trust me. All I can say is that you *can* trust me."

AJ Patel packed his tools, keyboard, and mouse back into his plastic case. "I'll be going now."

He turned and left the room. Miriam followed him out of her bedroom, down the stairs, across the main floor, and out the front door.

AJ Patel walked toward the fountain and then turned and said, "If I were to tell you where you could find such items, would you do me one small favor?"

"Yes. If I can," Miriam said.

"Call me AJ. Should we ever meet again."

"You got it, AJ."

3

MIRIAM WAS IN HER BEDROOM, staring at the blank monitor on the wall, thinking about how AJ Patel had accessed the operation system when a knock sounded at the door. "It's open," Miriam said.

Father opened the door but didn't step inside. "How is your communicator working?"

"It's fine," she said. "Why?"

"I received a message from Pacific Edge Technical Services, and a technician will be here tomorrow to complete the repair."

Miriam was smart but dense sometimes. Sometimes, even stupid. Currently, she felt both dense and stupid. Finally, she said, "Well," she paused, "it's kind of working but slow. A few stations are missing as well."

"Okay," her Father said, giving her a skeptical look.

Miriam sat on her bed, thinking. She couldn't get away with being sick again to be here when tech services, AJ Patel, arrived. But she had to be here.

Miriam joined her Father, Mother, and Derrick for dinner. She often skipped dinner, but not this time.

"Nice of you to join us," Father said as she sat.

"Sorry, I haven't been keeping much down all day."

Father nodded.

"She is still sick?" Derrick asked. "She should stay in her room, so she does not infect the rest of us with her illness."

"I don't think she is contagious," Father said.

Holding her plate, she accepted a slice of ham. "So, what did the tech people say?"

"The technician said he had a full schedule but would come by in the morning. I told him it was not urgent, but he insisted."

"That's nice of him." Miriam stuffed ham into her mouth. *That sounded lame.*

Father said, "Did you talk to the technician?"

"Not much. I was on the couch when he came. He didn't want to enter the house because I was home. I pointed to my bedroom and promised I'd stay put." She studied Father. "He finally agreed, and that's the last I saw of him. I fell asleep while he was working on the monitor."

Father stared at her and then returned to his meal.

Miriam said no more.

4

MIRIAM HOPED SHE UNDERSTOOD AJ Patel's message if, in fact, AJ Patel had made the appointment. As was their custom, Father and Mother left for work before she went to school, which contributed to her tardy violations. Typically, she walked to James Carver Academy, occasionally too preoccupied with her thinking to recognize the time, and more often, she knew the time but couldn't bear the thought of being at the Academy. But this morning, she called for a transport, scheduling it so she could leave at the last moment. Not because she had a sudden interest in the Academy, but because when she was tardy, the school attendance officer investigated the reason for her absence, checking surveillance cameras, the exact time she left her house, etc. Today, she wanted no investigation. She wanted no one to know that she had talked to AJ Patel.

A Technical Services transport arrived five minutes after Father's departure. She opened the door before the repairman activated the entrance request sequence. AJ Patel stood at the door.

"Hello, Ms. Miriam. How are you this fine morning?"

"I'm well, thank you," Miriam said, motioning him inside. Miriam scanned the street and the sky and saw nothing. Bird droppings, or what looked like bird droppings, covered the entrance security camera.

"You are still having problems with your communication device?" AJ Patel asked.

"It works fine, Mr. Patel," Miriam said.

AJ Patel raised his eyebrows and tilted his head.

"I'm sorry, AJ." Miriam corrected.

"That is much better. If I am to risk my job, at least we should be on a first-name basis."

"Where do you live?" Miriam asked.

"I live in the service area. But then you are not knowing about that, are you?"

"Where is it?"

"It surrounds Pacific Edge." AJ pointed. "Beyond the wall."

"I've wondered what was out there. Is it nice?"

"It's okay," AJ said.

"Is it safe?"

"Yes, it is safe." AJ paused. "Just not my first choice of places to live."

"Then why do you stay?"

"Did I say there were options?"

"You didn't. I am sorry."

"You need not be sorry. It's not your fault. Besides, what choice do any of us have?"

Miriam looked into AJ's eyes and saw a mix of sadness, softness, and something else. Courage maybe? But that didn't seem right. Or perhaps that's precisely what she saw. He was here, wasn't he? "You have something for me?" Miriam asked.

"No, well, yes. Sort of. Not with me. That would be too dangerous."

"What then?" Miriam asked. She checked the time. "I need to get to school soon, or I'll be late."

"I do not want you to be in trouble at school, so I'll be quick," AJ said.

"I'm not worried about being in trouble. If I'm late, they'll investigate my movements and see I was here when you arrived."

"Such a smart young lady," AJ said. "Listen carefully. I have a keyboard and mouse that I've disabled. Sabotaged is a more accurate description."

"But what good are they if broken?"

AJ held up his hand. "Please, just listen."

Miriam nodded.

"You can repair them. I placed a substance under some keys, so they didn't make a connection. I had to do this because the supply technician will confirm it does not work before replacing it. I did the same thing with the battery connections in the mouse. They will place the old items in the trash outside our facility tonight."

"How do you know it will be tonight?"

AJ held up his hand again. "Because they collect trash around 4:00 a.m., I will place a red plastic bag wrapped in yellow caution tape in the same trash receptacle. The bag contains a can of cleaner and several new batteries. The yellow tape indicates the contents are toxic. It is unlikely anyone will disturb it. You must go to the trash after dark and retrieve the red bag." He paused. "You must also find the keyboard and mouse.

I'm sorry, but you'll have to dig through the trash to find them. But don't worry, the trash is mostly cardboard boxes and such.

"Okay. Questions. One, won't they see me on the security cameras? Two, how do I fix the keyboard and mouse? Three, where is the trash?" Miriam ticked off each question with raised fingers.

"I'm trying to get there if you would stop interrupting." AJ tapped the side of his head in mock frustration.

"Sorry."

"So, to fix the keyboard, carefully remove the keys e, d, a, and i." AJ demonstrated using a fingernail as if he were pulling off the keys. "Also, on the underside of the mouse, open the battery compartment door. Now, take the spray and spray everything. Hold the device so the liquid pours off into a trash receptacle or, better yet, do it outside. The spray emits a strong chemical odor. Be careful not to get any in your eyes or on your skin. Then put everything back together."

"Okay. I can do that. Security cameras?"

"I have disabled the camera that overlooks the trash receptacle."

"Last question. Where?"

"The entry door is on the south wall of Pacific Edge. The trash receptacle is adjacent to the roll-up door. Technical Services is written on the walk-in door, so you'll know you are in the right place."

"I've seen the south side of Pacific Edge. I've not seen doors or trash bins."

"They are hidden from view. There is a second wall, same height, same color as the building. The wall conceals a roadway, trash bins, exits, etc. There are overlapping cuts in the wall. Start near the beach and go to the third cut, which is where you'll find Technical Services."

Miriam nodded. "I'll go when Father and Mother are asleep."

"Be careful. You realize your house alarm is set at 11 p.m., and if you open a door, the alarm will sound, waking your parents and summoning security," AJ said.

"Don't worry. I sneak out after 11 p.m. sometimes. Like I said, I am smart."

AJ nodded and started for the door. He turned before leaving and said, "I assumed you could get out undetected. I don't know why I'm doing this. It is dangerous for me. And the truth is, even if you figure out how to get into the OS, you won't learn anything valuable. You'll only end back where you started."

"Why are you doing it then?" Miriam asked.

AJ shrugged. "Not sure. Hope is the best answer I can give you."

AJ walked to his transport. Miriam followed him, walking to a transport of her own. Miriam said, "Thank you, AJ. I'll never forget this. Although I *have* forgotten your name." She winked.

AJ Patel smiled.

PART TWO

1

Saturday, March 15, One Day After Derrick's Exile

MIRIAM DIDN'T SLEEP WELL the night Derrick left. She wasn't worried about going back to the Academy. She wasn't worried about Marcus Carver. Worrying about that stuff could wait. She worried about Derrick. The commoner world didn't resemble what New America Media portrayed, but she didn't know the reality of it either. However, she knew Derrick would be terrified because he believed everything New America Media fed him.

On Monday, her first day back at the Academy following Derrick's exile, she planned to keep a low profile. She wasn't confident of success because she had also intended to stay out of trouble on Derrick's birthday as a gift of sorts. Unfortunately, her present didn't last long. It fell apart in New America History. Challenging teachers kept school interesting for her, and she did it regularly. Yet she tormented some teachers more than others. Mr. Jones, the New America History teacher, posed little challenge, and tormenting him would have grown boring except for two things: the subject was so phony, and Mr. Jones was a sanctimonious self-righteous dweeb.

New America History was the only class she shared with Derrick and Marcus Carver. The day that started what led to Derrick's exile, Mr. Jones started a debate with her. Mr. Jones usually started the debates, although, on that day, she had set him up by pretending to be daydreaming. Still, he started it.

Miriam felt up to any challenge he might toss at her. However, in that instance, he asked a question that was so stupid that it surprised her. She couldn't have asked for a better question to argue about. Also interesting, now that she thought about it.

Miriam had not witnessed Marcus Carver confront Derrick after class that day, but she had heard about it. At the time, she was unconcerned. Marcus Carver was a blowhard. She planned to confront Marcus the next day in class, where there would be a teacher and plenty of witnesses. Outsmarting Marcus Carver posed no challenge. However, her plan didn't work out because the Derrick-punching-Marcus incident happened before she had the chance to handle Marcus herself. Although she probably had the highest IQ at the Academy, sometimes she wondered why she was so stupid. Some of her actions backfired. Like the ones that led to Derrick's exile.

Her fault. Simple as that. It was unnecessary. It was stupid. She was stupid. She couldn't let it go. She knew why she disliked the curriculum. She understood why she harassed Mr. Jones. But to what end? She was not going to accomplish much. She was not going to change the information taught. She was not going to change the instructors. She was not going to change Pacific Edge or New America Media. So why? The answer to that question proved elusive. Elusive questions were a magnet to Miriam. Why? The question beckoned her.

Miriam knew the answer but didn't want to admit it. Tears formed in eyes she believed had been cried out. She and Derrick had never been close. Opposite gender, age disparity, different personalities, dissimilar thinking. Too unalike. She didn't like him. He didn't like her. Derrick only talked to her to criticize her. But most of the time, she felt as if she was invisible to him. Difficult as it was, she admitted to herself that she was envious of him. He was happy. He was pleased to go with the flow. She was not.

Everything Miriam did: the black clothing, hair, questioning, challenging, and arguing with instructors.

Everything.

Everything was aimed at getting Derrick to pay attention to her.

She didn't like him. But she loved him. She wanted him to open his eyes, because mostly, she wanted him to see her. Negative attention was better than none.

Stupid regarding personal interactions, yet she also knew she was smart. But she needed to get smarter to help Derrick. Yet she could no more increase her IQ than a mouse could kick a lion's ass. Yet, she had witnessed Derrick deck Marcus Carver, and had you asked her if that were possible, she would have said: "Right, as possible as a mouse kicking a lion's ass."

Something happened to Derrick that Miriam didn't understand. Perhaps a natural reaction for a brother will protect his baby sister, even if they don't get along. But not Derrick. The friction between Derrick and her wasn't mere sibling rivalry or the ordinary irritation between an older brother and his younger sister. The past few years as Derrick strove to be the perfect student and Chosen adherent, he had grown to loathe her. He would have booted her out of Pacific Edge himself were it in his power to do so. He didn't like admitting he even knew her. He would never protect her. Besides, he would never protect anyone because he was a complete and utter coward.

Reflex? No way. Derrick King's natural reactions to a confrontation were to run, cry, or faint. Take your pick. So, how in the hell did Derrick King attack instead of run? Avoiding conflict was as natural for Derrick as flying was for a gull. Furthering his image as a Creator-fearing, Chosen-worshiping brown-noser was the natural path for Derrick King. He would never put his own interests second. But he did. What happened to him? Merely turning 17 couldn't explain such a drastic change.

Miriam was three and a half years away from 17, so if his 17th birthday caused Derrick's miracle transformation, then she was out of luck for a few more years if another level of intelligence was coming her way.

She would need to figure it out with the brain she now possessed.

2

WHEN SLEEP FINALLY OVERTOOK MIRIAM, she dreamed about Derrick. She saw him in a dark place, alone, cold, hungry.

When her alarm sounded that morning, her mind cleared, and she realized it had just been a dream.

She would help Derrick, even if he didn't like her.

AJ Patel gave her a head start in December, exploring the computer system in her room. It had been informative, entertaining to an extent, but it was a closed system. It confirmed many things she suspected, yet offered no solutions to help Derrick. But it provided knowledge she hoped would prove useful. She didn't know what helping Derrick would look like. *Go there? Get him back to Pacific Edge?*

Miriam didn't start her quest on Saturday, although she wanted to. Fear didn't stop her but rather good judgment. Maybe she would start tomorrow.

Miriam had been wandering the streets of Pacific Edge after curfew for months before the Carver incident. She liked calling it the Carver incident. It sounded more mysterious than "when Derrick smacked Marcus." First, she had defeated the lock and alarm on her window. Then she learned how to shimmy down the chain that served as a downspout. She had covered the security camera with what looked like bird droppings but were mashed potatoes. It rarely rained, so one application lasted for months. Because security patrols had never been activated to apprehend her, and security officers had not arrested her after reviewing camera footage that would have shown her roaming about, she concluded that either there were virtually no staff members on duty after curfew, or they were otherwise occupied sleeping or playing at something.

Still, she had never illegally entered anything.

Until now.

The time dragged like a child's toy with a dying battery. That Miriam was anxious compounded the feeling that the clock had slowed. She was restless because soon she would break into the Technical Service Building. Not break in exactly because she had a code for the door if AJ Patel used the same numbers that he had used to access her computer. That was a big if.

* * *

That night at dinner, Miriam pushed food around her plate. Mother fought back tears from red eyes. Father remained silent. Miriam ate half of her rosemary-infused Cornish hen, most of her garlic parmesan asparagus, and all of her molten chocolate cake. The latter required no explanation. She ate because she needed nourishment for tonight. Upon finishing, she climbed the stairs to her room, where she slept.

Sunday, March 14, 12:15 a.m.

Just after midnight, her alarm, set on vibrate, erupted. She splashed cold water on her face and donned all-black clothing, including a black-hooded sweatshirt. Black-hooded sweatshirts were not available for purchase in Pacific Edge. She started with a white one. After experimenting with several things, she created black dye using a growth found on an oak tree. She didn't wear the black-hooded sweatshirt to the Academy because they would have confiscated it. She only wore it at night when she slipped into the darkness. Dark clothing for dark tasks.

A hint of fear coursed through her as she opened the window. The security system showed it as locked. The security system was wrong. She feared getting caught, but not for herself. Being discovered would make it impossible to help Derrick. However, excitement exceeded her fear. Not excited about leaving the house after curfew. That was not new. Excitement for what she would find in the computer network not designed to feed propaganda to the Chosen.

Into the night she went.

The streets were quiet. A half-crescent moon high above the horizon lit the sky, but it didn't change the illumination at street level, which streetlights lit as if it were daytime. Even in black, Miriam was visible. She did her best to walk in the shadows of bushes and trees. Instead of walking a direct route to the Technical Service Building, which was part of the outer wall surrounding Pacific Edge, which according to New America Media, protected the Chosen from the horrors of the commoner world, she took a route toward the ocean as she did when she retrieved the keyboard and mouse AJ Patel had gifted her. If they caught her, the destination wouldn't yet be obvious.

As she neared the cliffs overlooking the ocean, the salty scent rolled inland, carried by the low growl of crashing waves. Gulls called. A fog bank, which would have concealed her from the security cameras, hovered offshore. Maybe it would move in before she returned home.

Miriam liked the ocean. However, the Chosen discouraged spending time on the beach, and exposure of the skin was forbidden. Swimming attire covered most of the body if one were a girl. Too much danger from the sun's rays, they were told. Girls, apparently, were at higher risk of skin cancer than boys. The ever-present social norms of the Doctrine also apply primarily to girls.

The beach was open once per week under heavy observation. For their protection, they were told. Miriam didn't go to the beach on the designated days. She liked the beach at night, watching the relentless waves roll in, dreaming about what was beyond the horizon.

Hovercrafts are not loud. When she recognized the sound, the machine was close. She ducked under a bush just as the machine flew overhead. It paused. Hot-white light lit the grass around the bush, and slivers of light threaded through the leaves. She had never seen a hovercraft on her previous nighttime adventures. Typically, she left the house about 2 a.m., an hour later than she left tonight. She thought an hour wouldn't make a difference. She was wrong.

After a few minutes that felt like hours, the hovercraft moved on. Miriam remained concealed, watching as the machine searched the Pacific Edge streets. After 45 minutes, the machine disappeared over the exterior wall. She waited another 15 minutes. The thought of calling it off crossed her mind. She dismissed the notion—too many things to do and too little time in which to do them.

Pulling her hood up, she glided back onto the sidewalk.

Reaching the first wall that concealed the entrances, garbage receptacles, and other things deemed too unsightly for Chosen eyes, she hurried to the Technical Service entrance. A security camera overlooked the door. Miriam kept her face concealed from the camera. No reason to make identification easy. Now came the first obstacle that could doom the entire operation. Would the numbers AJ Patel used as a PIN open the door? Miriam, and determined PIN stood for personal identification number. She remembered the numbers. Miriam didn't forget numbers.

Fingers trembling, she keyed: 7, 23, 15, 4, 9, 77, then tapped: Enter. In the silent night, the latch clicked, and the door nudged open an inch.

Miriam eased inside. Then she froze. That might have been a mistake. What if the exit required a key or a second code? She turned and felt relieved. The door had a crash bar.

Her unauthorized entrance, break-in, was now a reality. A thought she had repressed, with some success, forced itself to the surface: she used AJ Patel's code to enter. That meant she put AJ Patel in danger. The stranger who had taken risks giving her an unauthorized keyboard and mouse, which granted her illegal access to the Pacific Edge computer system.

Green exit signs dimly lit the hallway. She had never been in a commercial building. The Academy was the closest thing she had experienced. She was never inside the Academy after regular hours. Yet something felt familiar, like a dream.

It was peaceful, yet the building hummed. Machines. Moving down the hallway, the absence of cameras was a welcomed sight. She walked past a door marked "Server Room." She perceived machines humming inside, and heat from electronic components scented the air. The door was locked. No keypad. The hallway emptied into a large open room with individual workspaces surrounded by short, cloth-covered walls. No doors. Lots of computers. She entered a workspace and moved the mouse at the side of the keyboard. The monitor lit up, and she saw a white rectangular box with a name, written as first initial and last name, no capital letters, no spaces. Below the name was a box named: Password.

Damn it.

She moved from computer to computer, hoping someone had left a computer in a status that didn't require a password. She found none. At the far end of the open room, another hallway marked: Field Service Division. The hall was lined with office doors. No windows. All locked. Each with a name at the side of the door. The name placard on the third door down the hall read: AJ Patel, Supervisor.

She tried the knob.

It turned.

3

Sunday, March 14, 2:15 a.m.

ENTERING AJ PATEL'S OFFICE, MIRIAM eased the door shut. The latch clicked into its metal receptacle. The room stood pitch black, save the glow from two red lights on electronic devices. She hesitated and then switched on the lights. AJ Patel's computer had three monitors, the one in the middle set horizontally and the two on either side set vertically. AJ Patel kept an orderly workspace. The keyboard and mouse were tucked away on a tray that slid underneath the desktop. The gray desk was clean and almost bare. One pen was placed atop a yellow notepad, next to it a picture displaying three people: AJ Patel, a woman, and a girl.

Miriam recognized the woman and the girl.

Samantha Bell and her mother. An attractive lady with a bright smile, blue eyes, and blonde hair. Samantha had her mother's eyes but a darker complexion and black hair. Her blue eyes and dark hair intrigued Miriam in grade school because they were unusual, which Miriam thought of as rebellious. Samantha inspired Miriam to change the color of her own hair to black, in contrast with her hazel eyes and pale skin.

Three people smiling. Two she knew from the past, and one she knew in the present. Samantha and her mother had been moved to another Chosen Community three years ago. Miriam tried to make sense of the photograph but came to the same conclusion: mother, daughter, and father. She didn't understand.

Miriam had never met Samantha's father. He didn't attend school functions, although her mother often did. Miriam tried to recall if Samantha had ever mentioned her father's name. Nothing surfaced. Miriam didn't know AJ Patel's ethnic heritage. They taught nothing in the Academy that provided such information. It was said that Black people originated in Africa and Oriental people, the Orient. But AJ Patel was neither. Dark skin, but not black, dark eyes, black hair. Ethnicity wasn't something Miriam had ever given much thought. Skin color didn't matter to her, never had, although it mattered to many people in Pacific Edge and to the Chosen in general. While mixed marriage was not illegal, it wasn't encouraged. Until now, Miriam had never seen a mixed marriage.

Because Samantha went to Pacific Edge schools, which meant she was Chosen, as was her mother, and to the best of Miriam's knowledge, regarding the norms of the Chosen, so was her father. But AJ Patel was a service worker, a commoner, and Samantha and her mother had been removed from Pacific Edge. Miriam thought they had been moved to another Chosen Community only because that's what the instructor had told the class the day Samantha was not present.

Now, Miriam assumed Samantha's father didn't attend school events because the Chosen frowned at their mixed marriage. Samantha and her mother didn't move to another Chosen community. They moved them to the commoner world. They must have demoted AJ Patel, yet they allowed him to be a computer technician in Pacific Edge. She wanted to know the entire story but had more pressing things to do.

Accessing the computer system was her best hope. Her plans had not evolved beyond a promise to help Derrick. She needed more information to make that happen. Moving the mouse brought the monitor to life, showing the same screen as the other computers except with a different name: Username—ajpatel and below that, Password. Miriam entered 723154977 and then Enter. The screen changed.

"Username or password is incorrect. You have two more attempts."

Miriam knew the numbers were correct. She didn't forget numbers.

Two more attempts and then screwed.

Thinking hard. AJ used this PIN to log in to the system at my house. He used the same PIN at the entrance door here. Either AJ Patel had a poor memory, which seemed unlikely, or he was a creature of habit and didn't like to change things. So, why did he use a different password to log in to his computer?

Those nine numbers were all she had. Same numbers at her house. Same numbers at the door. Same numbers here made sense. So, she reversed the numbers and entered 779451327. The screen changed.

"Username or password is incorrect."

"You have one more attempt. (click for password hint)."

Miriam smiled, positioned the mouse arrow over hint, and clicked. Then her smile faded. A cryptic message appeared: first+numbers. The numbers she knew. *But first, what? First date? First kiss?* Could be anything.

Stuck.

And then.

Voices.

4

RISING SLOWLY, MIRIAM MOVED CAUTIOUSLY. The voices grew louder. She looked at the bottom of the door and saw a slight gap. Turning off the lights might draw their attention. Two men's voices, getting closer. Almost to the door now.

From the hall, "Patel left his light on."

"Yeah, or he's working late. He does that sometimes. Gets called in."

"I didn't see his car in the lot."

"True."

"Might have walked."

"Maybe."

Miriam remembered she had not locked the door when she entered. She turned the locking device in the center of the door. Just as the lock engaged, she felt the knob move in her hand.

"Door's locked."

Three loud knocks startled Miriam.

"Patel! You in there?"

"I guess he forgot to turn the lights off."

"That's unusual. AJ is consistently consistent about such things."

"True."

"Should we get the master key and look?"

"Probably forgot to turn them off."

"But what if he's dead or something?"

"Well, his car would be here, right?"

"True."

"Should we get the key and check it out?"

"That's a lot of paperwork. Fill out the form to get the key. Write a report about what we found."

"True. Should we write up that he left the light on?"

"Paperwork."

"True."

"I'd rather eat lunch."

"Right, me too."

The footsteps moved down the hall. Miriam slid to the floor with her back against the wall. Her heart pounded in her chest, sweat trickled down her face. When the hovercraft came overhead, Miriam felt a hint of fear. When she first entered the Technical Service Building, her heart rate elevated a little. But this encounter brought the full meaning of her actions into sharp focus. It scared her. Not so much because of her personal risk, but because of the threat to Samantha Bell's father, AJ Patel.

After a few minutes, Miriam moved back to the keyboard. One more chance. First+numbers. First, what? First child? Think. Then, something occurred to Miriam, which was not logic but intuition. She didn't like intuition because it defies logic. Still, it was there. Who was AJ Patel's password hint meant for? Himself or Miriam? The purpose of the password hint was to help the user, not someone attempting to break into the system. Would AJ Patel need a hint? Maybe it was mandatory to complete the function before the system would work. Perhaps AJ Patel had a more complicated password to enter the system here. Perhaps that wasn't it at all.

One more chance.

Miriam's fingers trembled as she touched the keys and entered: aj723154977. With a finger touching the enter key, she paused.

Last chance.

Then, a thought: *What if this is all a trap?*

No other options. All or nothing. She tapped enter.

The screen changed.

5

BEAUTIFUL MOUNTAINS appeared on the monitors. A row of small images lined the bottom of the center screen: a funny-looking face, a colorful round sphere with a white squiggle line in the middle, a weird compass-looking thing, a small calendar, a musical note, a capital A, a gear, keys, and others. There was only one item on the screen itself. A folder: mking

Miriam opened the folder and found a single file, also titled mking. She opened it and read.

```
Miriam, if you are reading this, then
you've met my expectations. Good job.
Major challenges await you. You have
probably concluded the security at night
is complacent. You are correct, but that
doesn't mean they will not catch you. I
could help you with that, but I've decided
you need to do this on your own. Well,
mostly on your own.

I cannot leave my door unlocked all the
time. I hoped that the security staff
wouldn't check the door until you came.
There is a key taped to the bottom of the
desktop that unlocks my office. After
tonight, the door will be locked, so do
not forget the key.

Your first major task is learning to
manage the security cameras that will
reveal your trips here. You must also be
creating a PIN for the entrance door.
```

You must be setting up your own login information. If you are caught, it is important that they cannot link us. I will erase that you logged on tonight. We are okay so far. But next time you must be using your own password and login. I have created you a fake account: Maranda Kingston. Your password is password, which you must change the first time you log into the system.

I have made an e-mail account for you. E-mail is a system used to communicate when writing to other people on the Internet. You don't know that term, and it's hard to explain. For now, just think of it as a huge book of information stored electronically. Open the app that looks like a bird flying. To log into e-mail, use the same username and password. Your e-mail account is: marandakingston@techservice/admin.com

Derrick's e-mail is derrickking0312@Potterville.com. That Paul fellow set it up. Clever username, I'm thinking, because March 12 was an eventful day.

The system scans all employee accounts every 30 days. I must delete your account before the next scan, which is 29 days from today. Whatever you are doing must be completed by then.

The first security sweep in the building is between 2:00 and 2:30 a.m. If you are in before then, lock the door and work with the lights off. You should be okay, but it would be safer to come after the security sweep. You must decide when to

come. What you are intending and how
quickly you are learning will dictate
your schedule, I'm thinking.

If you can determine a way to manage the
security cameras and dodge the security
patrols, you are reasonably safe.
However, there is one system that poses a
problem. It is constant real-time
tracking of every member of the Chosen.
It is under a link called 1984. You won't
be understanding why that number is used,
but maybe someday you will. Security
personnel are not looking at this system
daily. You'll see why. They only use it
to track specific individuals. If you
come under suspicion, 1984 will betray
you as it sees your every move. Just as
it is tracking Derrick right now. This
system is not easily defeated. I was not
thinking ahead when I developed it. You
must incapacitate it to help Derrick.

Good luck.

Miriam stared at the screen. *Why had AJ Patel taken such a risk to help her?* She didn't know. It made little sense. One day, she hoped to understand and return the favor if possible. She still had accomplished nothing to help Derrick.

Miriam followed AJ Patel's instructions, setting up her own login information and then her e-mail. She studied the e-mail settings and found that she could send the e-mail encoded, which meant only the recipient could open it. She started to write to Derrick and then decided to wait. She had to learn about security cameras and how to defeat them. On the Technical Service page, she found a link titled Pacific Edge Security. On the next screen, there was a picture of smiling officers wearing tan uniforms. She had only seen security officers on hovercraft. Those officers wore helmets with mirrored face shields and black uniforms laden with weapons and other gear. Never smiling faces, never tan uniforms.

She clicked the employee login. A warning popped up stating that unauthorized access would result in corrective action up to and including termination, criminal prosecution, and civil judgments up to $500,000. They couldn't fire her, and she didn't have $500,000, so she clicked enter again and then filled in her username and password. The screen changed. She had entered the Pacific Edge security system. She found the security cameras and learned how to watch them in real-time. She could select several cameras, and they would appear on the monitor. She learned that she could drag them to one of the side monitors and arrange them. The need for three large monitors became apparent. Soon, the cameras from her house to the Technical Service Building were on the screen in order. She discovered she could view recordings and link them to the same timeline. Rolling the time back—the camera outside her house was blurred as if it had bird poop on it—the next camera showed her crossing the street. Then she moved through each camera's field of view. If security employees watched the recording, they would catch her. This wouldn't be easy. She never thought it would be.

She checked the time: 4:35. *Crap.*

Opening the e-mail application, she wrote a message to Derrick.

```
FROM:
marandakingston@techservice/admin.com

TO: derrickking0312@potterville.com

Subject: Your Number1 Pain in the Ass

Don't let my e-mail address fool you. It's
me, your number1 pain in the ass little
sister. Tell Paul that setting up your e-
mail as derrickking0312 was cool. Delete
this e-mail and then empty your deleted
e-mail too. I'm safe on this end for now.
I have a lot to tell you, but no time.
Got to run. Literally.

Love you
```

She shut the computer off.
She turned the lights out.
She unlocked the door.
She turned the handle.
She heard voices in the hall.

6

Sunday, March 14, 4:45 a.m.

"HEY, BRAD. WASN'T PATEL'S LIGHT on earlier?"

Miriam couldn't understand the reply.

She felt the knob turn in her hand.

She tightened her grip and then reached the lock with her left hand and forced the center button into the locked position.

"Door is still locked."

"That's weird. Should we have central-control check if Patel entered the building?"

"The entry door from our side isn't in the security log. Only the Pacific Edge side."

"Right. So, what should we do?"

Silence.

Finally, "Not sure. If we investigate, we gotta explain why we ignored the light being on when we saw it earlier. Lots of paperwork, interviews, performance reviews, none of that sounds good to me."

"But what if there's a problem?"

"Like what?"

"What if Patel is dead in there?"

"There are no witnesses. So, there's no problem. Plus, if he's dead, what are we going to do about it?"

"But they would review the cameras and see that we stopped here twice."

"It's a blind spot. Camera picks up at the cubical room."

"What if someone broke in during our shift? We'd have lots of questions to answer. We could get demoted or fired."

"Can't get demoted much lower than graveyard foot patrol. Getting fired might be an improvement. Besides, when was the last break-in? The Chosen are terrified of anything beyond their wall. Besides, they aren't smart enough to get in here."

"True. So, do nothing? How about sending Patel an e-mail? Ask if he came in last night."

"And if he didn't? Back to paperwork and questions. First question: Why didn't we follow protocol when we discovered it?"

How much time had passed? It must be close to 5:00 a.m. When do people start arriving? People would start moving around Pacific Edge anytime now, which was good because she would simply be out for an early morning walk. No worries. Except father would bang on her door soon, and she wouldn't be there.

"Let's forget it. No good can come of this now."

Miriam pressed her ear to the door. The footsteps faded, but she couldn't determine the direction, but she thought deeper into the building. Not sure. She waited for what seemed like an hour but was closer to five minutes. She moved the door lock slowly, silently. Eased the door open an inch. Nothing. Another inch. Still nothing. Inch by inch, she opened the door until she could see down the hall in one direction and then poked her head out enough to see the other direction. Nothing. She locked the door and stepped out of the office. Committed now. She moved into the open room with small workspaces. She tiptoed through the center of the room, watching the hall that led to the exit. It occurred to her that people wouldn't be coming to work from that direction. They would come in from behind her. She spun around and saw a woman in the hall, looking into a brown-leather bag slung over one shoulder.

Miriam ducked into a workspace. She strained to hear movements. Footsteps. Getting louder. Miriam ducked into the space where a worker's legs would be under the desk. Getting closer.

Then, a pair of red shoes at the end of two legs appeared in front of her. She pressed back against the wall of the workspace. *What are the odds of hiding in the space belonging to the first employee to arrive?* Within seconds, Miriam answered her own question by calculating the number of spaces in the room based on a snapshot in her mind. Sometimes her memory was a pain in the ass.

Still rummaging around in her bag, the woman muttered, "Crap." And walked away.

Miriam listened to the footsteps fade. She eased out of her hiding spot and peeked over the short fabric-covered wall. The woman was walking down the hall. Moving cautiously would be best. Miriam knew that. Be silent, be careful.

Miriam bolted toward the exit door.

No sirens or voices. She thought someone might hear her heart thumping louder than her footfalls. When she reached the exit door, she forced a more cautious exit than the voice in her head demanded. When the exit door opened, would it trigger an alarm? Maybe a silent notification to whoever monitored the cameras. She had no choice. Although she had not disabled the security cameras, she couldn't stay here.

She eased the door open. A morning breeze from the ocean mixed the smell of the trash with the scent of the sea. Not a pleasant odor. She peeked around the opening in the wall and glanced both ways. The streets of Pacific Edge remained quiet. In the distance, a solitary figure walking. Just someone out for an early stroll. The curfew had ended, and doors were unlocked, although most Chosen wouldn't venture outside until necessary. Miriam walked to the sidewalk, slipped off her hooded jacked, rolling it up and carrying it under one arm, and strolled toward home.

When Miriam got home, she scaled the chain that carried water from the rain gutter to the ground to the roof. Although the front door was unlocked, she couldn't risk Father or Mother seeing her come in. When she reached her open window, she heard a loud pounding.

"Miriam! Breakfast! Miriam?"

It was Father. He never yelled like that. How many times had he tried to awaken her? She scurried to the window, stuck her head inside, and said, "Sorry. Coming."

Miriam quickly stripped out of her black clothing, kicked it under her bed, donned her sleepwear, and opened the door. "Sorry. I was in the bathroom. Not feeling well."

"Goodness, Miriam. You look terrible."

No surprise. "I didn't sleep."

Father studied her for a moment and then said, "Good thing it's not a school day. You need to get some rest. Can you eat?"

"Maybe. If I can keep it down," Miriam said, although keeping it down wouldn't be a problem.

Miriam ate four slices of bacon, two eggs, and a pile of hash browns. She didn't say much. The New America Media Morning Report played on the large communication screen on the wall. Father had the volume turned down. Miriam watched the screen for any report of a break-in at Technical Services. She ate and watched and thought. She had really screwed up her first foray into the forbidden building. Braindead. That was her problem. She went at the wrong time, which almost got her caught before she even got there. Left the light on, which drew attention to AJ Patel's office. That could have gotten him fired or worse.

Accomplished nothing except creating her login information and setting up her e-mail account. She had to improve.

"What are you thinking about?" Father asked.

Miriam remained silent.

"Miriam?" Her Father paused. "Miriam?"

"What?"

"I asked you a question."

"Oh, sorry. Lost in my thoughts."

"Yes. That's what I asked."

"Asked what?"

"What's on your mind?"

"Oh, that. Nothing." Miriam rolled her eyes. *Braindead.* "I mean everything. Derrick. Everything."

"You need sleep. Worrying won't change anything."

"Sure," Miriam said. She drifted off again. I wonder what Derrick is doing right now. Will he have food? Is he still alive? Surely, he made it this long. He's safe in some type of housing Father provided.

"Miriam," Father said.

"Miriam," Father repeated.

"What?"

"You're doing it again," Father said.

"Doing what?"

Father shook his head. "Should I order you a sedative? You need to sleep."

"I can sleep. May I be excused now?" Miriam asked.

Miriam climbed the stairs, pulling herself along using the handrail. She fell onto her bed and slept.

* * *

She awoke in a familiar white room. Derrick was there, except his name wasn't Derrick. They called him Number Seven. He must have been about eight years old but large for his age. The Keepers, that's what the children called them, corrected Number Seven when he used his size and strength to take toys from others. Sometimes, Number Seven made other children cry. There were eleven other children in the room besides Number Seven. A total of 12, all about the same age. The only one Number Seven did not make cry was Number Six. Number Six was too smart for him. Sometimes, Number Six made Number Seven cry. Not with strength or size because, Number Six was a small girl. Number Six made Number Seven cry because she liked to trick him. Number Six thought it was great fun. Father was there too, but he wasn't Father then. Father would correct Number Six when she made Number Seven cry. Father, who wasn't Father yet, was Number Six's Keeper. Number Six didn't make other children cry. Just Number Seven.

Number Six watched Number Seven. He played with a small boy, Number Ten. Mother was there too, but neither Number Seven nor Number Six called her Mother. Mother, who was not yet Mother, was Number Seven's Keeper. Keepers were there five days a week until 5:00 p.m. After the Keepers left, more tenders came. Tenders didn't interact with the children like the Keepers. They ensured the children were fed, put to bed, and controlled when necessary. In her dreams, tenders were faceless or, at least, unrecognizable. Different people, as if rotating in and out of the job, but Keepers were always the same people. Each child had a Keeper assigned, but Keepers worked five days a week, eight hours a day.

The tenders were always there.

Always.

Number Ten had a toy. It was a shiny toy hovercraft with two figurines dressed in black. Number Seven watched every move Number Ten made with the shiny hovercraft toy. Number Seven's Keeper eased away from both boys. Neither noticed until she had left the room through a white door next to a large mirror. Except it wasn't a mirror. It was a window the children couldn't see through. Number Six had figured that out. None of the other children knew about it.

Number Six watched the boys and the shiny hovercraft. She giggled. She knew what was coming next.

7

Sunday, March 14, Evening

THE WHITE ROOM, THE ELEVEN children, the Keepers, the tenders, and Number Seven faded. Groggily, Miriam saw her room through half-opened, crusty eyes. A stale and slightly sour taste filled her mouth. On unsteady legs, she shuffled to the bathroom, where she drew water.

What time is it? She wondered as she drained the glass and refilled it and drained it again. She splashed water on her face, peered into the mirror, frowned, and returned to her bedroom.

Placing a mug under her espresso machine, "she said, espresso, please, double-shot, and a bit of hot water." She wondered if kids in the commoner world where they had sent Derrick had espresso machines in their bedrooms. Probably not.

"Your usual?" a disembodied voice asked.

"Yes. What time is it?"

"The time is 6:12 p.m."

"Damn."

"I do not understand your request."

"Nothing. Just coffee." The machine hissed, forcing steam through fresh grounds. The aroma cleared her head even before her first sip. Most of her peers, if one could call them that, didn't drink coffee, and the few who did add sugar, cream, flavored syrups, caramel, chocolate, etc. If Miriam wanted an ice cream sundae, she'd ask for it. She saw no reason to ruin good coffee with embellishments.

With the steaming cup in hand, she walked to the bay window, which was her favorite place in the world to sit and think and drink coffee. She sat on a thick cushion, put her back to the wall, pulled her knees to her chest, and looked out over the rooftops toward the ocean, which rolled with white-capped waves. This was not the window she used to escape. She used her bathroom window for that. It didn't have a view because the bathroom window was frosted. Typically, one wouldn't open the bathroom window, which meant it was unlikely anyone would check the alarm system there.

Her thinking station, as she called it, faced the backyard, 30 yards deep, landscaped with flowers and fountains and separated from the ocean by two blocks of homes, but the downward grade gave her an unobstructed view. She loved the sea, or at least the idea of it, as it seemed infinite, which she translated to mean endless possibilities, a contradiction to life for the Chosen in Pacific Edge.

She refused to ruminate about Derrick last night or her next move. For a moment, she forced everything from her mind except the ocean, the coffee, and the infinite possibilities. The thoughtlessness calmed her. However, the answers she needed were not rooted in the infinite possibilities of the sea but in the land of the commoners. Her mental barricade didn't last long. The weight of Derrick's situation and her lackluster performance invaded quickly enough. The situation felt daunting. She still didn't know how to help, but she promised she would. She promised she would come. But how she would escape Pacific Edge remained a mystery. She didn't even have a plan to get to the Technical Services building undetected. Father would soon call her to dinner. That was good because she was hungry.

At 7:00 p.m., Miriam walked to the dinner table before Father called her. She had downed another double shot of espresso, showered, and felt almost human. The table set, steam rising from prime rib, roasted duck, and turkey. Salads and side dishes galore completed the meal, and the table fully extended, as if guests were expected.

"What's the occasion?" Miriam asked, standing motionless near her chair.

Father said, "It is not a celebration. I wanted to ensure we had something you might eat."

"This is for me?" Miriam remained stationary. Her memory was virtually perfect, at least back to memories she didn't fully trust, and she remembered no special meals for her. For Derrick, yes, but not for her. She was not perfect like her brother.

"Sit, dear," Mother said.

Miriam stared at Mother for a moment and said, "Okay."

Miriam took thick slices of turkey breast and prime rib, a smaller wedge of duck, and added garlic mashed potatoes. Because Mother would chide her lack of vegetables, she added a few spears of asparagus topped with hollandaise sauce. She carved off a chunk of pink prime rib, soaked it a moment in au jus, and forked it into creamy horseradish before sticking it in her mouth. She closed her eyes as the succulent flavors flooded her palate. Every bite proved as good as the previous until she wondered if she was dreaming or if they had laced the food with drugs.

After eating in silence for several minutes, Father asked, "Did you sleep?"

Miriam chewed for a moment, swallowed, and said, "Yes. Too long, maybe."

"Too long, dear? What do you mean by that?" Mother asked.

Miriam took a bite of roasted duck, found it better than expected, studied Mother, and wondered, *what's up with calling me dear? That's a new one.*

"Hope I can sleep tonight," Miriam lied.

"I see," Mother said flatly.

Miriam looked at Father. He studied Mother and nodded slightly.

"Is everything okay? Has something happened to Derrick?" Miriam asked, putting down her fork.

"He is okay, as far as we know. We are not permitted to contact him. They allowed Mr. Jorgensen to send a message. He said they had arrived, and that Derrick was safe in his new housing."

"Where is he?" Miriam asked.

"We do not know."

"You don't know?" Miriam asked.

Father looked at the ceiling and scratched his chin. "It's better if you don't know. That's the Tribunal's decision, not mine. I can tell you it's about three hours to drive from here."

Miriam nodded and tried to picture the distance in her mind but failed. Nothing to attach it to. "How far is it?"

"I don't know. Does that make a difference?" Father asked.

"Just curious," Miriam said. "It doesn't matter. Ten miles or a thousand. He's gone." She felt water fill her eyes. She refused to cry. No time for it.

Miriam emptied her plate and, uncharacteristically, took seconds of garlic potatoes and prime rib, although smaller portions. Typically, she didn't eat generous helpings of red meat, but she felt like she might not see prime rib again. Her parents sat silently, watching her. When she finished, she said, "I'll help clear the table." She paused. "How is it done?"

Father said, "Help us carry everything into the kitchen. Put the dishes on the counter. Put food in the walk-in cooler. The help will take care of it in the morning."

Mother said, "That's a first."

Miriam said, "Sorry. I'm trying to change. For Derrick."

After dinner, Miriam would typically go to her room, where she would remain until morning or until she snuck out of the house. But today didn't feel typical. She sat on the couch in the great room off the entrance. Mother said she was going to her room and maybe take a hot bath. Father grabbed his pad communication device and sat opposite Miriam in his mahogany-colored leather chair.

"You're not going to your room?" Father asked.

"Not yet. I didn't want to be alone," Miriam said. She sat silently. Father read on his communication device.

"What are you reading?"

"A novel," Father said.

"A novel?"

"Yes. Fiction. That means it's made up, not true."

"Weird."

"Novels were popular in the old United States."

"Are they not forbidden?"

"Not forbidden. Restricted is more accurate. I applied and received authorization to read this one."

"How big is a novel?"

Father poked the screen of his device twice. "This one is 418 pages."

Miriam thought for a moment. "You read all that, and it's not even true?"

Father chuckled. "Sounds odd, doesn't it? This book is not entirely fictional. It's based on true events."

"I'm confused."

"Someday, when you're an adult, you should read novels. Then you'll understand."

Miriam nodded. I'll read one before I'm an adult if I can get out of here, she thought.

"What's the name of it?" Miriam asked.

"Zen and the Art of Motorcycle Maintenance," Father said.

Miriam wrinkled her nose. "What's a motorcycle?"

"There are no pictures, but from what I gather, it was an old-time form of transport, except it only had two wheels and carried only two people. Kind of like a bicycle with a motor."

"Weird. What's it about?"

"It's about a man and his son riding a motorcycle across the old United States. But it's about much more than that. It's like several stories within a story."

"Oh," Miriam breathed. After a moment, she asked, "What's a Zen?"

"I don't understand that part yet," Father said.

Miriam sat as Father read for 30 minutes. She had never asked Father, Mother, or Derrick for advice. She had never asked anyone for advice, although she would have happily dispensed her own had anyone asked. She now had a problem to which she had no answers, and that was no small thing.

On many levels, she thought of herself as stupid. She failed to understand social norms, social cues, and how others felt. For example, she didn't understand why people blindly trusted what New America Media told them. Why didn't they see the deceptions she saw so easily? Because she saw things others couldn't, she understood she was smart. Stupid and smart. That was her.

"Father," she whispered. "What is it you do?"

"At work? You know what I do. I'm an accountant."

"Yes, but what exactly does an accountant do?"

Father set his device in his lap. "Accountants do all sorts of things. Analyze expenditures, collectibles, and assets, reconcile reports and inventories, tax analysis. All sorts of things."

"Okay. But what do you do specifically?"

Father was silent for a moment before saying, "I analyze profit and loss. Why do you ask?"

"Just wondering. Do you solve problems?"

"Like mathematical problems?" Father asked.

"No, more like—people problems," Miriam said.

"People problems?"

Miriam hesitated, looked at the floor, and then looked at Father and said, "Like Derrick problems."

Father looked around the room. Bit his bottom lip. Finally, he said, "I wish I could give you an answer, but I can't. Derrick did something wrong and must pay the consequences."

Those damn watery eyes returned, which made Miriam angry. Father only confirmed what she had already suspected. It was not safe to talk openly. Watching and listening. Father said what was necessary to be safe. Still, that didn't help her. She didn't need a solution. She needed an epiphany. An idea. A starting place.

"You're right. There is nothing we can do. It's not about fixing Derrick's problem. Dummy Derrick created his own problems. I like to find solutions. It's what I do. There's nothing I can do for Derrick, but I want to analyze the problem. Kind of an exercise. But I can't find a starting place."

Father frowned and glanced upward and gave her a slight smile. "There's an old saying, not used anymore, but I read it in a novel. Derrick's problem must be solved the way one would eat an elephant."

"What does that mean?"

"One bite at a time."

Miriam smiled and stood. "Thanks."

She was off to eat an elephant.

8

Monday, March 15

AT THIRTY MINUTES PAST MIDNIGHT, Miriam, dressed in black, pulled her hood over her head, eased her window open, and crawled onto the roof. A full moon rose overhead, and in the distance, white-capped waves rolled onto the shore. The ever-present scent of the ocean cleared her mind. On the security camera aimed at the front of her house, she smeared more mashed potatoes she'd recovered from the kitchen. In her pocket, she had stuffed a prime rib sandwich for later.

Work to be done.

Despite the brightness of the lamps that lit Pacific Edge, sparkling stars spread across a flawless sky. She walked straight to the Technical Service Building. Tonight, she had to disable the security cameras, or this wouldn't last long. The sky was free of hovercraft. The streets contained no people. The brisk walk took her ten minutes and 35 seconds. The less time she spent on the street, the better her chance of reaching her destination undetected. Along the way, she studied the location of the cameras, which were mounted on the light poles. There may have been others she didn't see, but she would search for them using the computer. She noted a number-letter combination on each pole. Her street's cameras were identified chronologically, starting with the letter E—E-10, E-9, E-8. The pattern changed on the cross street using all numbers: 4-3, 4-4, 4-5. The next street running parallel to hers began with letters again: F-4, F-3, F-2. F-1 brought her to the wall. Cameras along the wall were just numbers 15, 16, 17, and 18. Under number 19 stood the entrance door to the Technical Service Building. She entered her new passcode, and the lock clicked. She eased the door open and listened. Silence. She stepped inside. Maranda Kingston was in the building.

The sound of machines murmured in the hallway devoid of humans. She passed the server room's humming door, eased through the maze of workspaces, and then down the hall to AJ Patel's office. Inside his office, she turned the lock and stood with her back pressed against the door. At first, the room appeared dark save for the lights on the monitors and computers, but her eyes adjusted until she saw the workstation and chair. Slow and silent, she moved to the computer. A wiggle of the mouse woke the machine. Pulling in a deep breath, Miriam typed in her Maranda username and password. The monitors came to life.

Good, so far.

She went straight to the security section and pulled up the cameras. She found the camera attached to the front of her home. Easy enough. It only required typing King into the small line titled search.

Finding the street cameras took longer until she found a drop-down menu listing the cameras by letter and number. She selected all the cameras that followed her route, dragging them to the screen on her left and lining them up sequentially.

With the clock rolled back to 00:30, she hit play. The first camera showed a blurry driveway. At 00:33, something, garlic mashed potatoes, to be precise, covered the lens and obscured the image. One down, 20 to go.

She watched herself walk from one screen to the next as she moved through each camera's field of vision. The first thing that surprised her, although she didn't know why it surprised her, was that the camera placement was not perfect. The cameras didn't provide complete coverage. She would appear in one camera, move down the street, and then disappear. But she wouldn't appear on the next camera for several seconds. On average, there was a 15-yard gap between cameras. She made a mental note of where each camera's field of vision ended and where the next camera's field of vision began.

Closing her eyes, she envisioned the street and the gaps and the trees and the shadows. Difficult, but not impossible. She could weave a course through Pacific Edge, remaining mostly in the blind spots. Calculating the time and distance, she decided that would take over an hour to navigate, and she would still appear in the cameras sometimes. Too much time, too much exposure.

She heard the same two voices outside AJ Patel's door. She eased around in his chair. Four dim shadows, representing two sets of legs, darkened the gap at the threshold.

"Light's off tonight. Did you learn anything about Patel being here last night?"

"Nope. No news is good news. Right?"

"I suppose. Should we check?"

"Negative. If there were a problem, we would have heard about it."

The voices grew quieter. "Sound's good to me. To be honest, I worried about it all day."

"We're in the clear now."

"Yep, I suppose you are right."

She couldn't understand the reply, but she smiled. AJ Patel had suffered no problems. That made her happy. Then her smile faded. The security guard's appearance meant it was after 2:00 a.m., already. Spinning around, the digital clock read 02:21. Over half of her allotted time, gone, and she had accomplished zilch. She had spent her time visualizing a serpentine route, weaving through the security cameras' blind spots.

What a waste of time. So damn stupid sometimes.

She clicked right and clicked left on drop-down menus, tabs, and icons. Nothing allowed her to delete sections of the security footage. Stumped, she opened the e-mail application, and as it opened, she realized she should have done that first. *Idiot.* Her heart dropped when the e-mail list appeared. One e-mail from ajpatel, one from someone called Human Resources, and none from derrickking0312.

Miriam read AJ Patel's e-mail first. She cursed under her breath.

This was not good.

AJ Patel explained that there were no controls within the security camera system that would allow her, or anyone else, to delete, pause, or manipulate the cameras or the recordings. To achieve anything, she would have to get into what he called the language, which he called E+++, of the operating system. He provided instructions on how to enter the OS language level but provided no directions on what she needed to do once she got there.

Thank you, AJ Patel.

Miriam felt flushed. Over half the night wasted, and she had accomplished nada. Patel's e-mail also said she must learn and then change the OS language. Almost three o'clock. Last night, she had decided that she had to be home by four to get a few hours' sleep so she could function in school.

School was not something she was looking forward to. She didn't want to talk about what happened to Derrick. She had never been a popular girl. But she was well known, an oddity to some, an abomination to others. Some students seemed supportive of her arguments with instructors, but she believed they just liked the entertainment it provided.

Miriam took a deep breath, rubbed her eyes, and followed AJ Patel's instructions to enter the hidden computer language. The screen changed from its colorful images to a black screen with plain white letters, numbers, and symbols:

```
venus[148]% CC -LANG:std IOpresent.cpp -
o IOmarandakingston

venus[149]% IOmarandakingson

$$$$$$$$$$$+1.00e+00

$$$$$$$$$$$-1.23e+00

$$$$$$$$$$$+2.35e+03

$$$$$$$$$$$+2.34e+01

$$$$$$$$$$$+4.53e+01

venus[150]%
```

Page after page of meaningless letters, numbers, and symbols. Miriam began crying.

Thank you, AJ Patel.

Jerk!

9

Monday, March 15, Morning

AT 3:32 a.m. MIRIAM LEFT THE Technical Service Building. She walked through the blind spots and ran, ducked, and dodged through the cameras' fields of vision. Two nights and she still had not dealt with the security cameras. She failed AJ Patel, who for no reason took a significant risk to help her. Or maybe he was just following orders to set her up. Her questioning nature had kicked in during the obstacle course to home. She hoped the first explanation was correct but feared the second was more probable.

The night air felt soft and still. The ever-present scent of the ocean settled on Pacific Edge, carried by a light fog. At this time of night, with no people, no transports, no hovercraft, Pacific Edge seemed idyllic, but that was not its true character. Pacific Edge was not what the Chosen were told.

Pacific Edge was darkest in full daylight.

At 4:06, Miriam crawled into bed fully clothed. She worried she couldn't sleep as her mind raced in many directions. She wondered how Derrick was doing and regretted that she didn't send him an e-mail. She speculated why AJ Patel had helped her, and the more she thought about it, the more outrageous it seemed. The most reasonable explanation? AJ was part of a trap to ensnare her.

She questioned her entire thinking at this point. She wanted to help Derrick, but if her performance the past two nights was any indication, she would only make things worse.

She envisioned how painful it would be returning to James Carver Academy. The computer language wove through her thoughts like a thread in a seam. She merely needed to learn the language, with no teacher, no key, no clue, and that was just to manage the security cameras. Lines and lines of nonsense floated through her thoughts.

And then she slept.

Children's voices woke her. White ceiling, white walls, tenders, Keepers, and eleven other children. Miriam sat up in her bed but found herself in a small chair. Number Seven floated toward her, his feet a few inches off the ground. He stared at her a moment and then said, "$$$+4.34f+01.11."

Miriam said, "What? I don't understand you."

"$$$+4.34f+01.11"

Number Seven held out his hand, which she took, and he helped her to her feet.

"Understand you must," Number Seven said.

$$$+4.34f+01.11

venus [200]% CC -LANG:off IOpresent.cpp -o

venus [151]%

$$$+1.00e+00

$$$-1.23e+00

$$$+2.35e+03

= false

$$$+2.34e+01

$$$+4.53e+01

=venus [150]%

= true

=venus [201}%

$$$+4.34f+01.11

venus[oo]% CC -LANG:on IOpresent.cpp -o

venus [000.02]%

$$$+1.00c+01

$$$-1.23c+02

= false

$$$+2.35c+04

$+2.34e+001

Miriam bolted upright. She grabbed the sheets with both hands. Sweat poured over her face. She gasped for breath. The dream, real, yet surreal. Looking around, she recognized her room. No Number Seven. No tenders or Keepers. The clock read 07:05. Her alarm would sound in ten minutes.

She became fully awake, but the dream remained as real as her room. The code streamed in her mind, floating before her eyes as if displayed on a transparent screen as large as the room before her. Line after line, as if scrolling through pages at AJ Patel's desk.

She understood.

All of it.

10

Monday, March 15, James Carver Academy

BEFORE FATHER CALLED, and before Father knocked on the door, Miriam came down the stairs, showered, dressed, and ready for school. She didn't look well-rested. Yet she didn't look like she had been up half the night illegally working at Technical Service, attempting to circumvent Pacific Edge Security either. Her fatigue masked her excitement, which would have been difficult to explain.

Miriam made herself a coffee, consisting of a double espresso shot into a splash of hot water. A covered plate awaited her at the table. Steam floated from the Eggs Benedict when she lifted the cover. Derrick's favorite breakfast. She looked at Father.

"I know. Maybe it's a mistake. I wanted to make it feel like Derrick was here," Father said.

Miriam swallowed and said, "It's okay. I understand."

"You look nice today," Father said.

Miriam wore black pants, the only color pants in her wardrobe, and a white blouse with a black ribbon at the neck. She only had two white shirts, and she wasn't sure why they were in her closet. She never wore them. While working last night, she decided to stay out of the spotlight at the Academy, lie low, make no waves. She had ordered new clothes of popular colors—popular colors here were boring as hell—before coming down to breakfast. Wearing white would increase her visibility today, so her transformation would, by necessity, be slow and, therefore, would never be completed because she didn't plan to be here much longer.

"Thanks," she said.

"What's the occasion?" Father asked.

"No occasion. I want to make some changes. It's time. It's what Derrick wanted."

Father patted her knee and said, "I'm proud of you, Miriam."

Miriam nodded, forked into the eggs Benedict, and wondered what Derrick was eating this morning. Probably not eggs Benedict. However, she would have never predicted it would be a sugary cereal, which contained little nutritional value except what the milk added and didn't exist in Pacific Edge. She ate silently, and what awaited her at James Carver Academy permeated her thoughts.

Miriam called for a transport. She had run, walked, and slithered her way through Pacific Edge enough recently. Also, walking, while not forbidden, was unusual, and she needed to stop being unusual. The less attention she drew, the better. She needed to be smart. Not intellectually smart, but people-smart, not her strong suit, and she knew it.

When it came to social norms, she was dense. Like her argument with Mr. Jones in New America History, which started the entire mess that Derrick was paying for. A complete waste. What did she hope to accomplish with that argument and hundreds of others like it? She wouldn't change Mr. Jones. She wouldn't sway students to her point of view. So why did she do it? Such a waste of energy.

Previously, she had refused to contemplate her motives. Now, she couldn't avoid the obvious. She did it for Derrick. She wanted him to see Pacific Edge as she did. For reasons she couldn't explain to herself or any other person, she felt the only hope was if Derrick saw the lies. That, too, was stupid.

Stupid girl.

Being bold, contrary, and peculiar had been her persona for so long that she harbored no illusion that going with the flow would be easy. Instructors would be pleased. She was certain about that, but it would prove to be an erroneous assumption. Some students seemed to relish her arguments with instructors. Yet none of them ever supported her position. She assumed they enjoyed the entertainment. Like watching a frivolous New America Media movie. Distraction worked like a drug for the Chosen. Miriam thought she understood why. Still, she admitted that understanding people was not her gift, so she might have misjudged the entire situation.

She had no friends, which didn't bother her. She sat alone at lunch, which suited her because it gave her time to think. Thinking was what she did best, and what she enjoyed most.

The transport arrived. Miriam pulled in a deep breath of air scented with the sea and flowers and resigned herself to her new role as the door opened and a disembodied voice said, "Welcome, Miriam King. I have arrived to transport you to James Carver Academy."

The transport itself cycled through a multitude of colors, capable of displaying a color of the passenger's choice or reading the passenger's mood. She often wondered if a transport could accurately sense what a person was feeling or if it just chose a random color, and then the person decided their temperament matched the hue the transport had selected. If it were a bet, her money was on the machine choosing the color at random. If the passenger requested the color be changed, the machine probably stored the response and used it on future rides, making the passenger feel as if it could sense moods. Miriam touched the transport roof. The transport turned flat black. Okay, so maybe it could sense her mood.

Miriam commanded the robot to change the color to sky blue, which the robot did without comment. Miriam saw no one walking. Only transports slipping silently down the streets with passengers hidden behind blacked-out windows. Were they accustomed to seeing her walking and now wondered where the weird walking-girl had gone after they exiled her brother? Or had she been invisible to them as they went about their lives, just like they were oblivious to the many contradictions that surrounded them? She didn't care what thoughts they had of her, yet she wondered how they could seem reasonably intelligent but not question the world around them. She wondered why she considered herself smart yet made so many poor decisions.

She wondered about a lot of things.

At the curbside in front of James Carver Academy, Miriam waited in the transport, watching students file into the building through the front passageway. Two security staff dressed in black, including black helmets with mirrored face shields, stood guard on each side of the sidewalk. The regular security officer in his gray uniform stood in his usual spot in the middle of the swarm, greeting students with his traditional smile. Why the extra muscle at the entrance? Had something else happened? Had someone threatened the Academy? Or were they mere theatrics to send a message that disruptions wouldn't be tolerated? Miriam judged the show of force to be the latter, but then what did she know?

She knew how to talk to computers. That was something, wasn't it?

After several minutes, the transport voice said, "Miriam King has arrived at her destination. Does Miriam King require any additional destinations?"

"Okay, okay. I'm going. Stupid machine."

"No need for hostility, Miriam King."

"Stupid machine," Miriam said as she exited the transport. Once outside the transport, she saw it had turned flat black again. *Stupid machine,* she thought.

Miriam blended into the crowd as best she could and moved into the building. Inconspicuous played like a mantra in her mind. No outbursts, no scenes in the halls, classes, or cafeteria. That was her only goal today, her first day back at James Carver Academy without Derrick.

Her success lasted three minutes.

Inside the building, at the far side of the atrium, near a hallway that forked from the center like spokes of a wheel, stood Jana Somersworth. Jana was on Derrick's list of girls from which he would choose a wife. Not the right person for Derrick, but Miriam was sure that he planned to pick her. That moment was the first time Miriam realized that exile was not a complete disaster for Derrick.

Jana stood with her arms folded over her chest, her red eyes laser-focused on Miriam. Jana, who typically wore stylish clothing, wore all black, not a Miriamistic, all-black-like-statement-of-rebellion black, but a full-length black dress as one might wear to a funeral.

Miriam considered ducking down a different hallway and then circling back. But that would only prolong the inevitable and probably make matters worse. *Might as well get this over with,* Miriam thought as she dropped her eyes, slowed her pace, and walked toward Jana.

"You wanted to talk to me?" Miriam asked before Jana spoke.

"You got that much right, you little witch." Jana's neck turned red to match her eyes.

Miriam dug her fingernails into the binding of her electronic tablet. "I'm sorry about what happened to Derrick. I feel terrible."

"You feel terrible? *YOU* feel terrible? Oh, that's rich. Ruined my life, and *you feel* terrible."

Miriam's grasp tightened on her tablet, threatening to snap it in two. "He's my brother."

"I was on his list. You knew that, right? Now, I must start over. And I'm certain he was going to pick me." Jana started to cry.

Miriam saw a crowd forming around them. "I know you were on his list," Miriam said truthfully.

"Had he made his choice?" Jana sobbed.

"I don't know," Miriam said.

"Was he going to choose me?"

"I don't think so. I'm not sure though," Miriam lied. No one should have expected perfection regarding her ability to keep a low profile with so little practice.

"Why did he throw his life away? He was so thoughtless. Such a stupid thing to do."

Miriam wanted to slap her. The realization that she couldn't help Derrick if she succumbed to temptation stabilized her. "He was protecting me. He was neither thoughtless nor stupid."

"You are awful, just awful. So damn thoughtless, just like your brother."

With that, Jana Somersworth stomped off. With any luck, it would be Miriam's last encounter with her. Jana had to concentrate on getting on another boy's list and focus her mind, body, and soul on being picked in the first round. Miriam turned slowly to a group of students staring at her with blank faces. Ducking her head, she eased through them without speaking. Someone—she didn't know who—touched her softly on the shoulder as she moved through the crowd. It felt like a touch of understanding, perhaps one of kindness. She wanted to turn and see who had touched her in such a manner but did not.

In Mr. Jones's class, she sat with downcast eyes, hoping to avoid speaking. Mr. Jones said little and avoided asking Miriam questions. He gave the class a pop quiz, which had never happened before. The questions made her angry, but she answered each question with a predictable Chosen answer. After the last quiz had been handed in, Mr. Jones told the students to read the next chapter until the end of the class.

When green light bathed the classroom, and students rushed to their next class, Mr. Jones said, "Miriam, a word before you leave, please."

Miriam stood at the front of the room, waiting. Instructors did not intimidate her. Certainly, Mr. Jones did not. He was small in stature and mind. But something had changed inside her, and Mr. Jones didn't seem as small or unintelligent as before. She dreaded what was coming. Maybe because she knew she was defenseless. Her intellect, which was her only defense, was locked in a prison of her own making.

When the last student had left, Mr. Jones closed the door and stepped toward Miriam.

She took an involuntary step back and held her tablet close to her chest with folded arms.

"I'm sorry about what happened to Derrick."

Miriam surprised herself when she relaxed a little and whispered, "Thank you."

"Derrick was one of my favorite students," Mr. Jones said.

"I'm sure he was," Miriam said.

"Not for the reasons you might think. Yes, he was easy, compliant, or maybe a more accurate word is culpable."

Miriam knitted her eyebrows but said nothing.

Mr. Jones held her gaze for a moment and then lowered his eyes. "I feel responsible. I should not have argued with you that day. That's what started it, isn't it?"

Miriam noticed a tear in Mr. Jones's right eye. She surprised herself for a second time by feeling sorry for him.

"It was my fault," she said. "I started it. I should have just given you the answer you were looking for."

Mr. Jones looked up, locking eyes. The tear still there. He glanced up at the corner of the ceiling, covered his mouth with his hand, and whispered, "Never. Never blame yourself. I must do what is expected of me. But you are the only student who challenges the status quo. You, Miriam King, are my favorite student. Never change."

11

MIRIAM COULDN'T SUPPRESS A smile, wiping a bit of water from her eye, nor dismiss the bewilderment she felt as she entered the hallway, which was empty, except for Mr. Jones's next class waiting in the hall. Plus, one girl who Miriam only knew as Candice, who was also in Mr. Jones's class with Derrick and herself. No doubt Miriam would be late to her next class, as would Candice.

"May I walk with you?" Candice asked, coming alongside Miriam.

"What is your next class?" Miriam asked.

"Geology," Candice said. "I followed Derrick there every day. That's why I saw what happened."

"Saw what?" Miriam asked.

"I don't mean to make you feel worse," Candice said. "Marcus Carver grabbed Derrick right after Mr. Jones's class that day. Marcus got right in Derrick's face and threatened him."

"Threatened him?" Miriam asked.

"Yes. Marcus said, if Derrick couldn't get control of you, someone else would. Or something like that. I'm not blaming you. But you see, Derrick already thought Marcus might hurt you before the lunch thing happened."

Miriam turned right at the end of the hall. "Let's go to your class first."

"Okay. Thanks," Candice said. "I wanted to let you know. Plus, there's one other thing."

They arrived at the door to Geology. "Many of us look up to you. We're too frightened to say it."

With that, the light turned red, and Candice disappeared into the classroom.

Miriam walked to her next class. She should have hurried, but she didn't. She was already late. Nothing would change that. Her next class was literature, with Mrs. Springfield, a perpetually melancholy lady with long grayish hair worn in a bun. The literature available to Chosen students consisted of the James Carver Doctrine, various works by members of the Carver family, and a few selections written by noted members of the Chosen Hierarchy, past and present. Miriam lingered in the hall just outside the door. The door would be locked. Miriam had been late enough times to know that. Finally, she rapped lightly, and a few seconds later, Mrs. Springfield opened the door.

She smiled and said, "Come in, dear. Mr. Jones called and said he had held you over. No problems for you here."

Miriam walked in, head down, but she glanced up a few times as she made her way to her desk. A few students met her eyes: some smiled, and some glared.

"Miriam, allow me to catch you up on our discussion," Mrs. Springfield said.

"Yes, Ma'am," Miriam said, although she knew the subject was an ancient book written by a distant relative of James Carver about how to close deals. The most boring book she had ever read. It was compulsory reading. The writing was well below the grade level. She remembered the book well, like she remembered everything, which she assumed was just how everyone remembered things. This class would be easy. She could coast. No arguments.

"We were having a discussion regarding fiction. Have you heard of fiction, Miriam?"

They had never discussed fiction in literature. It had briefly been mentioned in History of New America class and only as one of the many forbidden relics of the old United States, which commoners still read. Odd that Father had mentioned it just yesterday. Miriam remained frozen, mesmerized by the eyes of peers staring, as if they were about to witness something miraculous or disastrous. Miriam was certain this was a trick, trying to get her to launch into one of her rants about how the Chosen restricted freedom and withheld truth, but she would not fall for that. Not today. Never again.

Finally, Miriam said, "It is a form of literature used in the old United States."

"Thank you, Miriam," Mrs. Springfield said.

Miriam saw the changed expressions on the faces of her peers. She was not good at reading such things, something Derrick had pointed out many times. Therefore, she didn't know what thoughts lurked behind their faces. She placed her tablet on her desk and adjusted in her seat. Still, the others stared. Those in the front twisted their positions to face her as if she might have mutated into an alien from a distant planet.

Mrs. Springfield chuckled. "That sounds like a textbook response from New America History. Not what I expected, yet understandable, given the unfortunate circumstances you have faced the past few days. We have been discussing the concept of fiction. What is it? Why was it so popular for hundreds, if not thousands, of years? Why was it bad? Was there any good in it?"

Miriam adjusted in her seat. "Okay."

"It was unfair of me to put you on the spot like that, dear. I'm sure you'll catch up with the class quickly enough." Mrs. Springfield moved to the middle of the room and faced the class. "We've talked about how fiction might be bad. Now, was there any good in it?"

Mrs. Springfield gestured to someone sitting behind Miriam.

"There was nothing good about it. That is why it is banned."

Other voices erupted, a jumble of words, which Miriam could usually sort out well enough in such situations, but today her mind drifted back to what Candice had said. *If Marcus had threatened Derrick. It was as if Marcus had set Derrick up for the courtyard encounter.* Miriam played the entire courtyard scene back in her mind. It had not escaped her at the time that Marcus had been ranting on and on. Marcus kept glancing back at the entrance as if he were waiting for someone. *Derrick was late coming to lunch. Marcus was waiting for Derrick.*

"Miriam? Miriam?" Mrs. Springfield stood over her.

"Oh, sorry, Mrs. Springfield. I didn't sleep well last night," Miriam said.

"I understand. I was asking what you thought."

"About what?" Miriam asked.

"Could anything good come from fiction?" Mrs. Springfield asked.

"I don't know. I've never read fiction." Miriam paused, then, despite promising herself she'd lie low, said, "Fiction is not banned."

Murmurs passed through the room.

"That is not what I asked," Mrs. Springfield said with a smile and then continued. "Someone said there was nothing good. That's why it is banned."

"She's a liar!" someone said from the back of the room.

Miriam couldn't associate the voice with a face, nor did she try.

Mrs. Springfield held one finger to her lips. "Let's listen to what Miriam has to say." Mrs. Springfield nodded to Miriam to continue.

"Since I've never read fiction, I don't know if there is anything good about it. But fiction is not banned. It is restricted. I do not know how it is accessed or how such a request is approved. I do not know how many fiction books are available or who decides what can be read. But I know it is not banned."

"She's a troublemaker!" This came from the same voice. Others joined.

"Silence!" Mrs. Springfield's voice rose above the din. Her placid demeanor changed. Her eyes opened wide, and her nostrils flared.

Miriam shrank back in her chair. This was the second time she had felt intimidated by an instructor, both of which occurred on the same day. First, Mr. Jones and now, Mrs. Springfield, of all people.

"That I allow spirited and open discussion does not mean I will tolerate personal attacks. Is that clear?"

Miriam swore she heard heads nodding.

"What is particularly egregious is that Miriam is telling you the truth. Which should give you pause to consider why you're attacking Miriam."

The room grew silent. Miriam resisted the urge to look around to identify the person who had called her a liar. Part of her wanted to lash out, verbally confront that person with her narrow, erroneous thinking, and part of her felt a tinge sorry for the girl, so brain-washed she couldn't think objectively. And then Derrick came to her mind, and a tear formed in the corner of Miriam's eye.

"Miriam," Mrs. Springfield said gently. "Can you think of anything that might be good about fiction?"

This was not a topic Miriam had given much thought. And right now, she had more important things to think about. Yet she sensed Mrs. Springfield was not going away quietly on the topic and wondered why. Miriam sat straight and leaned forward, elbows on her desktop, chin in her hands, thinking. *Whatever made fiction good was probably also why it was restricted.* She wondered how many fiction novels had been written and how many were available to the Chosen.

After a few minutes, Miriam lowered her hands to the desk, cleared her throat, and said, "Imagination?"

"Go on."

"In fiction, a writer could imagine things that are not true or that are not yet true."

An almost indiscernible smile emerged on Mrs. Springfield's face as she motioned for Miriam to continue.

Miriam glanced to her right and then continued, "We have not been taught much about ancient history, so now what I'm about to say is fiction." Miriam paused, thinking, then said, "But just because it is fiction, meaning that I'm making it up, does not mean that it is not true or close to true. Civilization must have been much different a long time ago. People couldn't have started with transports and flying machines or even novels. People must have shared stories verbally. Storytellers must have imagined things that were not yet real. Maybe a storyteller imagined a day when a story would be contained on the wall of a cave, and then maybe another storyteller imagined a story etched on small stones so it could be carried with the people as they moved. Maybe another person began to think of how that might look in real life and wrote the story on small flat stones, and then later, another person thought of a way to make the story easier to carry by writing it on a piece of bark or a tough leaf. And that spurred an idea and then another idea until someone had learned to make paper."

Miriam's thinking was fully engaged now. She twisted around in her seat and looked students in the eye. "Perhaps a person lives in an unpleasant situation and imagines a better life. That person can't say things are bad because people in control won't tolerate any challenge to their authority. In such a place, speaking the truth could be dangerous. So, instead, the person imagines a better life and describes it in a story so that others can share the dream, and upon seeing it, they can make it come true."

"Excellent, Miriam," Mrs. Springfield clapped her hands. "I have an assignment for the class. You shall each write a brief fiction story. Between 500 and 1000 words."

A murmur drifted through the room. A boy raised his voice behind Miriam. "Fiction? How do we do that?"

Mrs. Springfield laughed. "You make it up! Use your imagination."

"Imagination?" asked another.

"Yes, yes. Maybe you're a young girl who meets a friendly dragon."

"Dragon?"

Mrs. Springfield raised her arms like wings and hissed. "It's a large flying lizard that breathes fire!"

Mrs. Springfield floated across in front of the room, spinning a circle. "Maybe space aliens attack the planet."

"Space aliens?"

Mrs. Springfield waved at the ceiling. "Creatures from other planets. Or maybe someone builds a sailboat and sails to faraway lands. Have fun with it. No one will see it except for you and me."

"Is this even legal?" The first girl asked.

"No one will see it except you and me."

The students were to work on their fiction stories during the rest of the class. Miriam, like others, sat thinking, but Miriam's thoughts differed from those of her peers. She worried about the dangers of this assignment, and she never thought about making stuff up, lying on purpose. She only thought about exposing lies. Lies were bad. Yet maybe she had not analyzed that thoroughly. Lies that were portrayed as truth were bad. But that wasn't quite right because all lies were used to distort the truth. Perhaps fiction isn't the same as lying. That sounded right. Fiction wasn't true, yet it was just imagination.

She pondered this. But why? Entertainment. That made sense. It could be entertaining.

That explained it. Yet, somehow, she sensed there was more. She had said in some situations, a person might tell a story because it was too dangerous to confront those in power. She dwelled on that for a moment. So, fiction could be used to communicate forbidden thoughts and ideas. Miriam believed that what they showed on New America Media wasn't accurate. That meant it was fiction but was presented to be truth because it served a purpose for those in power. Fiction could also be used to tell the truth through stories. This felt important and deserved more thought.

However, she couldn't shake her apprehension regarding this assignment. Normally, she would have been thrilled to make up a story, perhaps exposing a New America lie in a way that made others think. That was what she wanted. For people to think.

This was no coincidence. Miriam was sure of that. But how could Mrs. Springfield know Father had told her about novels? One of the favorite phrases of the Chosen is that everything happens for a reason. The Chosen have been told that everything, every day, their entire existence, had all preordained. If they just went with the flow, did what they were told, asked no questions, they couldn't go wrong.

But that wasn't true. Things could go wrong. Become ill, get injured, get exiled like Derrick, but when any unpleasant events occurred, it was because the person had gone astray. That's what they were told. Miriam didn't buy it. And she didn't buy that this fiction assignment was a coincidence or fate or that it would work for good should she submit a story that reflected what she believed. It must be a trap. Now, she had to determine how not to be ensnared.

When the room glowed green and the students stirred from their chairs, Mrs. Springfield stood near the door, smiling, and said, "Have fun with your assignment. And avoid discussing this assignment outside of class. Okay?"

Miriam, determined not to linger, uncharacteristically edged herself into the horde streaming from the room. Before she could ease through the door, Mrs. Springfield said, "May I speak with you, Miriam, before you leave?"

Miriam extracted herself from the throng and stood by Mrs. Springfield's desk. Mrs. Springfield continued, smiling and nodding to the other students as they passed. Miriam wondered what trouble she was in now. Second class, second teacher who wanted to speak with her privately. She hoped this didn't continue all day. The word of her private teacher conversations would get around the school quicker than rain wets a road, and with as many theories as to the reasons for those conversations as there are raindrops in a storm.

When the last student had left, Mrs. Springfield closed the door and whispered, "Don't be frightened, Miriam, but be careful what you say in your story. Keep it non-accusatory, low-key. Bland might be the right word. Do you understand? The assignment is not for you. It's for the others. Just a little nudge, if you know what I mean."

Miriam studied Mrs. Springfield's face. Her smile seemed genuine, flowing not only from her mouth but from her eyes. Miriam couldn't recall Mrs. Springfield ever looking so thrilled with something. It was weird. "Uh, sort of. Maybe."

"I just don't want you taking any unnecessary chances, my dear. Maybe just a children's tale. Something light-hearted. Okay?"

"Sure," Miriam said.

"I know you don't understand this, not yet anyway, but in this small introduction to fiction, thinking outside the ordinary, my goal is for the students to begin understanding what some of us yearn for in Derrick and you. Been yearning for… well, for years."

"What? What do you want from Derrick and me?"

"Hope. For the first time in a long time. Hope."

12

MIRIAM SELDOM FELT CONFUSED. She might lack knowledge, but that meant she had not yet found specific information. But as she moved down the hall to the next class, she felt confused as hell. Two teachers, one who she thought hated her, the other as benign as a bare white wall, had chameleoned right in front of her eyes. The most likely answer to this change in behavior was to trick her into saying or doing something the Tribunal could use against her. A plot. That made sense. It didn't even anger her because it was the logical thing to do. She couldn't be angry about logic.

Logically, neither Mr. Jones nor Mrs. Springfield could genuinely express support. Genuine things must be based on facts, data, and logic, all of which told her that Jones and Springfield were setting her up. Miriam didn't enjoy basing rational decisions on feelings. Feelings were for abstract things. She understood that. What she didn't understand was why she felt Mr. Jones and Mrs. Springfield were being honest in their show of support.

The rest of the morning passed without incident. She strove to be invisible and settled for being silent. She planned to skip lunch and spend that time in the library with headphones and the volume set at zero while some lame New America Media educational video played. But when lunchtime came, she was starving. Starving was not the best condition in which to confront the rest of the day, so she went to lunch. On the way, she realized that Marcus Carver was not in the first period, which provided a little comfort, albeit unwarranted.

Miriam grabbed a tray, selected a sandwich and salad, and went to the far corner of the courtyard, where she sat alone with her back to the shrubs and flowers. Eating alone was Miriam's regular and preferred routine. Given the events of last week, she was sure that eating alone wouldn't prove difficult. Once an unpopular girl, she was now a pariah. Then she saw Rebekah Ford walking straight toward her.

Rebekah skipped the part where one asks if she can join, omitted the part where one exchanges pleasantries, dropped her tray on the table, and then plunked down opposite Miriam. Rebekah's eyes were red and her nose raw. Reading emotions had never been Miriam's strong suit, yet she didn't think Rebekah's feelings were like those of Jana Somersworth. Miriam took a bite, studying Rebekah with curiosity.

Rebekah took a drink of her soda, and then said, "Anything from Derrick?"

Miriam swallowed. "No."

"Nothing?"

Miriam shook her head.

"Damn it," Rebekah said.

Miriam said, "Honest, I have not heard anything."

"That wasn't directed at you. I hoped you might know something. Do you know where he is?"

"No."

"Damn."

They ate silently for a few minutes. Studying each other as if trying to make a decision.

As Rebekah finished her salad, she said, "Do you think he's okay? They would tell your parents if something happened, right?"

"I think so. He's okay. At least, I feel he is." Miriam wondered why she had said that last part.

It made no sense to say something like that. Feelings again. Damn it.

13

Monday, March 15, Evening

AT DINNER, MIRIAM CONTINUED HER new practice of keeping her mouth shut. Father and Mother cooperated, remaining quiet themselves, as deep in thought as she was. However, she was running the computer code in her mind, prewriting the script she believed would eliminate her image from the security cameras, allowing her safe passage to and from Technical Service. She assumed her parents were thinking about Derrick. If she could have read their thoughts, it would have saved her a lot of time. After dinner, she went to her room. She wanted to sleep before she left but was sure she wouldn't rest. She fell asleep when her head hit the pillow.

The sound of Mother's voice calling her name, floating like a dandelion seed, drifted into her consciousness. The room wasn't right. Not her bedroom. Not Mother, her Keeper. Mother before Mother became Mother. A dream, yet she felt as if she awakened in the dream and the dream became reality.

Mother stroked her hair. "You slept so soundly."

Miriam pushed the Keeper's hand away.

"I've asked them to let us take you home. Would you like that?" The Keeper asked.

Miriam tried to speak but couldn't. She shook her head.

"No? Oh, but we would have so much fun. You are a special girl, Number Six. When we leave here, you would have a name. I'd call you, Miriam."

Miriam sat straight up in her bed. Her nightshirt soaked. The room, dark except for the clock's glow, 11:45 p.m. *Damn dreams. Why did she keep having them? Was Number Seven in her dream? She didn't remember seeing him.* That caused her stomach to twist into a knot. *Why was her Keeper Mother? Her Keeper had always been Father. Number Seven's Keeper had always been Mother.*

She stumbled to her sink and splashed water on her face. She stared at her reflection in the mirror as her mind cleared. *Stupid dream.* The dream faded. Miriam tried to hang on to it, analyze it, but it disappeared. It seemed real, but now she couldn't remember it. Something about a Keeper taking her home. But this was her home. Always had been her home. Except in the dreams.

It was a little early for her trip to Technical Service. She ordered coffee, changed into her black clothing, and donned her black hooded sweatshirt. It wouldn't hurt to be early. She was confident she understood how to write a code that would eliminate her image from the security cameras and recorded data. That would be a good night's work.

Tuesday, March 16, 12:05 a.m.

Miriam crawled through her bathroom window, dropped to the driveway, and made her way to Technical Services. She pulled the hood of her sweatshirt up, even though she didn't think it would matter after tonight. She entered the code at the door and eased the door open. With the door cracked open, she listened. All was quiet except the machines. She tiptoed to AJ Patel's door, inserted the key, and stepped inside. She logged into the computer as Maranda Kingston.

She checked her e-mail. There was one message. Not from Derrick, which she didn't expect, but still felt disappointed. The message was from AJ Patel, who wanted to know if she had fixed the cameras. She closed it and moved deeper into the computer's system until she found the code for the security cameras. On the other monitor, she opened the security camera recordings and found the recording from the first camera on the first day she entered the Technical Service Building.

Concentrating on the code, Miriam didn't hear the voices until they were just outside AJ Patel's door. The lights were off, and she hoped the light from the monitors was not noticeable at the door's threshold. She stopped typing. Held her breath. The doorknob rattled.

"Looks like Patel shut off his lights."

"Yep. No problems noted. We're in the clear."

"Door's locked."

"We deserve coffee. I'll buy."

"I'll take you up on that."

Miriam breathed and returned to the code. It was taking her longer than anticipated. If she only deleted the few seconds when she appeared on the street, it would be simple. But, if she did that, the clock would jump forward several seconds and the camera would be out of sync. Not a big problem, unless someone watched it. Then it would be a problem. Low risk of that happening. But Miriam decided shortcuts were a bad idea. She had one shot at this. If they caught her, Derrick was screwed. She had to make her image disappear while the clock continued to run. That took more code.

She started the recording and watched herself walking on the street. The hood kept her face concealed. She must be the only person to have watched this recording, or security would have been going crazy. Then, she updated the system with the new code. She refreshed the video recording, held her breath, and tapped play. She watched the clock glide through the time during which she had moved through the camera's field of view. No hooded girl in black. She'd done it.

Now, she needed to do the same thing to the other recordings and then write the code into the system so she wouldn't be recorded on her way to and from her new job. Lots of code. It was exhausting. She wouldn't learn how to copy and paste for a few days yet. The writing got faster, but she could have limited the changes to only a line or two had she known about copy and paste.

When she entered the last line of code, she was 30 minutes late heading home. *Damn it.* She moved through the building silently, hearing voices but not encountering anyone. She wrote the code for a narrow window in time, which meant she must come and go at specific times, which she screwed up this morning, and she would have to fix again tomorrow night. *Damn it.*

The morning air felt cool and smelled of the ocean. She tugged her hood up, covering her head. If she had been faster, she could have left the hood down. If she had left on time, there would be no recording of her movements. Because she was late, there would be more code writing for that again tomorrow. If she had been faster, she would be invisible to the cameras right now. But she was not invisible to the cameras this morning.

And she was not invisible to the eyes watching her from a second-floor window.

14

Tuesday, March 16, Morning

MIRIAM SLEPT AN HOUR AND then got ready for school. Her image in the mirror revealed bloodshot eyes with darkened areas underneath. She looked like she felt, or did she feel like she looked? Laboring down the stairs, she took a piece of toast from Father's plate, gave him a crumb kiss on the top of his head, headed out the door, climbed into the awaiting transport without selecting a color, and rode to school. The first call for class was in progress as she exited the transport. In an entirely un-Miriam-like fashion, she ran to avoid being late.

Marcus Carver sat in her first-period class. He didn't look injured. Medical procedures for the Chosen, they were told, were quite advanced compared to the old United States or the commoner world. Still, she wanted him to be injured. Marcus glared at her as she entered the room. She could not see her own scowl but thought it likely surpassed the loathing displayed in his eyes. Because she had work to do to reach Derrick, she hoped he didn't start anything with her. Yet she hoped he did. She was unsure what she would do but was certain it wouldn't be pretty.

Glancing to her right, she saw Mr. Jones standing at the front of the room. Mr. Jones was a weaselly sort, which was the best description Miriam could muster. But this morning, he looked like a rabid weasel who might inflict a brutal wound if challenged. Jones focused his newfound animalistic intensity on Marcus Carver. When Jones noticed Miriam enter, the corner of his lip turned up, and his eyes warmed. She felt as if she had awoken in an alternate universe. She took a seat in the back of the class, which forced Marcus to twist around to see her. While maintaining a low profile, she intended to make Marcus Carver uncomfortable in every way imaginable whenever the occasion presented itself. She suddenly questioned whether both were possible.

In accordance with her plan, Miriam remained silent.

Then Mr. Jones said this: "A few days ago, Miriam and I had a, let's call it, a spirited discussion about the age of the Earth."

Jones stepped to the back of the room and stood behind Miriam. She felt him there, within inches of her. *Please don't do this. Not now. I have too much to do. Too much to lose.*

"I followed Academy teaching guidelines. However, I didn't handle the discussion well. I became defensive. I do not want to discourage questioning minds. Our very survival may depend on them someday." Jones paused and then moved in front of Miriam. "Miriam, I want to apologize for how I handled our discussion."

Miriam said nothing. She nodded. Mr. Jones smiled. Something had changed. From that moment forward, Miriam could not reconstruct how Mr. Jones had ever seemed weaselly to her.

Mr. Jones returned to the front of the class. "For the remainder of the class. I want you to review your digital New America History textbook and formulate a question. The question must be something that you do not understand or have never heard asked or answered, or something that does not make sense to you. For example, Miriam asked why we can't read what scientists in the old United States thought about the age of the Earth. I may not answer your questions, but for this exercise, the answer is immaterial. It is the question that's important. Because without questions, there can be no answers. Would you agree, Miriam?"

Everyone twisted in their seats and looked at her.

Miriam said nothing but nodded in agreement.

A girl named Julie raised her hand at the front of the room.

"Yes, Julie?"

"Mr. Jones, is it okay for us to ask such questions? Uh, we have been told that questioning the Chosen Doctrine is heresy."

Mr. Jones rubbed his chin with his left hand and nodded. "I understand your concern."

Another student said, "Are we going to be in trouble if we do this assignment?"

"No one will be in trouble. Tell you what. If you are uncomfortable with the assignment, you do not have to voice your question. If you ask a question, it is merely a question. You are not challenging the Chosen Doctrine, only formulating a question. For example, you might ask, 'Why is it called the Chosen Doctrine? Why not the Preferred Doctrine or

Assigned Doctrine or Controlled Doctrine?" We will not debate. It's only a question. Does that help?"

Whispers drifted through the room. Mr. Jones made no attempt to stifle the discontent. Instead, he rocked slightly from heel to toe, smiling.

Miriam stared at her desk but didn't scroll through the pages of New American History. She could recite it even if she didn't believe it. Perplexed, she wondered how to comply with Mr. Jones's assignment without asking a question that was too controversial. Every question circulating through her thoughts was like a ticking bomb. *What percentage of scientists agreed on things like the age of the Earth? Scientists must be responsible for the technology we use in Pacific Edge. Why are we not taught about it? Why are the Chosen leaders afraid of science?* Tick, tick, tick.

When the class ended, students seemed reluctant to leave, except for Marcus Carver. He stood, turned, glared at Miriam, and acted as if he were about to say something. Then he turned, pushed a kid out of his way, and headed for the door.

Marcus had just reached the door when Mr. Jones said, "Marcus, a word, please."

Miriam was the last person, other than Marcus, to exit the classroom, which was by design. She looked back at Marcus, his face red. She glared. She wondered what Mr. Jones would say to him. Perhaps let him in on the trap that was being set? The door closed, and Miriam turned into the hallway to see Jana Somersworth leaning against the hallway wall, clutching her tablet against her chest. Jana's eyes were no longer red. She pushed off the wall and walked toward Miriam. Miriam thought for a moment that Jana intended to slam into her, but Jana veered at the last moment.

Jana leaned in and said, "Witch. You'll get yours."

Heat rose in Miriam's chest, and she started to respond and then stopped herself. *Not worth it. Selfish bitch.*

Walking behind a trio of giggling girls, Rebekah Ford came alongside Miriam.

Give me a break, Miriam thought. Stealing a sideways glance, she recoiled because Rebekah looked like hell. Her hair was unwashed and showed minimal effort from a brush or comb. Her eyes had black bags underneath, as if she had not slept in days.

"Sit with me at lunch," Rebekah said. It was not a request.

"I want to be left alone," Miriam replied.

"Sorry. That's not going to happen. Sit with me. I'm not going to bite."

"You say that now."

Rebekah smiled, just a little. "See you at lunch."

* * *

Mrs. Springfield smiled as Miriam walked in. Miriam thought Mrs. Springfield looked different. Younger, prettier, but that didn't seem possible that the woman could have transformed overnight. Perhaps it was Miriam who had changed. Students paused in front of her, tapping on their tablets and then handing them to Mrs. Springfield.

Oh, crap. The story. I forgot about the damn story.

When Miriam stood before Mrs. Springfield, she said, "Sorry, Mrs. Springfield. I didn't write my story."

The smile faded. "I so looked forward to your story. You are not the only one. I'll give you and the others time today while I look at the ones that have been turned in."

Miriam took her seat. She opened the word processing application. It would have been much easier to have dictated the story. Now, she would have to type it on the screen. That was not a problem. She had become good at typing. She had been typing all night in a different language.

Fiction. That, too, seemed like a new language. Facts were her native tongue. Not make-believe crap. She had no idea what to write. And whatever she wrote, it had to be safe. *Trap. Springfield and Jones had conspired to set a trap for me. Or maybe the Tribunal had assigned the task. Possibly, the Tribunal offered a reward.* Then Miriam had an idea.

She started to write.

At lunchtime, Miriam didn't see Rebekah Ford, which offered her some relief. Miriam sat as far from others as possible, with her back to the wall. Her relief didn't last long. Rebekah entered the courtyard. She didn't go for food but walked straight toward Miriam.

"You're not going to eat?" Miriam asked, hoping Rebekah would go for a tray and reduce the time they spent together.

"I don't feel well."

"You don't look well," Miriam said a little too quickly.

"Thanks."

"You should go home."

"I plan to, but I had to talk to you first. This seems like a good way to do it. You don't have many friends, so we should always be alone here."

"Thanks," Miriam said.

"What are you going to do?"

"Do about what?" Although Miriam was not good at reading people, she was sure Rebekah meant what was she going to do about helping Derrick, but there were so many other things Rebekah could ask about: what are you going to do about your fiction story, what are you going to do about the trap Jones and Springfield are setting, what are you going to do about Marcus Carver, what are you going to do at Technical Service. Fortunately, Rebekah didn't know about Technical Service.

Rebekah rolled her bloodshot eyes. "About helping Derrick."

Miriam took a bite of the tuna sandwich she had selected from the lunch buffet. She didn't like tuna. She wasn't sure why she had taken it. After a few moments and a swallow, she said, "I don't know."

"You have no plan?" Rebekah's voice rose an octave on the word plan.

Miriam considered her response. This was starting to feel like another trap. Perhaps Rebekah had offered her services to the Tribunal as revenge. If Miriam were in Rebekah's situation, it would make sense to do that. "I want to help him, but I don't know how."

Rebekah's jaw muscles tensed. She stood and said, "Someone has to help him. If not you, then who?" Rebekah walked away. After a few steps, she turned and said, "See you at lunch tomorrow."

15

Wednesday, March 17, 12:01 a.m.

MIRIAM CLEANED THE POTATOES OFF THE camera, pointed at the driveway, and then scrambled down the rain chain and onto the driveway. She breathed the crisp night air. Pacific Edge rested silently, except for the crashing waves to the west. She loved that sound and the sight of the ocean, which offered a sense of freedom she had not experienced. Derrick was free now, although he probably had sealed himself in the living area that Father arranged, yet freer than he had ever been in Pacific Edge. She wore the same black clothing, including the black-hooded sweatshirt, but did not pull the hood up this time. No need. She was on time, and the cameras were ignoring her. Invisible. Or so she believed.

Intellectually, she knew that believing something didn't make it so. Later, she would understand it in practical application. She thought about her primary focus after she erased her image from yesterday's trip home. Options swirled in her mind like a kaleidoscope until she couldn't focus on any of them. *Keep it simple,* she told herself. *One bite at a time.* Get out of Pacific Edge, but on her own terms, and then she could help Derrick. Time was important, but this wouldn't happen fast. The Tribunal gave Derrick 30 days. He would be safe during the study period. Twenty-five days remained before Derrick was thrust into the commoner school.

But how to help him? She knew nothing about commoners or the world in which they lived. She had as much to learn about the commoners as did Derrick. Still, she didn't know what she needed to learn. You can't know what you don't know. Consumed by spinning thoughts, she almost smacked into the wall. She remembered nothing about her walk there. A security patrol could have flown right over, and she wouldn't have known. One mental note made. She had to pay attention. A slip could end her plan, which wasn't a plan yet, just a vague notion of helping her brother. The one who didn't like her.

The back door clicked open. Miriam eased her head in. Silent. She made her way to AJ Patel's office, making note of details she had previously overlooked. For example, down the adjacent hall from the common work area was a room with an espresso machine and snack and soda vendors. *Cool.* She made herself a double-shot espresso and got a bag of mixed nuts. Apparently, they provided snacks to employees, which technically included her as Maranda Kingston. She saw no cameras in the room. Evidently, employees didn't have a limit on snacks and sodas.

Back in Patel's office, she sipped espresso and wrote code. Eliminating her image from the trip home yesterday morning took an hour and two minutes. Not bad. When she finished her first task, she made her second decision regarding priorities. She had to learn more about what the computer system did besides sending electronic messages and monitoring security cameras. First, she needed another espresso, which she fetched, along with a candy bar she had never seen. Back at the computer, lights off, door locked, she rocked back in AJ Patel's leather chair and studied the monitors. She opened the e-mail application and found an assortment of messages that went out to all employees. She scanned them but found nothing interesting because she was only concerned about getting out of Pacific Edge and finding Derrick. As a temporary employee, she wouldn't make it to the summer picnic, although she found it interesting that the employees had such an activity. For a moment, she thought about what it would be like to be there, chat with AJ, meet his family, reunite with Samantha Bell. *"Hi, great to see you. Sorry, they booted you out. Me? Not much, just breaking into buildings and trying to escape."*

There was a round blue thing that looked like a compass she had seen on maps. She clicked on it. A plain white screen with a drawing centered over a white rectangular box appeared. Under the box, the word search. What would a person search for on a computer? It turned out quite a lot.

First, she typed the word map. A list of options, different maps, she assumed, were listed. Over four billion in 22 seconds, according to the screen. Who needed four billion maps, it didn't say. She picked one, and a map opened as if one were looking down on the Earth. The map showed a blurred image of a small city on the coast and superimposed the words Pacific Edge over the city. Miriam thought it was a poor map service to produce such a blurry image. Using the mouse, she zoomed the image in. Still blurry, there was a blue dot that appeared to represent the Technical Service Building. Then she zoomed out. Once the image expanded, everything beyond the city of Pacific Edge became clear.

She zoomed out farther. The coastline expanded. The map filled with a spiderweb of yellow lines and green blotches. The green areas were labeled as either a national forest or a national park. The names of towns popped up on the map. She wondered if Derrick lived in one of them. She would e-mail him tonight and ask about his location.

She saw Pacific Edge was in an area called California, which was a name she did not recognize. Zooming back in, Miriam studied the area around Pacific Edge. There appeared to be three roads entering Pacific Edge: one north, one east, and one south, where the ocean created the western border. She already knew that. The wall surrounding Pacific Edge appeared to be a single continuous building, except for the western border, which was guarded by the ocean. She was in the southern part of the building. Beyond the building, on all sides, was a town larger than Pacific Edge. This must be where the commoners lived who provided services for the Chosen. However, the size of the city seemed larger than the number of people needed for Pacific Edge.

In the bottom left-hand corner, she saw a small box titled satellite. She clicked on it and the map changed. It filled with colors and looked like an actual picture. She could see details, and the yellow lines became streets. Names of streets and buildings appeared. She moved the map around and saw schools and hospitals and parks and even weird-looking transports on the streets. Fascinating. When was this picture taken? The city appeared to be intact and orderly. Not the bombed-out visions shown on New America Media. She had concluded that New America Media was fake. This map supported her conclusion.

She heard voices in the hall and recognized them to be the same two security guards. Right on time, but today, she relaxed. The door was locked, and the lights were off. No worries, except she was ready for another espresso, and now she'd have to wait. She typed the word satellite into the search box. There were images and explanations. Small flying machines orbiting the Earth. They took pictures that made the map and many other things, such as communications, military applications, media, etc. Word after word, Miriam explored the world outside Pacific Edge with this astonishing application.

Thirty minutes had passed, and she thought it was safe to get another espresso. Sleeping didn't concern her, and coffee didn't keep her awake. She didn't know what to expect when she started, although she had anticipated there was much to learn. However, she didn't foresee what she had found. The amount of information appeared to be infinite. *Who wrote all this stuff? Where was it stored? Why don't the Chosen have access to it?* She knew the answer to the last question but still found it hard to comprehend.

She eased the door open. Silent. The security guys were gone. She walked to the common area, paused, and scanned the cubicles, listening for sounds of others being present. Silent. She hurried to the room that contained the snacks and coffee. Thinking hard again, so many things to do and so little time. Although there was a small window in the door to the coffee room, she didn't look inside. She threw the door open and strode to the espresso machine.

Halfway across the room, she froze.

Two uniformed men sat at a table.

Staring at her.

16

MIRIAM TOOK A DEEP BREATH and proceeded to the espresso machine, hoping she looked more confident than she felt.

"You startled me," Miriam said, filling a cup with a double shot.

"Who are you? What are you doing here?"

"I'm Maranda Kingston. I work here."

"You look too young to work here."

"Yeah, I get that a lot everywhere I go. Part of the reason I'm here only at night. Easier that way."

"Okay," one man drawled. "Working on what, exactly?"

"Uh, well, secret stuff. That's the other reason I work nights. Easier that way."

One man stood up. "Can I see your ID?"

Miriam sipped the steaming espresso. Thinking. "My bad. I forgot it at home. I'm bad about that. Because I work at night, on secret stuff, I rarely wear my ID."

"You're supposed to always wear your ID. It's the policy."

Another sip. "True. But because of the secret stuff, it's better if people don't know I'm here or who I am."

To make this work, Miriam needed to act the opposite of a person there illegally. She walked to their table and sat down.

"Hope you don't mind. It gets kind of lonely being here alone."

The standing man sat. "I suppose it would."

"So, here's the deal. This is a problem. I should have checked the room before I walked in. Sorry."

"What's a problem?"

"That you know I'm here. Because of the secret stuff. I'm supposed to report it. They will probably move you both to another town. Sorry."

"Move us? Who will move us?"

"Headquarters. Because of the secret stuff. Not your fault. They'll take care of everything. You'll probably be back on the job someplace else tomorrow night."

"You mean someplace else, like another duty assignment here?"

Miriam shook her head. "No, probably across the country. Because of ..."

"The secret stuff." The man finished her sentence.

"Yep. Sorry, guys." Miriam sipped coffee.

Both men turned pale. The fellow who had remained seated stared at the table and said, "I can't. I can't move. My daughter is playing the lead role in the school play. It will break her heart."

Miriam thought she saw tears in his eyes.

The other man said, "Can't we keep this between us? A secret. We don't care what you are working on. And we can help you. Warn you if someone comes in during the night. That sort of thing."

Miriam sat back. "Not sure. That would be against policy."

"Like not wearing your ID?"

"You got me there."

"You could take your break with us. That way, you wouldn't be alone. What do you say? Moving would be hard on our families."

"You guys can keep a secret?"

"Hey, we're security people. Secrets are our business."

"You can't tell anyone. Not a supervisor, not your wives, nobody. And if anybody ever asks, you never saw me. Because if you admit you knew I was here and didn't report it, you'd be worse than fired."

Both men nodded as if they understood what worse than fired meant. Perhaps they did.

"Right," one man offered. "We're screwed either way. If we report you, then they'll move us. If we don't report it and admit it later, well, we all know what that would mean."

Miriam nodded, although she did not know what that meant but accepted it wouldn't be good.

"Deal," she said. "Now, I need to get back to work. I need both of your e-mail addresses."

"What do you need those for?"

"Because I'll send you both an e-mail to prove that I'm Maranda Kingston. Because you are security people." She winked.

Both men relaxed and recited their e-mail addresses.

"You want to write those down?"

"No, I've got it."

"Are you one of those child prodigies?"

"Something like that."

Back in AJ Patel's office, Miriam collapsed in the chair, placed her elbows on the desk, and cradled her head in her hands. She trembled, and for a moment, thought she might heave the coffee. After a few minutes, she started to sob. Tears ran freely down her cheeks, landing on the desk. Her carelessness had almost ended any chance of helping Derrick. However, the opportunity may have ended, and she just didn't know it yet. The security guards seemed to buy her subterfuge, but they might have been going along until they could report her presence to the proper people. No choice now but to move forward.

Miriam wiped her tears. She opened the e-mail application and addressed an e-mail to both men.

```
TO:
bradhendricks@pacificedge.com/security
martywashington@pacificedge.com/security

Gentlemen,

Maranda Kingston here. Sending you this
e-mail to confirm that I am legit. Feel
free to e-mail me. Or if you're ready for
coffee, just rap on AJ Patel's door. I'm
here from 12:15 a.m. to 4:30 a.m.

It was a pleasure to meet you. Glad I'll
have someone to chat with on break.

Maranda Kingston
```

Miriam had lost her train of thought. She was not sure what to do next. She opened the search thing and stared at the empty box. And then a thought occurred to her. She typed fiction in the search box. The first item on the next screen was a definition:

```
    Fiction:
    Noun
    Literature in the form of prose,
 especially short stories, and novels,
 which describes imaginary events and
 people.
```

Miriam wondered if commoners had access to fiction or if that was another myth. She went back to the search page and entered: fiction novels. The next page showed a line of pictures, which were book covers. There seemed to be no shortage. She typed: where to find novels. The search results indicated commoners could find fiction novels in many places. There were stores that had nothing but books. Miriam read the descriptions of several novels. Some places even let one read the first few pages. To read more, purchase was necessary.

She lost track of time.

When she glanced at the time on the top right-hand side of the screen, her mouth fell open: 4:20. She almost missed her deadline, which would have screwed up her security camera fix. And what had she accomplished? Virtually nothing, except walking in on security guards during their break. Determined to have done something worthwhile, she went to the security page and found an icon labeled 1984. When she clicked on the link, a screen showed a line drawing of Pacific Edge. Glowing green dots filled the town. She zoomed out enough to include the surrounding commoner community.

The surrounding community had no green dots, except one.

A single green dot inside the Technical Service Building.

The clock read 4:30.

17

WITHOUT CHECKING FOR SECURITY STAFF, Miriam rushed to the exit. One minute and 45 seconds late, which didn't seem like much, but she had a two-minute window per camera. Walking from one camera's field of vision to the next took one minute and 52 seconds. When she modified the computer code that operated the security cameras, it seemed best to keep the time span short and her movements precise. Not a smart decision.

A million stars glistened above her as she jogged through the first two cameras and then slowed to a fast walk. A cool breeze caressed her hair and carried ocean mist that saturated her face, wrapping her like a soft, moist blanket. On a normal day, the breeze and the ocean scent would have lifted her spirits. Today, she thought nothing would lift the weight that felt like it would crush her flat. She wanted to be with Derrick. She would find a way to help him if she could find a way to get to him. The only accomplishments she had made so far were to cause his exile, walk-in on two security guards, and almost miss her scheduled time to avoid detection.

Stupid girl. How is such a stupid girl going to help anybody?

Then there was 1984. Had she not goofed around looking up stupid stuff like fiction, she would have found 1984 earlier and learned more about it. Speaking of fiction, she needed to finish her story for Mrs. Springfield's class. *Stupid, stupid, stupid.*

Beyond looking up irrelevant stuff like fiction, she had spent her time making a half-assed fix on the security cameras, only to learn 1984 was tracking her 24 hours a day, seven days a week.

Then she stopped. Right in the middle of the street.

Was 1984 tracking Derrick?

For a moment, she considered running back to Technical Service to see if Derrick showed up in the 1984 program. She wanted to go back but realized that would be dumber than the other things she had done tonight. She checked the time and jogged to the middle of the next block. She quickened her pace, but not because she was behind schedule. She felt as if someone had lifted a boulder from her shoulders. If 1984 was tracking Derrick, she could learn his location. An involuntary smile formed on her face. The ability to learn Derrick's location comforted her. She wouldn't have felt comforted had she known about the eyes watching her.

If 1984 was tracking Derrick, she needed to warn him. She had planned to send him an e-mail tonight, but no, she wasted time looking at fiction instead. Her mood darkened again. That she wanted to e-mail Derrick but had failed to do so made the hole in her chest grow a little. That she was having too much fun playing with crap on her new computer filled her eyes with tears. Up onto her roof, through her window, and onto her bed, she sobbed until she slept.

Wednesday, March 17, James Carver Academy

Miriam sat in a transport outside the Academy, watching students enter the building. Best to wait until she had just enough time to reach her first class without being late. That would limit anyone's ability to intercept her before class. She had no strategy for walking from class to class or during lunch. One step at a time. Scanning the students, she didn't see Jana Somersworth, Rebekah Ford, or Marcus Carver. Because she planned to torment Marcus Carver, his absence was a small letdown. Miriam didn't think she'd see Rebekah Ford until lunch. That's when Rebekah said they would meet. Miriam thought that when Rebekah said she would do something, it would happen.

Miriam left the transport and entered the building. Outside her first class, she saw Jana Somersworth laughing and talking with a boy Miriam didn't know. *Looks like they assigned Jana a new potential husband,* Miriam thought.

Jana glared at Miriam.

"Good morning, Jana. Surprised to see you in such good spirits so soon," Miriam said.

Jana said nothing.

"Good morning, Miriam," Mr. Jones said.

"Morning," Miriam said.

Marcus Carver sat in the second to the last row this morning. The last row was filled. He had learned his lesson yesterday and wouldn't give Miriam an advantage this morning. Marcus had outsmarted her, or so he thought.

Miriam walked toward Marcus but didn't make eye contact. She stopped beside the boy sitting behind Marcus. She stared at the boy. His name was Mike or Michael or Mitch, something like that. Mike/Michael/Mitch glanced at her. She nodded her head to one side: *Move it.* After several seconds, Mike/Michael/Mitch slid out of his seat and Miriam sat.

Marcus squirmed. Miriam smiled.

Mr. Jones showed a New America documentary, or propaganda reel, in Miriam's opinion. She'd seen it before. She didn't need to see it again, which was good because it gave her time to work on her fiction story that was overdue in Mrs. Springfield's class. Yesterday, she started but didn't like where it was going. Now, she didn't have a single idea of what to write. She liked facts. Plus, she had never read fiction until previewing novels during her last technical service visit. But she had watched a lot of fiction. Like the documentary Mr. Jones was playing.

When the New America documentary ended, Mr. Jones asked, "Miriam? Any thoughts on this story?"

Miriam looked up from her tablet. "I'm sorry, Mr. Jones. I wasn't paying attention. To be honest, I was working on an assignment for the next class."

Mr. Jones nodded, rubbed his chin, and didn't speak for a moment. "How about you, Marcus? What are your thoughts?"

Marcus set his tablet on his desk and sat up straight. "It shows that commoners are savages. It demonstrates that were it not for the protection provided by New America, we would all die painful deaths." Marcus twisted his head, looking at Miriam from the corner of his eye.

A voice in Miriam's head said, *don't do it*, but her hand raised anyway.

Mr. Jones smiled and sat on the edge of his desk. "Yes, Miriam."

She wondered why Mr. Jones was acting so weird. Normally, he avoided Miriam rather than seeking her input. She considered asking if she could use the restroom.

"Miriam? You had a comment?"

"Well, I was thinking. Is there any way to corroborate the documentary?"

"Interesting question. Class? Anyone wish to comment on Miriam's question?"

The hands of a third of the class shot up.

Mr. Jones pointed at a boy in the front row.

"Textbooks. The textbooks corroborate the documentary."

"Thank you, Tim."

Mr. Jones pointed to a girl.

"Daily news stories. We see them all the time. A person would have to be completely stupid not to know the savagery of the commoners is on the news all the time." She turned in her seat and glared at Miriam.

Miriam saw several heads nod in agreement.

Mr. Jones beamed. "Thank you. Miriam? Care to comment? Seems there is corroboration. Doesn't it?"

Miriam took a deep breath. She considered agreeing and letting it go at that. She had more important things to accomplish than playing mind games with Mr. Jones. Time to stop challenging the status quo. Time to move on. It occurred to her that her combative style was not only to get Derrick's attention. She had also hoped that thought-provoking dialog would cause others to start thinking for themselves. Start a movement of truth-seekers. That was her dream, and she wanted Derrick to be in that dream, like he was in her dreams of the Keepers and the tenders. Staying out of it wasn't going to happen. Let it go, move on, get out. But Miriam couldn't abandon her true nature. However, perhaps she could domesticate it a little. "The documentary, the news, and the textbooks are all New America Media. Correct?"

Mr. Jones stood. "Excellent point, Miriam."

Light from the ceiling turned green, signaling the end of the class. Students stood, but Mr. Jones held out his hand and said, "Not so fast. Assignment. Ten percentage bonuses to final grades of any students who can think of a source that corroborates the documentary, independent of New America Media."

Murmuring filled the room as people started moving again. Marcus Carver held up his tablet over his shoulder so Miriam could read it. Large red letters read: YOUR NEXT.

Miriam chuckled. Apparently, English was not Marcus Carver's strongest subject. Miriam considered that tormenting Marcus was too easy to be fun. She dismissed the notion. Easy or not, he would pay before she left Pacific Edge. She hoped to leave on her own terms but was not above smacking Marcus Carver alongside the head with a blunt object if the opportunity presented itself.

"You'd better go for that ten percent bonus. You likely need it," Miriam whispered as she passed.

Miriam surprised herself, smiling at Mr. Jones near the door. "That was brilliant."

"Thank you, Miriam. I thought so, as well," Mr. Jones said.

* * *

Mrs. Springfield stopped Miriam just outside her classroom. "Do you have your story today?"

"Yes."

Mrs. Springfield smiled.

Mrs. Springfield didn't ask Miriam to read her story. Springfield called on five other students first. Four were ready, and one was not. A girl named Anna read her story about a pink dragon that came from the mountains. The girl made friends with the dragon, and the dragon carried her away. A boy named Peter talked about building a raft out of limbs from trees, and he sailed away to a faraway land. A boy named Ted discovered a tunnel that led under the wall. He escaped, never to be seen again. A girl named Jesse wrote about being chosen by a nice boy and living to be 200 years of age and never leaving Pacific Edge. Three of the four wrote about getting out of Pacific Edge. That surprised and didn't surprise Miriam at the same time. The last girl wrote a fairytale about doing exactly what they expected of her. Maybe too afraid to write anything else. Maybe as deluded as Derrick.

Miriam took a different approach. Because making something up seemed impossible, she wrote something rooted in fact, mixed with dreams, experienced by an unnamed girl who might or might not be Miriam King. Not an escape. Not an exhibition of imagination. Not a departure from what she had always done. Attempting to get people to open their eyes.

"Miriam? Will you read your story, please?"

Miriam didn't stir. She thought about saying she had not finished it, even though she had told Mrs. Springfield that she was ready. It occurred to her that her story could create problems. Those problems could come back to haunt her. As much as Miriam wanted to help Derrick, she found denying her passion difficult. Maybe impossible. Miriam stood and read.

```
     A girl lived in an ordinary house on
an ordinary street in an ordinary
Chosen community. The girl was like
every other girl, mostly. But there
was one thing about her that differed
from the other girls. Curiosity.
Sometimes her inquisitiveness caused
problems. One rainy day, she lay on
her bed, staring at the ceiling.
Boredom caused her mind to drift like
a cloud on a breeze. She was about to
```

tell her communication monitor to turn on when a question entered her mind. In a drawer beside her bed, was a small black device about four inches long and two inches wide. It had buttons that controlled the communication device. Everyone had one of these remote devices, but no one used them as far as she knew. Everyone merely said aloud what they wanted, and the monitor implemented the command. It was easier that way. People liked easy. She retrieved the unit from the drawer and studied it. She pushed a button labeled on, and the monitor came to life. She pushed a button labeled off, and the monitor turned black. She played with the device, making the sound louder and then quieter and changing channels. But that was all the unit did. Boring.

She shut the monitor off and started pushing combinations of buttons. On and off at the same time. Nothing. On, Off, and Volume Up. Nothing. She pushed Volume Up, 5, 0, Channel, On. The monitor came to life. But something was different. A box labeled MENU appeared in the center of the screen. Below MENU two options: ENTER, EXIT.

She sat up in bed. She selected the word ENTER. A list appeared: Search, Recordings, Password, Parental Control, Security Level.

She selected Recordings and learned that there were no recordings. She selected the word Search and found she could search for programming based on title, subject, or date. If the

program was in the future, an option
to record appeared. She selected the
words Parental Control, and the screen
asked for a password. Password? What
is a password and who makes it?
Parents? She tried their names in
different combinations, added their
address, birthdays, etc. with no
success. Frustrated, she entered the
word password, and the screen changed.
She saw there were five levels of
Parental Control. It was set at level
two. She changed it to level three.
One step at a time, she thought. She
selected the word Security, the last
option. She was asked for a password,
and she entered the word password. The
Security screen looked like Parental
Control. Five levels, and it was set
at level one, which she changed to
level five.

The ordinary girl living on an
ordinary street in an ordinary Chosen
Community now had an extraordinary
secret. She wondered, what shall I do
with this secret? Share it with my
friends? In the end, she decided the
secret might be dangerous. So, she
kept it to herself, at least for now,
at least until she could learn how
dangerous this secret might be.
Because someone had gone to great
lengths to keep this secret. A Keeper
of Secrets. The Keeper might not want
the secret shared. The Keeper might be
angry that the ordinary girl had
discovered it. Keepers are not
parents. But parents might be Keepers.
It is not safe to share secrets.

The room remained silent after Miriam stopped reading. She took her seat. Her heart pounding. Mrs. Springfield stood at the front of the room, staring at her. Then Mrs. Springfield did something she had not done for the other student's stories. She clapped her hands. Some students joined her. This puzzled Miriam. Her story was not that good and not even fiction. Miriam had discovered the secret code of the remote after AJ Patel gave her a keyboard. She thought many of the students would go home and play with their remote-control units. She doubted any of them would remember the sequence that would grant them access to the menu system, little risk. Still, she had a queasy feeling.

"Miriam, I liked your story," Mrs. Springfield said.

"Thank you," Miriam said.

"Do you know why I liked it?"

"I do not."

Mrs. Springfield smiled. "Because it sounded true."

"But fiction is not supposed to be true. It's supposed to be made up."

"That is correct. But what makes fiction interesting is when it sounds as if it actually happened. Even if the story is farfetched, when it takes the reader to a new world, makes them believe, that's what makes it good."

The room turned green, but the students didn't move.

Mrs. Springfield said, "Remember. Just because fiction is made up, doesn't mean it doesn't contain truth. Do you understand?"

Miriam stood. She glanced at a tablet on the desk. It belonged to a girl named Anna, a shy, bookish girl who had never spoken to Miriam. Anna wrote the story about the pink dragon that carried her away from Pacific Edge. Miriam saw what Anna had written.

Volume Up, 5, 0, Channel, On.

18

THE NEXT TWO PERIODS PASSED as slowly as the last day of school before vacation. Miriam vanished into her thoughts. She wondered what Derrick was doing. She wondered if he was afraid. She wondered if he missed her. But mostly she worried about what Anna had written on her tablet. The secret code of the remote control that gave access to a hidden menu, which if used skillfully revealed that New America Media told lies about the commoner world.

Why had she used the actual sequence in her story? Her story contained more facts than fiction, but she didn't think anyone would believe it. Why would they? It was fiction. The bigger question—*why am I so stupid?* She considered herself smart. She remembered things. She remembered the details of her seventh birthday. Mother and Father threw a big party. Derrick, being the older of the two, already aloof, kept asking why she got a big party, but he ate his share of cake and got a present. White cake with pink frosting, her favorite, and she remembered that seemed strange because she didn't remember having it before.

Why am I so stupid?

The question haunted her. She had pushed Derrick away by continually proving herself to be the smarter of the two. Yet she wanted to be closer. She suspected so many things about New America, James Carver Academy, and Pacific Edge, and she wanted to share them with Derrick. She trusted no one else and admitted, begrudgingly, that she didn't trust Derrick either. Still, she wanted him to be her brother. When Derrick hit Marcus Carver, Miriam felt like Derrick's sister for the first time.

At lunch, Miriam loaded her tray. Long days and long nights required food for energy. She walked to the table in a far corner of the courtyard. Rebekah Ford sat waiting, bloodshot eyes set deep in dark circles, watching as Miriam approached.

"You look awful," Miriam said, settling across from Rebekah.

"Thanks," Rebekah said.

"You should go home. I hope you're not contagious."

"I'm fine. Just not getting much sleep. You look as if you're not sleeping well yourself."

"I'm getting by." Miriam took a bite of food. "Sorry, you can't sleep."

"I'll be better tomorrow. I think I have something figured out now."

Both girls ate in silence for a few minutes. Miriam had nothing to report and wasn't sure she would tell Rebekah if she did. She had no reason to trust her. Miriam sensed that someone had walked up behind her. Rebekah's eyes affirmed that someone had joined them.

"What are you two talking about?" Marcus Carver's voice was unmistakable.

Miriam didn't turn to look at Marcus. She didn't want to give him the satisfaction of looking down on her.

"None of your business," Rebekah said.

"What if I make it my business? You were on Derrick's list for Choosing, right? I think I'll request they put you on my list. Then what you do is my business."

"Piss off, Marcus," Rebekah said.

Although Rebekah still looked like warmed over death, her eyes narrowed, emitting darkness that scared Miriam a little. And Rebekah wasn't even looking at her.

"Or what?" Marcus asked, his voice sounding as if he had somehow stuck his head in an empty barrel.

"You don't want to know. Jerk."

Marcus stood there for a moment and then walked away, mumbling. Miriam giggled.

"Jerk," Rebekah repeated.

"Thanks," Miriam said.

"For what?"

"Getting rid of him."

Rebekah took a bite of her sandwich, talking with a full mouth. "No thanks necessary. I can't stand the jerk. I didn't do it for you."

"Okay."

"Anything from Derrick?"

"Nothing from Derrick."

"You're sure about that?"

Miriam glared at Rebekah. "I would know if I'd heard from him."

"That doesn't mean you would tell me."

Miriam studied Rebekah and decided Rebekah Ford was dangerous, possessing a ferocity deep, hard to calculate, and easy to underestimate. Miriam said, "I don't think Derrick was going to pick you." Miriam instantly regretted saying that and wondered what possessed her to say such a thing, especially since Rebekah appeared on the verge of a mental break.

Rebekah's neck turned red. "I know that. I'm not stupid."

"I'm sorry. I should not have said that." Miriam took a bite of food and then, after a moment, said, "But if you knew, why do you want to know if I hear from Derrick?"

Rebekah stood. "Figure it out. You're smart, right?".

19

Thursday, March 18, 12:01 a.m.

THE NIGHT AIR, THICK WITH salt-scented fog drifting from the sea, revived Miriam as she stepped onto the driveway outside her home. She was still adjusting to her school-eat-sleep-work-sleep-school-start-over schedule. Difficult, but it worked. It would have worked better had she gone to sleep right after dinner instead of lying awake thinking about 1984.

When she finally slept, Rebekah Ford crept into her dreams, demanding to know what Miriam had heard from Derrick. Rebekah said she knew about the e-mails. Miriam kept telling herself it was just a dream, but even now, the lingering angst was not easily shaken. It was as if Rebekah had crawled into Miriam's brain during the night. Walking down the deserted street, the haloed lights struggling to illuminate the foggy air, Rebekah Ford's last words at lunch haunted her: "Figure it out. You're smart."

Miriam walked with her hood down. She had fixed the security cameras. Tonight, the dense fog prevented recognition, even if the cameras still functioned properly. Yet, halfway to Technical Service, she felt uneasy. Sometimes, Miriam acted on intuition, like when she put AJ in front of numbers that comprised AJ Patel's password. She didn't like intuition. She didn't like dreams. She didn't like fiction. She liked facts. Something solid she could get her mind wrapped around, like getting her hands wrapped around a cup of coffee. Dreams and intuition were no more substance than the fog that hung in the air: there yet not there. That's why she tried to fight off the feeling that someone was watching her. It wasn't real, and it didn't make sense.

Miriam pulled up the hood of her sweatshirt and snugged it tight, all but covering her face.

She went straight to the break room for an espresso, half hoping Marty and Brad, the two security men, were there, yet she didn't know why she wanted to see them. It was not logical, and the feeling angered her. She was not lonely. She didn't need them. She didn't need anyone. The break room was empty. She shivered.

Espresso in hand, she walked to AJ Patel's office, logged in, and then checked e-mail. Someone in the human resources department encouraged her to attend the retirement seminar scheduled in the afternoon, delete. Another e-mail reminder about the employee association picnic on Sunday: delete. Delete, delete, delete. She sipped the rich espresso and considered the fact that it was good. Surprisingly good, given that it was for service workers, commoners. She took another sip, rolling the rich nectar over her tongue. Rich but not bitter, burned, or acidic. *Wasn't all the good stuff reserved for the Chosen?* She navigated to the Pacific Edge Security page, hovered the mouse icon over 1984, and took another sip. *This is better than the espresso at home.*

The screen changed and filled with green dots in homes. Sometimes two together, sometimes one in a room, and only one displayed outside the perimeter of Pacific Edge, inside the Technical Service Building. The dots didn't move, which made sense because everyone was asleep. She stared at the screen, wondering if the dots would move if the people were awake or if the screen was a snapshot, updated periodically but not displayed in real time. Given the time of night when she could observe 1984, she might never know.

She took a deep breath. She had planned her next task yesterday and at the time, certain it was the right thing to do, yet now she hesitated, not sure if she dared learn what 1984 might tell her. With her index finger, she rolled the wheel on the mouse, making the map expand. As the perspective of the map enlarged, it revealed a city surrounding Pacific Edge. There were no green dots in the city.

She sipped her espresso. It had turned cold and bitter. At the top of the 1984 screen, a search window opened. To test the search function, she typed: Miriam King. The arrow icon turned into a colorful spinning wheel, and the word 'Searching' appeared below it. Then, the screen zoomed in, isolating one green dot in the Technical Services Building. A window opened:

```
Miriam King
7 Circle Court
Pacific Edge
Status: current
TS-#6
```

Her name and her address. But what did TS-#6 mean?

Knowing the search function worked as she assumed, she typed the next name: Samantha Bell. The spinning wheel spun.

And spun.

And spun.

An error message appeared: a red octagon with an exclamation mark in its center, and written to the right of the message:

```
Subject not found
Status: Terminated
```

Status terminated. What did that mean? Not exiled? Why no green dot?

Then, an obvious question surfaced in Miriam's mind, and she wondered why she had not asked this question previously. *How does 1984 work? What is it? What sees it and transmits its location and information to the computer?*

Miriam looked at her coffee cup. Empty except for black sludge at the bottom. *Terminated.* It could mean terminated, as in, fired, rejected, dismissed. It could mean something Miriam refused to consider. Maybe Samantha was alive, but she had been turned off in the 1984 system and could be reactivated with a click of the mouse if one knew where to click. However, Samantha Bell was not Miriam's concern, not that she wasn't concerned about Samantha, but there was someone more pressing.

Miriam placed the cursor in the search window again and typed: Derrick King.

The colorful wheel spun.

20

Thursday, March 18, 2:31 a.m.

MIRIAM STARED AT THE COMPUTER screen, and the colorful wheel had been spinning for a few seconds that felt like years.

A wrap at the door, "Maranda! Are you in there?"

Miriam recognized the guard named Brad. She paused, then said, "Yes. I'm here. Just a minute."

Miriam minimized 1984 and pulled up her e-mail screen.

Easing the door open a crack, she peered out and said, "What's up?"

"We're headed to lunch. Want to join us?"

Miriam had far too much work to do. No need to have excessive contact or risk raising suspicions regarding the legitimacy of her presence, yet she said, "Sounds good."

Miriam followed Brad and Marty down the hall, wondering what the hell she was doing. The two guards didn't speak as they walked. *Maybe they were leading her into a trap. Maybe they were all talked out.*

"How's your night going?" Miriam asked.

"Slow as usual. Boring as hell. Makes for a long shift." Brad looked over his shoulder. "Glad you're here. Gives 33% more people to engage with."

Miriam smiled. Brad didn't want to report the light on in AJ's office on her first night. Didn't want the paperwork. She liked him.

Miriam allowed Marty and Brad first turn at the vending machine. Each selected a sandwich, a bag of chips, and a candy bar. A few of the candy bars offered were available in Pacific Edge; most were not. Miriam selected a roast beef sandwich, potato chips, and a candy bar she had never seen before. She made a cappuccino, feeling she'd had enough black coffee for tonight. The security guys preferred sodas.

Miriam joined them at a table near the vending machines. Although the room was empty, the boys enjoyed being close to the food. Miriam took two deep breaths to settle her nerves as she sat. "I'm starving. Thanks for inviting me."

"No worries," Marty said as he carefully unwrapped his sandwich and emptied the bag of chips beside it.

No worries seemed an interesting phrase, Miriam thought. She wondered if she would ever feel it appropriate for her use.

"What are you working on in there?" Brad asked, signaling with his thumb toward Patel's office.

Miriam chewed a bite of roast beef. "Can't tell you. Secret stuff. Remember?"

"Right. Sorry, not looking for details. Thought you could give us a general idea. Like, are you working on computer programming, system integrity, audits? You know, the 10,000-foot view."

Ten-thousand-foot view. That might explain it.

"Yes," Miriam said as she took another bite.

Marty laughed.

Brad said, "Okay. Secret stuff. I got it."

Wanting to redirect the conversation, Miriam said, "So, only the two of you here at night? Things must function well."

"It is quiet. That's for sure. The day guys see more action," Marty said.

Brad laughed. "If riding around in their sky bucket is what you call action."

"Well, it beats walking around this place all night," Marty said.

Miriam watched the back and forth, hoping they might offer up some information that would be of value without her asking too many questions.

"I suppose," Brad said.

"You cover the tech building then?" Miriam asked.

Both men stopped eating and looked at her. Brad's cheeks swelled from the bite he had taken.

"That would be a small job," Marty said.

Miriam forced a chuckle. "I suppose it would be. Right?"

Brad and Marty stared at her.

Miriam squirmed in her seat. "You guys don't take a joke very well, do you?"

Brad started chewing again and nodded his head.

"You got us on that one," Marty admitted.

Brad swallowed and took a drink of soda. "We patrol the entire building. Even then, it's not a big assignment, as security details go. Pacific Edge is a small Community and on one side is the ocean. The only smaller security ring is in New York, isn't it, Marty? What's the name of that place?"

Marty looked at the ceiling. "Riker's Island? Is that the place?"

"Yeah. That sounds right." Brad looked at Miriam. "You been there?"

Miriam shook her head and took a drink of her cappuccino.

21

WRAPPING THE REMAINING HALF OF her sandwich in its paper, Miriam stood. "I'll eat this at my desk. I got to finish what I've started before I leave. Nice visiting with you, boys. Same time tomorrow?"

Miriam returned to AJ's office. She flopped into the chair, shoulders slumped. She opened 1984 and stared at the spinning disc, still searching. *What hope was there, really? Too many obstacles. Too little time. Too little reality. Too much fantasy.* She wasn't smart enough to figure this out. She had no plan. She didn't even know what she was trying to accomplish. Help Derrick. That sounded all noble and everything, but help him, what?

She dragged the 1984 screen to the left monitor. She entered the commands necessary to access the computer programming level. Moving through pages of code, she searched for anything related to 1984. Determined to do something worthwhile that night, she lost track of time. She found nothing about 1984, except the commands that allowed users entry to the system by clicking on the 1984 icon. She found coding related to e-mail, archive storage, and personal data storage. Those could prove useful, but she had no time to research further. Remembering how to find the areas of interest was not a problem.

Miriam closed the operating system code window and dragged the 1984 map back to the center monitor. Still spinning. Stuck. She closed the program and then opened it again. With a deep breath, she rolled the wheel on the mouse. The map on the screen expanded. A cluster of green dots in the center. None elsewhere. She rolled it again. The map expanded. One big green clump was now in the middle of the screen. She rolled the wheel. The map continued to expand.

In the upper right-hand corner of the screen was a solitary green dot in a place called Potterville, California. She moved the mouse and hovered over the dot. To the side, a window popped open.

```
Derrick King
501 Main St.
Potterville, California
Status: Exile
```

TS-#7

Miriam reached up, touched Derrick's name, and whispered, "Number Seven."

22

WHEN MIRIAM LEFT THE TECHNICAL SERVICE building, mist cloaked Pacific Edge like a thick soup. The streetlights created murky gray clouds so dense the houses stood like ghosts. She walked with her hood down, certain the cameras were blind and her programming unnecessary. Still, the feeling of being watched didn't leave her entirely. She supposed it never would. She focused on the sidewalk, only able to see a few feet in front of her. Miriam crossed to the side of the street on which her home was located, hoping she didn't miss it.

She walked straight to the rain gutter chain, climbed onto the roof, through the window, and then crept to her bed. It was as if her mind recalled the exact route home, although she had never thought about memorizing it. Settling in, she pulled the covers to her chin. She was beyond tired. She felt like someone had beaten her. Every muscle hurt. But she couldn't sleep. Derrick was in a place called Potterville. It was right there in his e-mail address. Yet she had missed it. She had never heard of Potterville. She did not know the name of a town might be used in an e-mail address. She did not understand how e-mail worked. None of that helped. She had missed it, plain and simple. What else had she missed? Plenty, she was certain.

Her 1984 profile ended with TS–#6. Derricks ended with TS–#7. Number Six and Number Seven. She didn't speculate what TS stood for, mostly because she was afraid to know. Her dreams of children, known only as numbers, seemed different from other dreams. More like looking through a window of memory than random firing sensory neurons in her brain. Concentrating hard, she tried to recall her earliest memories of living here with Father and Mother. She remembered the first day of the second grade and the party that followed. Mother had bought her a new dress for school. She couldn't remember having any other clothing before that. Her first dress. She remembered Derrick wearing a white shirt and black pants at the breakfast table. It was the first memory she had of Derrick.

* * *

When her alarm sounded, she wanted nothing more than to turn her brain off and go back to sleep. She wouldn't function well in school today. She showered, which woke her to a degree, and dressed. At the breakfast table, she smiled at platters of bacon, ham, eggs, potatoes cooked crisp and well-seasoned, toast, blackberry jam, and coffee.

"You look tired," Father said.

Miriam loaded her plate. "I didn't sleep well."

"Do you want to stay home today?"

Miriam took a bite of bacon, followed by a fork full of potatoes. *Absolutely,* she thought. If it were possible, she would stay home every day until she devised a plan to help Derrick. That's why she surprised herself when she said, "I'll be okay. I should not miss more school."

Father nodded and said, "I'm proud of you, Miriam. That is a responsible thing to do." He didn't add that he thought Miriam was irresponsible most of the time, other than being responsible for getting Derrick exiled.

Miriam ate in silence. No reason to argue with Father. It wasn't about being responsible. She didn't want to be alone with her thoughts any longer. At least school provided some distraction, although being distracted might be dangerous. The real problem was that if she was awake, she was thinking. Always thinking.

Miriam had time, so she walked to school. The fog still pressed down on Pacific Edge like a thick white blanket, as it had not yet retreated to the sea. It would pull back off the coast by early afternoon but would lurk there all day and return tonight, which suited her because it made her walk to the Technical Service Building feel less dangerous. Rebekah Ford stood on the sidewalk about halfway to James Carver Academy. Miriam didn't want to talk to Rebekah, but she knew that Rebekah wouldn't ask permission.

Rebekah fell in beside Miriam. "You look awful."

"Nice of you to notice," Miriam said. "You look closer to human this morning."

"I feel closer to human," Rebekah said. "I found a system that works better for me. What happened to you last night? Couldn't sleep?"

"What was your first clue?"

"Sorry. Just making conversation, I guess."

"Well, try not to."

"Try not to what?"

"Make conversation."

They walked in silence for two blocks. James Carver Academy appeared in the mist like the hull of a ghost ship lost at sea.

"What have you learned?"

Miriam stopped, pivoted toward Rebekah, and said, "What do you mean, 'What have I learned?'"

"I mean, have you heard anything about Derrick?"

"No. I told you I'd let you know if I did. So how about you leave me alone, and when he contacts us, I'll let you know." Miriam felt her face flush red. She reminded herself that today was not a day for confrontation.

Rebekah stared at Miriam. Miriam couldn't discern Rebekah's thoughts. A mix of anger and pity, perhaps. Finally, Rebekah turned and walked toward the school. With her back to Miriam, she said, "That doesn't work for me. See you at lunch."

As Miriam approached the front doors, she saw Jana Somersworth talking to Rebekah. They seemed to argue. Jana glared as Rebekah leaned close to Jana, whispering in her ear. Jana spun on her heel and stomped into the school.

What was that about? Miriam wondered.

* * *

Mr. Jones stood at the door, as was his custom, greeting students. He was smiling. Miriam noticed he had been smiling a lot lately. She was on time. No need to rush. As she approached, Mr. Jones' smile faded.

"My goodness, Miriam. You look ill, child. Are you okay?"

Miriam furrowed her brow. Mr. Jones had been acting stranger than usual, but his concern for her seemed crazy. "Didn't sleep well last night."

"I'm sorry. I'll make the lesson easy today."

Miriam took her usual seat at the back of the room. The seat that Marcus Carver occupied set empty. She hoped it remained empty. Red light bathed the room, signaling the start of class. This is when Miriam used to slip through the door. Her little protest. A dig at Mr. Jones, hoping to start a debate. None of that now. She wondered why that fight had once seemed worthwhile. Miriam drifted off in her thoughts, remaining half alert, sure Mr. Jones would try to draw her into one of their infamous debates, all part of some elaborate plot to exile her. Miriam was certain that if they exiled her, it would be to a distant location, so she and Derrick couldn't reunite. Mr. Jones had made an unnerving transformation to a kind and supportive teacher. He had the monster hidden, but she was confident it was still there. A monster in a Mister-

Nice-Guy skin suit. If fiction were allowed, she would write a novel about this two-faced character: Mr. Jones and Dr. Skin, she would call it.

Mr. Jones, true to his word, kept it light. He announced a New America History video followed by a short Q & A. A few groans drifted through the room, which was unusual because Chosen teenagers, Miriam being the exception, didn't complain about what instructors did. The groans were well-founded because the video was a tired, overused piece of New America propaganda that every student had seen dozens of times since grade school. Miriam remained silent, which, upon reflection, was so unusual that in itself made her stand out.

She couldn't have asked for a better class. She zoned out during the video but could recite every word if Mr. Jones asked. But he didn't ask. However, she was certain that Mr. Jones saw her malaise, which ordinarily would drive him crazy. But not today.

Her mind drifted to Rebekah Ford. Miriam didn't know what to do about Rebekah. She was becoming a pain in the ass. Miriam was unsure where she had picked up that expression, but it fit the occasion. *What were Rebekah and Jana talking about?* Must have been about Derrick or herself or both. Miriam was unsure if Rebekah was an enemy or a potential ally. The safest guess? Enemy or, at a minimum, a pain in the ass who would make things difficult. She had hoped her rebuke this morning would give Rebekah pause, but Rebekah seemed unphased by it.

She would have said that her mind then drifted to Derrick, but that was inaccurate, and she knew it. Derrick had been there all morning since she located him using 1984. A more accurate description was that her mind did not drift to Derrick. No drifting or other casual thoughts occurred. Instead, Derrick was front and center, occupying 98% of her thinking, if thinking could be so measured.

TS–#7, Number Seven was her peer in the place of Keepers and tenders. A real place, she felt certain now, not merely a dream. Her memories of that place were obstructed, but the memories leaked through when sleeping. Focusing all her mental energy, she tried to resurrect those memories but failed. It was as if a wall had been constructed in her brain. She only remembered the dreams, and dreams didn't restore her past. Only fragments. Fragments of dreams. Maybe it was a coincidence with a simple, benign explanation. Miriam didn't believe in coincidences. What did TS stand for? She would find out tonight. It became the most important item on her list of-very-important-items-that-must-be-accomplished.

***

Miriam walked into Mrs. Springfield's class and noticed whispering students fell silent as she neared them. Some offered her weak smiles. Others stared as if she had a bug on her forehead, which was feasible because she felt like the walking dead.

Mrs. Springfield sat at her desk as students entered. She looked up at Miriam, pressing her lips into thin lines and furrowing her brow. When red light bathed the room, Mrs. Springfield didn't stand to shut the door. Instead, she asked a red-haired boy named Alex to close it. Alex sat stunned for a moment and then did as instructed.

Mrs. Springfield sat, drumming her fingers on her desk as if lost. Unsure of what happens next. After a few moments, she said, "I'm giving you a free period to read or work on other homework."

Students fidgeted in their chairs, uncertain of what to do in this abnormal situation.

Then, Mrs. Springfield sat up a little, looking over the students. "Yes, Anna?"

"Mrs. Springfield, I was wondering, since it's a free period, if I could, and I'm not asking for extra credit, read another piece of short fiction that I wrote. I think it's better than the one I read yesterday."

Mrs. Springfield smiled. "That would be wonderful. Please come to the front of the class."

Anna walked to the front, looking down at her feet. She faced the room and then cast her eyes to her tablet.

"Go ahead, Anna. I'm sure we will enjoy your story."

Anna looked at Mrs. Springfield and then turned her gaze to Miriam as if asking permission. At least Miriam felt Anna was looking at her, so Miriam gave Anna a slight nod. *Go ahead. I'm listening. We all are.*

Anna cleared her throat and began:

```
Dana was an ordinary girl, living in
an ordinary house, on an ordinary
street, in an ordinary Chosen
Community. Dana was not brilliant or
brave. But she was curious. Because
Dana was not brilliant, she had only
questions with no answers. Because
Dana was not brave, her questions
remained unasked.
```

Then one day a Magical Girl gave Dana a Magical Phrase. Unlike Dana, the Magical Girl was both brilliant and brave. The Magical Girl said, be brave, be careful. In the quiet privacy of her room, Dana spoke the Magical Phrase. With a low growl, then a whoosh, and a blinding light, a portal in her bedroom wall opened. The portal revealed a magical world.

At first, Dana feared for her life because real magic was forbidden in her ordinary house on an ordinary street in the ordinary Community, so she closed the Magic Portal, crawled into bed, and pulled the covers over her head.

Dana remained silent, staring at the spot on the wall where the Magical Portal had appeared. No sirens sounded in the night. No knocks came at the door. The ordinary house seemed extraordinarily quiet. As if secrets had escaped from the Magical Portal and set up an invisible shield to protect the Magical World from ordinary people. Dana wondered if the Magical Portal would open again. The magic that had escaped might have sealed the portal, so no invasion from the ordinary world could occur.

Dana eased from her bed and ambled toward the spot where the Magical Portal had appeared. She spoke the Magic Words. The portal opened. Dana considered for a moment, closing the portal, and never opening it again, shoving the memory of its existence and the key to its opening far into the caverns of her mind, where they

```
would remain buried forever. But then
she wondered. Why did the Magical Girl
entrust Dana with the secret code? Did
the Magical Girl see something in Dana
that she didn't see herself? Was there
something   extraordinary   in   the
ordinary girl?
     Dana took a deep breath and crossed
the threshold through the Magic Portal
into the Magical World. Dana knew that
there would be much to learn, but one
thing she knew instantly. She could
never return to the ordinary house on
the ordinary street in the ordinary
Community as an ordinary girl.
```

Anna stopped reading. She looked up from her tablet. She looked at Mrs. Springfield. She looked at Miriam. Miriam understood what Anna had done. Anna had used the code on her remote to enter the first level of control behind her communication screen.

Anna was in a dangerous place.

The sound of clapping broke the silence. Mrs. Springfield must have started it, but it soon spread through the room and grew louder as some students joined her. One-third of the class joined Mrs. Springfield, clapping, one-third sat stunned, and one-third glared at Anna. Miriam memorized them all. Anna ran to her seat, and her eyes shifted to Miriam. When she saw Miriam was not clapping, Anna started to cry.

"Anna," Mrs. Springfield began, "that was much better than your first story. More details. I believed Dana had found a magic portal. I won't give you extra credit, but I will accept that story in place of yesterday's story."

A boy named Harold jumped up from his seat. "Why does she get a second try at it? That's unfair. And her story seems inappropriate. She should be punished instead of rewarded."

"Harold, please sit. We still raise our hands before we speak in my class."

"Yes, Ma'am," Harold said, taking his seat.

"Harold, would you like to write another story to replace the one you did?"

"No, Ma'am. I don't like fiction."

"If you don't want to write another story, why are you concerned if Anna does extra work? I don't see that it affects you unless she is getting an unfair advantage, which she isn't. Besides, I just gave you an opportunity to do the same, which you refused."

Mrs. Springfield continued. "Harold, why do you think the story is inappropriate?"

Harold twisted in his seat. Every eye riveted on him. "I don't know. It's not true. Magic and magic portals do not exist."

Mrs. Springfield laughed. "Of course, they don't. This is fiction, or did you forget? I'm no expert, but I'm sure pink dragons don't exist, yet you didn't complain about Anna's story yesterday."

"I didn't like that story either."

"Not liking something and making unfounded accusations are quite different things. Aren't they?"

"Yes, ma'am," Harold whispered.

"Bearing false witness is what, Harold?"

Harold stared at the top of his desk. "A violation of the Chosen Doctrine."

"That is correct. Do you want to file a complaint regarding Anna's story? I have the form here and would be happy to forward it to the Tribunal."

"No, Ma'am."

"Do you have anything you want to say to Anna?"

"I'm sorry."

"I doubt she heard you. When you apologize, look at the person and speak loud enough that she can hear you."

Harold stood and turned to Anna. "I'm sorry."

Anna nodded, her eyes still moist.

"Does anyone else have anything to say about the story?"

The room fell silent. Miriam noted those who had glared at Anna had assumed the stare-at-the-desk position, same as Harold.

A girl named Julie raised her hand.

"Yes, Julie."

Julie turned in her seat toward Anna and said, "I liked your story, Anna. I'd like to know more about what Dana finds beyond the magic portal."

Several others spoke simultaneously: 'me too', 'I liked it', 'it was awesome'.

"Class," Mrs. Springfield stood.

The class fell quiet. Mrs. Springfield tapped a small device on her desk. Miriam noticed a red light on a small camera in the corner of the ceiling.

"I want to make this clear to the class." Mrs. Springfield was staring at Anna. "This assignment is now concluded. Fiction books are not permitted at your age. When you become adults, you may read fiction books the High Council has approved. This was a writing assignment that gave you a bit of freedom of expression. Some of you took better advantage of that freedom than did others. However, let me be clear: there will be no more fiction written or read in this class. Does everyone understand?"

Miriam noted nods and wide eyes around the room.

Mrs. Springfield moved her hand back to her lap.

The red light disappeared.

"However, I have no control over your thoughts or actions outside my classroom." Mrs. Springfield returned her gaze to Anna and smiled. "I encourage comprehensive study and pursuit of knowledge. Be aware that knowledge is a powerful thing. It sheds light on darkness. Some hate the light and will attempt to extinguish it. Therefore, one must be careful. Do you understand?"

Anna nodded her head.

Mrs. Springfield smiled.

Miriam thought, what in the hell have I done?

23

WHEN MIRIAM LEFT SPRINGFIELD'S CLASS, a knot of students blocked the hallway. Everyone was talking at once, making it difficult to pick out a single voice. A few kids were forcing their way past the crowd, edging along the wall nearest to the classroom, which made leaving difficult.

As Miriam neared the door, Mrs. Springfield said, "What's the hold-up?"

When Miriam joined the stream of students, she heard her name, so she forced her way into the crowd to see what they were looking at.

Upon wedging between two large boys, she saw what caused the stir. Someone had taped a professionally made white banner with bold black lettering to the wall. It read:

MIRIAM KING YOU ARE NEXT

Anger rather than fear flared, and Miriam started toward the banner, intent on ripping it down. Then she stopped. Would ripping it down show courage? Or fear? Miriam had never thought of herself as brave. But it was not fear that stopped her. Her next move would put things in motion that she couldn't control or predict. Still, her nature dictated she examine the benefits and disadvantages of her actions. She could tear the damn thing down and drag it straight to a teacher. But to her, that projected fear and fear was what someone wanted.

She thought about screaming and demanding to know who was responsible, but that seemed desperate. In the end, she walked away. Let the teachers find it and deal with it as they see fit or not. She was unsure whether any of them cared what happened to her. As she forced her way back through the throng of students, someone said, "She'll get what she deserves."

Miriam didn't return to that hallway to see if they had removed the banner. She was not called to the administration office, nor did any teacher mention it.

At lunch, she resigned herself to seeing Rebekah Ford.

"I heard about the sign," Rebekah said as Miriam sat. "How are you feeling? Any news about Derrick?"

Miriam said, "Nothing has changed since this morning."

"Right. Sorry."

Miriam took a bite of some sort of breaded chicken with a sweet red sauce. She chewed deliberately, thinking about the question. *Why is Rebekah so insistent? More specifically, why does she seem to think I know something rather than have heard something?* "What makes you think I know something? I told you I'd let you know. I feel you don't trust me."

"I don't trust most people. Don't take it personally."

As had become their custom, both girls ate silently for a few minutes. Miriam felt like hell, so it was no surprise that she looked the part. The combination of weariness, the banner, and what she had learned last night suffocated her. Miriam decided to go to the headmaster after lunch and tell him she was going home. She needed rest. Tonight, she needed to be productive.

"Who do you think did it?" Rebekah asked.

"Did what?"

"Put up the sign."

Miriam took a bite. "I don't know."

"Must be Marcus."

Miriam shrugged. "He's not here today."

Rebekah pushed a chunk of lettuce around her plate in a bath of ranch dressing. "Then one of his minions. Probably why he's absent. So, he won't get blamed."

"Could be. Makes sense. Doesn't matter."

"No, I suppose it doesn't. I might kick his ass before this is done."

Miriam thought about asking what she meant by before this is done and decided against it. Things were too complicated as it was. She didn't need further entanglement with Rebekah.

Miriam stood. She was ready to go home and get some sleep.

Rebekah grabbed her by the arm and pulled her back into her chair. "What did you give Anna?"

Miriam was seldom confused, but this time she was. "I haven't given anything to anybody."

"Cut the crap. Anna got something from you in Mrs. Springfield's class."

"I didn't give her anything. I read a piece of fiction. It was an assignment."

"I know it was an assignment. I'm not stupid, you know."

"No offense intended. I'm not feeling well. So, with your permission, I'm going home."

Rebekah removed her hand. As Miriam turned to leave, Rebekah said, "Her name is Anna Ford. She's my sister."

24

MIRIAM WALKED OUT THE FRONT doors of James Carver Academy, where a transport awaited. She had called her Father on her family communication device. He didn't pick up, so she left a message telling him she had left school and asking that he call to okay her release. Sorry that she didn't go to the administration office and get permission before leaving, but she felt too sick to do so. She didn't think Father would be upset or lecture her for leaving without permission.

"Did Miriam King check out of school?" the bodiless driver asked.

"None of your business."

"Pacific Edge Transportation Service is responsible to ensure that its transports abide by Pacific Edge rules and regulations at all times."

"Just take me home. Stupid machine."

"I have no feelings. You cannot insult me."

"I just did."

"Did Miriam King check out of school?"

Miriam sighed. "No, I'm sick. I contacted Father, and he'll call the school."

"Confirming Miriam King contacted her father." A couple of minutes passed. "Mr. King does not respond. Confirmation incomplete. Returning Miriam King to James Carver Academy."

"Just stop."

"Miriam King did not properly check out of James Carver Academy."

"Stop."

"Must return Miriam King to James Carver Academy. Miriam King is absent without authorization."

"Emergency stop. Full override command."

The transport stopped, and the doors popped open. Miriam got out.

"Miriam King used an unlawful emergency stop. Miriam King is absent without authorization from James Carver Academy. Must report Miriam King to proper authorities."

Miriam stuck her head into the transport. "Knock yourself out. Stupid machine."

Miriam walked home. She tried the front door. It was locked, which meant Father had not yet received her message. That sucked. She thought about climbing up to her window, but that posed some risk. What if Father didn't get her message and came home to find her asleep in her bed? He would know she had defeated the lock system, which wouldn't be good.

She put her back to the door and slid into a sitting position. Resting her head against the door, she closed her eyes and hoped the sound of the lock disengaging would awaken her. If the tribunal security jerks came looking for her, she'd be easy to find.

Tap, tap, tap.

She awoke to the sound. Not loud. Wood on wood. Her eyes felt scratchy, and her vision cloudy, as if someone had put a glob of oatmeal in each eye. She didn't like oatmeal.

Tap, tap, tap.

She knew that sound. Number Seven attempting to do a lesson the Keepers required of him. She understood she was dreaming, except not dreaming. Remembering. Aware, yet unaware. It was a feeling she fought until she could pull herself from the world of dreams. But that was before, and this was now. She relaxed and focused on what she could see.

The room came into focus. The lesson consisted of putting wooden pegs into matching holes in a wooden board. The board was painted white, and the pegs and corresponding holes were painted red, green, blue, purple, orange. They gave the student a wooden hammer painted black. But the hammer was unnecessary. The pegs fit if the right peg was placed in the right hole, and since the pegs and holes were also color-coordinated, the test seemed too simple to be of value. Miriam passed the lesson within seconds on her first attempt.

Number Seven was trying to put a triangular peg into a round hole. Tap, tap, tap with the wooden hammer. Miriam wanted to help him, but she couldn't move. She couldn't speak. Only watch.

Two Keepers stood nearby, watching him.

Neither Keepers nor tenders had ever spoken in previous dreams, but one Keeper said to the other, "What are his settings?"

The second Keeper said, "Compliance is set on five. Restraint is set on four."

"You told him to put that peg in that hole?"

"Correct."

"How long has he been at it?"

The Keeper looked at the device in her hand. "Twenty minutes."

"Excellent. The Founder will be pleased. Set restraint on 2."

"Are you sure you want to do that?"

"Yes."

The Keeper touched a device with her finger.

Tap, tap, TAP

TAP, TAP, TAP

TAP, TAP …

Number Seven pounded at the peg, forcing it into the hole an inch before the hammer splintered. Then he grabbed the board and threw it across the room, hitting a tender in the back. The tender screamed and fell to his knees. This was not the first time Number Seven had hit a tender with something. Probably wouldn't be the last.

"Excellent," the Keeper said.

25

FATHER TOUCHED HER SHOULDER. "MIRIAM, MIRIAM. Have you been sleeping here all afternoon?"

Miriam looked around and then realized she was sitting outside with her back to the door. "Uh, I guess. You're home early?"

"Not early. I thought you'd be in bed." Father helped Miriam to her feet.

"The door was locked when I got here," she said. "Sat here thinking if I fell asleep, the sound of the door unlocking would wake me."

"Are you hungry? Do you want a snack from the quick-serve machine, or should I order an early dinner?"

"I'll eat something, but I won't ruin my appetite. I'll take it up to my room if that's okay. I might sleep more before supper."

"I'm sorry you're not feeling well. I called the Academy and cleared everything up, so you don't have to worry."

Miriam wasn't worried. She went to the kitchen. Father went to his bedroom, which suited her. She was not interested in additional conversation. She asked the snack machine for clam chowder and a hot chocolate, which was ready in three minutes. She went up to her bedroom and sat at her desk. The scent of the soup rose in spiraling whiffs of steam. She sipped her hot chocolate and then tasted the chowder, marveling at the quality despite the fact that it came from a machine. Derrick loved food, and she felt guilty because he probably hated what he had to eat in the commoner world. Miriam believed New America Media's portrayal of the commoner world was erroneous, but she didn't know what it was actually like out there. However, she assumed commoners didn't eat well. She ate and thought and grew depressed. The obstacles seemed endless, like the ocean.

After finishing her soup, she lay on her bed, hands under her head, staring at the ceiling, unable to sleep. Many problems and little time. *And to what end?* Miriam had no answer. One bite at a time. Keep it simple. 1984 created a huge problem. Telling Derrick would only increase his paranoia. She would confirm what they had assumed. They are watching. Perhaps add that it's worse than expected.

Hacking 1984 seemed impossible, and AJ Patel said as much. Learning more might provide a solution. Derrick would never be safe as long as 1984 functioned. Her priority solidified: understand and deactivate 1984.

Friday, March 19, 12:01 a.m.

From the roof, Miriam stared at the fog, standing offshore like an army awaiting invasion authorization. Miriam no longer cared if the fog stayed at sea or poured over Pacific Edge like a wet, heavy cloak. She snugged the hoodie around her head and then shimmied down the waterspout made from a heavy chain. She walked with purpose toward Technical Service. Her thoughts laser-focused on 1984, and well-rested. Leaving the Academy early was genius. She would thank Rebekah Ford on Monday, or not, because Rebekah was a complication she didn't need. Nor did she need a complication caused by Anna Ford, which was Miriam's fault for providing Anna a code to get into the first level of the wall monitor's menu. Sometimes, she was so stupid. No wonder Derrick didn't like her.

Miriam stopped at the employee break room and made a double-shot espresso. Brad and Marty weren't there, but she realized the benefits of meeting them. When it first happened, she thought her rescue attempt would end before it started, but instead of an end, it proved to be a beginning. Now, she moved about the building without worry. First, she checked e-mail, saw none of interest, and then plunged into research. On a shared drive, she found hundreds of documents concerning 1984.

She learned that 1984 is a global positioning system or GPS device that tracks people—Chosen people to be precise. Doctors implant a chip in each Chosen baby. They deactivate it when a Chosen person leaves the Community. However, Derrick's device remained active. Deactivation was password-protected. This, however, might be the answer. She just had to hack the password. A training manual provided simple instructions. Once inside, a grade school student could deactivate it.

However, a problem with that solution appeared on the next page. It's as easy to reactivate 1984 as it is to deactivate it. Plus, if she deactivated it, an investigation might lead them to her, which would cause her exile, which wouldn't be bad, except they would put her on the other side of the continent.

Why were they still tracking Derrick? She found no one other than Derrick being tracked outside Pacific Edge. Many others had left, and they tracked none. *What made Derrick special?* Many people left Pacific Edge, like AJ Patel. Possibly, AJ deactivated 1984 for his family, and no one cared that he did.

Why were they tracking Derrick?

Perhaps the person assigned to deactivate Derrick had forgotten or had not gotten to it. Possibly, they wanted to know if Derrick stopped moving. Or maybe Derrick's exile was not permanent. Miriam smiled. *Maybe they have people protecting Derrick. Maybe his rescue is unnecessary.*

A light knock came at the door. "Maranda, are you there? We're going to lunch if you want to join us."

Time had evaporated. "Go ahead. I'll be there soon."

It occurred to Miriam that she needed to understand the Tribunal's intentions regarding Derrick. She was unsure how to learn that. Possibly e-mails between the Tribunal and others. But she didn't know how to hack into e-mail accounts.

Deep in the system, she found a folder titled: e-mail, which provided a list of additional folders, including a folder titled: Users. She opened it and saw a list of e-mail addresses. This would take time, and she was hungry. She minimized the folder and headed to the lunchroom.

"There she is," Brad said as Miriam walked in.

"Hi guys," Miriam said. She selected a turkey sandwich from the food machine and a mocha. She had developed a broader vision of espresso beyond double shots.

"Why so glum?" Marty asked as Miriam sat with her food and drink. "You have problems?"

"Oh, it's nothing. Just thinking about a work problem. It has me stumped," she said, taking a bite of her sandwich.

"That's what is good about our jobs. We don't have many problems to solve. Just walk around the complex. Nothing ever happens. Staying awake is the toughest part. But we never nap, right Brad?"

Brad sprayed soda from his mouth and then laughed. "Right."

Miriam smiled. Not because Brad sprayed his drink, which was funny, but because Brad and Marty trusted her. And she liked them, although she couldn't say why. They were not the smartest guys in the world. They were, by their own account, lazy. Still …

"I'll figure it out. But I'm feeling stressed."

"What makes it so stressful? If you can tell us, without the secret stuff," Brad asked.

"Time. I don't have much time to finish. And I'm stuck. Which equals stressed." Miriam regretted saying that. She didn't need to reveal things to these guys. They were still Pacific Edge Security, and they would arrest her if they knew the truth.

"Are you leaving? We had hoped you'd be here a while. It's been nice having you join us for lunch. We've never had anyone here on a special assignment. Have we, Marty?"

"Nope. Never. I've been here for ten years, and you've been here longer. So, yep, real special, having someone new here."

Brad scratched his chin. "What you're working on must be important. I mean, particularly important. Because you are the first person here on a special assignment, working at night. Strange indeed."

Miriam sensed some mistrust in Brad's voice. "I'm the first one you've discovered. Had I been paying attention, you'd be unaware of my presence."

Brad looked at Marty. Marty shrugged.

"So, here's a secret I will share. I'm not supposed to come out of the office except to come and go from the building, and I'm to check security cameras to ensure the path is clear. I'm not supposed to come in here, but I have a weakness for the espresso. You may have noticed."

Brad furrowed his brow a little and then laughed. "See there, Marty. That's why I like her. Bends the rules and loves coffee. How can you not like a person like that?"

Marty laughed and then said, "Right on, bro. She's cut from the same cloth as us."

Miriam didn't know what cut from the same cloth meant for sure but thought it meant she was like them, although she was not, and they didn't understand how unalike they were. She laughed with them.

"We will miss you. How much longer do you have here?" Brad asked.

"Not sure. A few weeks. Depends."

Brad's face turned serious. "I hope you can tell us before you leave. We'll have a little going away party. I'll have my wife bake a cake or something. Just the three of us. It will be our secret." Brad winked at her.

Miriam fought back a tear. "I'll try. But I don't have control over the timing."

"You're done when you solve the problem? And they will pull you out quickly?"

That seemed as good an explanation as any. Miriam nodded, sipped her mocha.

"I hope this doesn't sound too personal, but you seem like family. Like a daughter or niece. And family is the most important thing. Sometimes, family isn't even a blood relation." Brad looked at Marty. "Right, brother?"

"Right, brother."

The two men slapped their hands together above their heads.

That's when an answer came to Miriam. Right then. Right there.

Miriam stood and gathered her dishes. "Well, I'll see you guys tomorrow."

"Tomorrow is Saturday," Brad said. "We are both off. Mike and Henry will be here tomorrow. Should we tell them about you?"

Miriam stood motionless. *Crap. What to do? I needed to work. I don't need more exposure.* Miriam tapped the side of her head. "I lose track of the days when I'm on these assignments. I won't be here tomorrow either. See you on Monday."

"Maybe we'll see you in town this weekend," Marty said.

Miriam paused at the door. Looking back, she said, "Maybe. Have a great weekend."

She stepped into the hall, hoping neither man followed to ask additional questions or ask where she went during the weekend in the town outside the perimeter walls.

Weekend? I should have realized they'd have the weekend off. Why am I so stupid?

In AJ Patel's office, she sat and stared at the monitors. She should have made a double espresso before she left the lunchroom. She contemplated the weekend. Taking the weekend off was a non-starter. Yet, getting caught posed a risk too great to take. She addressed an e-mail to Derrick. She considered telling him about getting into Technical Service but decided against it.

She opened Derrick's last e-mail and thought about the address: derrickking0312@Potterville.com.

They sent Derrick to Potterville, California. Thinking about how she'd not realized the town was right in front of her the first day she came here caused her stomach to churn bile, which felt as if a volcano was about to blow, which wouldn't be good in AJ Patel's office. She pulled the trash can from under his desk to be safe.

What is Potterville.com?

Her e-mail address, marandakingston@techservice/admin.com, was associated with Technical Service. Other organizations and towns must have independent e-mail systems. AJ Patel told her that e-mail was used to communicate with people on the internet. *So, what is the internet?* She had used it to research fiction but didn't know how it worked. It might be like an enormous book with lots of information. Typically, she would study until she understood it. But there was no time for that. A clock counted down in her head. Derrick had a few safe weeks remaining, yet with each passing minute, the need to act felt more urgent.

She brought up Potterville on a map, noting its relationship to Pacific Edge. Opening the internet application, she typed Potterville into the search box. A list appeared about Potterville, California. At the top of the page was written: About 332,000,000 results (0.55 seconds).

Fascinating.

She didn't have time to read 332,000,000 articles and couldn't imagine needing to do so. She returned to the original screen and typed in Potterville.com.

Potterville.com appeared at the top of the list. On the Potterville.com page, she found an e-mail tab, and there, she found she could create a private e-mail account. It was free. She liked the internet. She wondered if having an e-mail address that didn't originate at Pacific Edge Technical Service would be safer. She filled in the information. Using her fictitious name and an address in Potterville. It asked for a phone number, which she didn't understand, so she entered some random digits until the format was correct. The next screen asked for her e-mail name. She entered Maranda Kingston. That name was taken. She thought, and then she smiled and entered, number1sis.

```
Friday, March 19

TO: derrickking0312@potterville.com

FROM: number1sis@potterville.com

Subject: It's me

I have a new e-mail address, but it's me,
you know, your pain-in-the-ass sister. I
hope the new e-mail address is safer.

Problems here, but more on that later.
You wouldn't believe what I'm doing. It's
crazy.

I hope you're okay. I worry about you. I
am making progress. I've learned a lot,
```

and it's worse than I thought. I can't go into it now. I don't have enough answers.

You probably don't trust that this e-mail is legit. Ask me a question only I can answer.

Later, Brother

26

AFTER THE E-MAIL TO DERRICK whooshed its way through whatever electronic wizardry dispatched e-mail from one place to another, Miriam's mind cleared. She wondered how long it took an e-mail to travel to Potterville—seconds, minutes, hours, days, or instantaneously? Didn't matter. Derrick would be asleep, and he liked to sleep, so she would be home when he saw it. She wouldn't see his response until next week. That decision was made. She couldn't risk coming to Technical Service over the weekend. She couldn't take the weekend off. She needed to work at home. How to do that remained a mystery.

At the bottom of the center monitor, a funny half-white, half-blue face thing was called Finder, which she assumed might be another internet application. She opened it and learned it was a search type of application but for computer folders and files.

Excellent. Too bad I wasn't smart enough to find this sooner.

There were thousands of folders. In the right-hand corner was a search text field. She typed in 1984. A list appeared. She scanned through it: 1984 data, 1984 documentation, 1984 bugs *(that made no sense)*, 1984 fix, 1984 AJPATEL…

Miriam pulled the storage device AJ Patel had provided—when he commissioned her illegal keyboard and mouse—and stuck it in a port on the computer. She didn't know the device capacity or the size of the files. She dragged them to the device. A window said, copying 1092 files.

Watching the window update as the files were copied, she wondered what she should look for next. It took a few minutes to finish copying, during which she thought of several other items of interest. She typed TS-#6 into the search field. Nothing. She typed TS–#7 into the search field. Nothing. Maybe if she knew what TS stood for, but she didn't.

Thinking. She typed Derrick King into the search field.

A list of files filled the screen.

The most recent file, according to the date, was created just yesterday. She clicked on it, and a small window opened, requesting a password.

Damn.

The filename suggested it was an e-mail. She closed the window and scanned the list of files. There were files dating back years. She stopped scrolling and pulled the sidebar down toward the bottom of the screen. Then she stopped.

Test Subject #7: Derrick King.

"Found you," she whispered.

27

March 20, Saturday, 12:01 a.m.

MIRIAM AWAKENED AT HER REGULAR time. No reason to change her schedule. Mother or Father might discover her in the kitchen making an espresso or snack, no big deal. Finding her working with her monitor in computer mode, different deal, door locked. Using the tools AJ Patel had given her, she opened the computer access panel, inserted the storage device, and pulled her keyboard and mouse from their respective hiding spots. The storage device appeared on her screen as Unknown Drive. She contemplated where to begin. This thing lacked the applications of AJ Patel's computer. It was not a device intended for work. They meant it for propaganda delivery.

Determined to learn something useful over the weekend, Miriam started opening folders and files. Or, more accurately stated, she tried to open them. Each wanted a password she didn't have. Or did she? She had set her profile as an administrator. She didn't know if that was important, but administrator was top of the system hierarchy, so why not? In the password window, she typed Maranda Kingston's password. The file opened. She scanned through the information but found nothing helpful. She opened 1984 documentation, which contained an extensive list of files. A file named Operation Manual seemed promising.

When Miriam finished reading the 384-page Operation Manual, two things had occurred: she was hungry, and she knew a great deal about 1984, except how to defeat it. In the kitchen, using the manual setting, she made a double espresso, added to equal parts of hot water, and from the snack dispenser, she selected a meat pie, which came out two minutes later with steam wafting through the flakey pastry.

Taking her drink and food to her room, she thought about the file titled Test Subject #7, which was password-protected, and she had not tried to open. Part of her longed to understand their origins, and part didn't. Although difficult, she pushed her desire to learn about Derrick and herself to the back of her mind. Their past was not the key to the present; 1984 was. The meaning of Test Subjects #6 and #7 might, however, be the key to their future if they had one.

She had learned that 1984 was a global positioning system (GPS) that used a tiny transmitter implanted in all Chosen at birth. The preferred implant location was in the middle of the back because, although small, it was possible to detect it under the skin. Miriam felt her back. She couldn't find it at first, but with much stretching and poking, she found a small square hard spot.

The standard procedure was to turn the transmitter off when they removed a Chosen person from a Community. Tracking them was no longer important. It didn't say why tracking those living inside the walls of Pacific Edge was necessary. Since no one seemed to be actively monitoring 1984, Miriam assumed that the necessity of the system had diminished. If that was true, it was not so stated in the manual.

Also, not stated was how to disable the damn thing. Knowing what it was and how it worked was great, but it didn't help. Miriam spent the rest of the night reading files and documents about 1984, and when the sun rose, she had found nothing that would defeat the system. She was down to the last folder, titled 1984 Bugs. She had no interest in insects. Her eyes grew heavy. She felt defeated. She stumbled to her bed and slept.

March 20, Saturday, 7:00 p.m.

Miriam awoke to heavy pounding. After several seconds, her mind cleared enough to understand what was happening.

"Miriam! Are you in there? Are you okay? Miriam!" Father yelled.

Miriam crawled off the bed. Still dressed, she staggered to the door, opened, rubbing her eyes. "Yeah. What do you need?"

"It's dinnertime. Have you slept all day?"

"Dinner time?"

"Yes. It's on the table." Father studied her for a moment. "Are you okay?"

"Yeah. Couldn't sleep last night. I'll be down in a minute."

Damn. Dinner time. I lost the entire day.

She ran a comb through her hair. Brushed her teeth because it tasted like a herd of camels had marched through her mouth while she slept.

"There she is," Father said as she descended the stairs. "And she looks almost human."

Miriam gave a slight smile. She would accept looking almost human as a compliment because she felt like a bear emerging from hibernation. Looking almost human had not been difficult. Eating like a human might be more challenging.

They ate in silence. Miriam concentrated on eating like a normal person but had a second pork chop and a third dinner roll. She appreciated the silence. She didn't want to talk. She couldn't grasp how being Test Subjects affected her relationship with Mother and Father, but she assumed she would never see them the same way upon learning the truth. Eventually, she would have to talk to them. Unfortunately, that time came sooner rather than later.

Father pushed his plate away. "We need to talk, Miriam."

"Okay," she said, still chewing a chunk of pork.

"Mother and I are worried about you. You said you didn't sleep last night and slept until dinner. That is unusual, even for you."

Miriam nodded.

"Dear, this thing with Derrick has been hard for you. It's been hard for all of us. You cannot help Derrick. But you can help yourself," Mother said.

That's what you think, Miriam thought but didn't say.

"Miriam, we know what you're doing," Father said, staring at her.

Finally, after several silent moments, Miriam said, "You do?"

"Of course we do," Father said.

Miriam washed the meat down with a swig of milk but said nothing.

Mother touched Father's arm and said, "You're trying to think of a way to help Derrick. Worrying yourself sick. Blaming yourself for what happened. But you cannot help him. None of us can. Father has worked tirelessly to get the Tribunal to lessen his sentence but to no avail. Derrick is on his own now. And he's doing okay."

Miriam felt the heat rising in her face. "What do you mean he's doing okay? What have you not told me?"

Mother glanced at Father. Father nodded. "We need to tell her. She deserves to know."

Miriam stood. "Know what? What are you keeping from me?"

"Calm down, Miriam. It is not acceptable for you to talk to us with that tone," Father said.

Her chest heaving. *I'll give you tone,* Miriam thought. However, although she wanted to scream at them, she wanted information. Venting her rage wouldn't achieve the best results. So, she sat and said, "I'm sorry. I just want to know. It would help me, I think."

Mother patted Father's hand and said, "It's okay. Tell her."

Father nodded and said, "The Tribunal changed the conditions of his release. He starts school on Monday."

"Have you talked to him?"

"No," Father said.

"Honest?"

"Honest. I have talked to Paul, and he said Derrick is doing okay and should be okay at school. He said Potterville has a good school. No big problems other than typical stuff for that age group."

Miriam nodded. She wondered what typical problems the age group had in the commoner world. She wanted to bolt to her room and get to work. The fast-ticking clock was spinning now.

And that's when Miriam knew what she had to do.

Her only option, escape from Pacific Edge.

28

EXTRICATING HERSELF FROM THE Father-and-Mother lecture had taken longer than she had hoped. She didn't argue. She nodded, punctuating with "I'll do my best" at the appropriate times. Having endured Father and Mother's best advice, it took all her strength to ignore folders and files regarding Test Subject. She had to focus on priorities, and the priority was defeating 1984. She couldn't escape when it would be so easy to locate her, and neither she nor Derrick would be free until they were free of the omnipresent GPS trackers implanted in their backs. One folder remained, but she didn't see how information about bugs could be helpful. What bugs had to do with GPS tracking was a mystery, yet mysteries begged exploration.

Miriam opened the bug folder and scanned the files. The information was not about insects. Instead, the documents detailed glitches, anomalies, problems, hiccups, snags, irregularities, abnormalities, idiosyncrasies, defects, malfunctions, fails, and flops. Crap that goes wrong. Bugs. Duh. She should have known.

She scanned the list of files, which was long because there had been many problems associated with 1984 beyond the obvious that it was extraordinarily authoritarian and a big pain in the ass for someone trying to flee a place that seemed impossible to escape. It occurred to Miriam that Pacific Edge might not have always been as secure as it is today. At one time, this system was essential. Now, not so much.

Looking for files that might describe conditions under which the system stopped functioning, she scanned to the bottom of the list and then started over at the beginning. About a third of the way down the list, she saw a file she had missed: chip failure.

Inside the chip-failure file were 76 documents. The chips stopped working sometimes for no apparent reason. Therefore, doctors used a scanner during annual checkups to determine if the chip still worked. The scanner didn't give the doctor information, but it relayed it to the 1984 system, and then the system alerted the appropriate authority if any problems were detected. Then, the hospital contacted the person with the failed transmitter. A doctor told the person that a small skin cancer had been detected during the checkup. The person reported to the hospital, and then, under a mild sedative, a new chip was implanted. Rate of occurrence: 1 in every 5000. No solution. Unless she could find a doctor to remove her chip.

Many documents described problems with the system. All had been fixed. Miriam had read or scanned 64 of the 76 documents and was discouraged because nothing she had read proved helpful. One document title then caught her attention: AJ Patel microarchitecture_design_parameters. The mouse icon hovered over the document. Until now, she had ignored AJ Patel's role in 1984. In his first document to her, he mentioned the existence of 1984 and that she would need to defeat it. He also said that would be difficult because he worked on and refined the program. Miriam learned that AJ Patel was instrumental in the most recent improvements of 1984.

Why am I so stupid? AJ Patel could be pretending to help but just waiting for the right moment to have her arrested.

There was no obvious connection between AJ Patel giving her a keyboard and mouse and Derrick's exile unless it was all part of an elaborate setup. A test like they had often forced on Number Seven. And she was part of it, part of the plan that sent Derrick into Exile. She spun off her chair, ran to the bathroom, and threw up her dinner.

Miriam sat on the floor next to the toilet. Thinking. If this was a setup, an experiment with Test Subject #6 and Test Subject #7, it didn't change the situation. Derrick remained exiled, and she had to escape. However, it presented additional problems. She needed a better plan, which made it difficult because she didn't have the first plan yet.

That's when it happened.

It was as if she felt the pieces in her mind click into place.

29

IF IT WAS A TEST they wanted, she would show them their test had been poorly designed. With a glass of water, she rinsed the bile from her mouth. At her monitor, she read the Patel_microarchitecture_design_parameters document. Line by line, word by word. AJ Patel would help her escape. He just didn't know it. Or maybe he did.

An explanation of why she could not see the path forward moments earlier failed her. Sometimes, it seemed a fog clouded her mental foresight. Like she had 20/20 vision but wore dirty sunglasses. Somehow, she felt that she had overcome something, but she couldn't say what that something was. But it was not gone. More like she had shut the door, holding fast to the doorknob, so it didn't come back. She didn't know how long she could keep it out.

The overview didn't help but established the extent of the challenge that stood before her. The 1984 transmitter, or Orwell Transmitter as they originally called it, now in its eleventh generation, had undergone extensive testing and upgrades. Although a few still had a tenth-generation transmitter, most people were implanted with the newer version. Based on the dates of release, Miriam and Derrick had version 11.4 implanted in their backs.

If nothing else, AJ Patel proved to be a thorough man, documenting everything in precise detail. He started each test sequence with an overview of the test, the rationale, and a summary. Although the summary often said the transmitter withstood all testing, she read each word anyway, refusing to let any detail go undetected.

Patel tested the transmitter at different temperatures, even though a human could only survive a narrow range. In his opening narrative, he explained the temperature test was important to ensure the transmitter survived from fire to artic, even though the host didn't. They used the transmitter in combat situations where bodies, or more accurately, the person's equipment, needed to be recovered. The transmitter withstood temperatures from -75 to 5000 degrees Fahrenheit. No solution there.

Patel tested the chip in a substantial number of solutions, even though the chip was implanted in a human body. Water, saltwater, chlorinated water, six strong acids, five alkaline solutions, antifreeze, various forms of alcohol, urine, and heavy water (which pertained to nuclear reactors, whatever those were) failed to shut the damn thing off. Patel rattled on for several pages about reactors, how they functioned, and how the water became heavy. Miriam read every word. The transmitter didn't survive in the strongest acids, but then neither would she nor Derrick.

Miriam read with no success until she was about three-quarters through the document. And then she saw something. The transmitter failed at 98% when subjected to high voltage. AJ Patel tested the transmitter using different voltages, starting at 1.5 volts to 50,000 volts. The failures occurred above 220 volts. The test included increasing amounts of amperes at each voltage. AJ Patel included many graphs that showed the relationship between voltage and amperes, how each test affected the Orwell Transmitter, and whether the shock killed the host.

She read each page, studied each graph, wondered how this might help because the amount of electricity needed to kill the transmitter also killed the host. But then, at the high end of the voltage tests, she saw that with high volts and low amperes, the chip failed, but the person lived, usually. The Orwell failed 89% of the time. Not bad odds. People survived at a much higher rate. The number of people who might die from exposure to this voltage was so small that AJ didn't provide a percentage.

AJ Patel's summary caused Miriam to dance around her room. When the Orwell Transmitter was exposed to a security staff stun device, it failed 89% of the time.

She only needed a device.

She knew some guys who would help her get one.

30

A MINOR CELEBRATION WAS IN order. Miriam trotted down the stairs—having lost most of her dinner—a mocha and a pastry would help commemorate her discovery. Humming, she looked up halfway down the stairs and saw Father and Mother staring at her like she had sprouted lacy wings and emanated a cloud of fairy dust. It was one of those rare moments when Miriam did not know what to say.

"Hi," she said, wondering what time it was.

"What are you doing up?" Father asked.

His question stung, innocent as it was, seemed more like the inquisition of a Keeper than a parental concern.

"What are you doing up?" She asked and added, "I'm getting something to drink."

"You are in a much better mood. Why is that?" Mother asked.

Miriam looked at the ceiling and said, "I don't know. Getting news about Derrick, I guess. It wasn't good news, but it was something. And you said he was okay. That was huge right there."

Father and Mother looked at each other as if passing an unspoken communication. Father said, "Glad you are in better spirits. Don't stay up too late. You need to get back on a regular sleep schedule. This won't go on much longer."

"I'll work on it," she said. "Anything else?"

Neither Father nor Mother said anything. She walked into the kitchen, which was open on one side to the great room where they ate dinner and gathered to watch New America Media, although Miriam seldom joined them. Derrick had often watched the news and documentaries with them, talking about the blessings of being Chosen and the horrors of the commoner world. On many occasions, Father had tried to encourage her to spend what he called family time but gave up when she was ten.

She ordered a hot chocolate from the machine, a good drink if one wanted to sleep. Father and Mother whispered for a few minutes, watching her, and then retired to the master suite, which occupied half of the main floor. She had never seen the inside. To the best of her knowledge, neither had Derrick.

Once they were gone, she dumped the chocolate in the sink and rinsed away the evidence. Then she ordered a double espresso in a splash of hot water and a pastry filled with fruit. She giggled at Father's statement that her schedule wouldn't last much longer. *No, it won't last much longer, and if he only knew my real schedule, he might have fainted, and if he knew why it would end soon, he might have had a heart attack.*

But she stopped smiling.

Why did he say, "won't go on much longer" instead of "cannot go on much longer?" Mere semantics or a mental slip?

Cannot indicates the condition is not sustainable. It must change to regain a healthy balance in life. *Won't* indicates the condition could continue, but external forces will not permit it. *What if Father knows what I've been doing? I think I'm getting away with it, but what if it's a setup? Some sort of test. Test Subject #6.*

Miriam climbed the stairs, looking back over her shoulder to see if Father or Mother were watching from their door. She scanned the room, wondering if they were monitoring her with hidden cameras, and realizing that if they were, the cameras would be nearly impossible to see. Only the outside cameras were easily seen. At least the ones she knew about were easy. To understand how complex and to what extent this entire situation might be a test, she had to understand who she and Derrick were. She needed to understand who the people she knew as Father and Mother were as well.

Father was right about one thing. Her schedule had been disrupted. She set her coffee and pastries on her Cherrywood, bedside table. She didn't need sugar and caffeine. She needed a few hours' sleep and then work the same schedule as she would during the week. Coffee and sugar would be waiting for her when she awoke.

March 21, Sunday

One minute after midnight, Miriam awoke to the alarm. As the sleep cleared from her eyes, she realized there had been no dreams about Number Seven and Number Six. She didn't think the dreams would continue because the door to those memories was open. She could begin accessing them without the help of her subconscious. In her bathroom, she splashed water on her face and considered taking a shower but didn't. No time for that.

After reheating her coffee, she sat and opened the first of many files dated 12 years earlier, titled: TS-#7 program overview.

31

THAT SUNDAY, MIRIAM MAINTAINED A disciplined schedule: read, sleep, eat, read. She came to meals, so Father didn't need to beckon her. At the table, she spoke when spoken to but otherwise remained silent. She had learned a great deal about her and Derrick's status as test subjects, and now it was vital she disclosed no sign of her awareness. During these limited encounters with Father and Mother, she thought their attentiveness was too attentive, as if they were studying her. She wondered if they had always studied her, but she had failed to notice.

In the early afternoon, she went downstairs for food, selecting a chicken pot pie from the machine and hand-making a mocha with two shots. The automated setting made decent drinks, but something about tamping the grounds by hand comforted her. Perhaps because she controlled the entire process.

Before she could head back to her room, Father stepped in and said, "Join us in the great room. Leave your food."

Mother sat on the fireplace hearth, dressed as if she and Father might go to a dinner affair. A knot formed in Miriam's stomach. *Something happened to Derrick. Maybe commoners learned he was there. Swarmed the building and took him.* Her thoughts angered her because, like it or not, she was surrendering to New America's propaganda.

"What's happened?" she asked.

"Good news," Father said.

Miriam realized she had been holding her breath. "Good news?"

"We get to communicate with Derrick. Just a brief conversation, but we'll get to see him," Mother said.

Father raised his hand. "Strict rules, though, as you might expect. No discussion about the Tribunal changing Derrick's conditions. No questions about where he is."

"Better than nothing, I guess." Miriam shrugged.

The home communication system sounded a tone signaling someone had arrived in front of the house. "Visitors have arrived in front of the King residence," a disembodied voice said throughout the home.

Father opened the door. Three men wearing identical black suits walked in. Miriam didn't recognize any of them. They didn't introduce themselves. They repeated the rules that Father had already stated, stretching the explanation to 15 minutes by adding lots of "if any of the rules are violated, the transmission will end immediately, no future communications, severe penalties for all parties, etc., to ad nauseum."

One man positioned the family so they could see the monitor screen. Then, two men stood on each side of the family, but Miriam was certain they were just far enough back so Derrick couldn't see them. The third man positioned a camera, which seemed much larger than necessary, on a tripod in front of them. He turned on the family's communications monitor, and the family appeared in a small box in the upper right-hand corner of the screen. The camera operator spoke into a communication device, stating they were ready.

Derrick's face filled the screen.

Miriam glanced from side to side. The men watched with stares of steel. As subtly as possible, she sent Derrick a message she hoped he would notice, pointing to her chest she held up one finger and mouthed: number1sis.

* * *

At dinner, the last time she would spend more than a passing moment with Father and Mother until tomorrow, she asked if they had heard anything additional about Derrick. Father said they had not. Miriam didn't believe him. She was certain they knew more.

She had read many, but not all the files copied to the storage device. After dinner, she focused on more recent documents, mostly e-mail messages. She learned the Marcus Carver incident was a test for TS-#7. But it did not go as planned. Notes indicated TS-#7 had not met standards. The test had been carefully designed and rigorously monitored. In another document, she learned that they had been testing TS-#7 for years, which surprised her. It was important that she read more, but now she had to move on to more urgent matters.

Although she didn't completely understand the purpose of the testing, that didn't affect her decision. She needed to escape, and the impossible would be even more difficult if they knew what she was doing. A game of chess where the opponent controls all the pieces is not easily won.

She considered conceding defeat. At least that would give her some sense of control. Unless they had predicted she would discover they were monitoring her, and upon learning the futility of her quest, she would give up, which would prove their theories correct.

Screw that.

After dinner, she felt compelled to read further, but she needed sleep because she was returning to Technical Service tonight. They would expect her to do that. She lay on her bed staring at the ceiling in the dim light, but she couldn't sleep. Instead of forcing sleep, instead of compelling her thoughts, she let her mind drift, and she emptied the thoughts. In the silence of her mind, something might come from beyond her natural thought process. Why she believed that was never clear to her, but it worked just the same.

Drifting.

Drifting.

Drifting.

March 22, Monday, 12:01 a.m.

The alarm sounded. She didn't know when sleep overcame her. She shuffled to the bathroom and splashed water on her face. Thought about showering but didn't want to risk awakening Father and Mother, although she was now operating under the assumption that they knew what she was doing. The reason for not showering was to avoid letting them know she knew they were watching. She now understood what she must do. She had to remain visible in her quest to help Derrick yet ensure her true intentions remained hidden at the same time. She had no idea how to accomplish that.

Down the drain chain and onto the driveway, she pulled her hood over her head. No change. *Still hiding from you guys.* She realized she had not accomplished anything that would help her escape. At least, that was how she felt. Halfway to Technical Service, she felt as if someone were watching her. However, feelings mean nothing. Only facts. She dismissed it as paranoia. She had an abundance of that.

Miriam entered the building as warily as the first time she arrived, uncertain if Brad and Marty had returned from their weekend. However, if it was a set-up, the weekend guys had also received instructions same as Marty and Brad. *Those two are convincing actors,* she mused. A slim chance existed that her assumptions were wrong, so she still needed to be careful.

She wondered if they had a program that monitored her every keystroke. She logged into the computer and began her search. She found a utility that listed every running program. She scrolled through the list, not knowing what she was looking for, memorizing each application. She saw one that looked promising or threatening, depending on one's point of view: SnoopKey.

She shut the machine off and unplugged all the cables from the wall, hoping that would disconnect the machine from the network and the elimination of electricity would cause any programs still running to stop. She did this understanding that hoping accomplished nothing. Programs wouldn't care what she hoped for. She plugged just the electrical cord in and restarted the computer. The opening screen appeared, and she logged in using AJ's username and password. Not wanting to leave more digital tracks than necessary, she went straight to the application monitor. She scrolled to the bottom of the screen, and SnoopKey was not running under AJ's login. Did it run when any user logged on, or did the user have to start or stop it? She didn't know, but she'd find out.

Snoopkey wasn't running under her login either, so that made her feel better, sort of. She had started getting used to the idea that someone was monitoring her every move. However, she thought it changed nothing.

She had an idea. She inserted her storage device—she learned they called it a flash drive—into the machine, found the folder she wanted, and saved a copy of everything pertinent to the subject. Then she shut the machine down again, restarted it, and logged in as Maranda Kingston. She opened the file search application and searched for TS-#7, TS-#6, Derrick King, and Miriam King. A list of folders appeared. She wanted to read the e-mails before and after the Marcus Carver incident, but she resisted the urge. Once opened, those watching her would know that she knew. If they were watching her. See how it confused things?

To be safe, she read some old stuff. She had already read enough to understand. Still, as she had when she first started reading documents at home, she cried. She was angry and scared. She smiled when a tap came at the door, and a familiar voice said, "Maranda? Are you working tonight?"

Miriam closed the file and sprang to the door. "Hi, guys. Lunchtime already?"

"Yep. We'll see you there soon?"

"I'll walk with you if that's okay."

"Sure is."

Miriam closed the door but didn't lock it because that would be weird. Still, it made her nervous. Anyone who walked in could see what she was looking at. But they already knew what she was looking at, unless they didn't. Anxieties based on emotions and speculation, not on facts. Not good.

Miriam walked between the two men who accepted her as a peer or at least pretended they did. That thought made her a little sad. She hoped that while incompetent; they were honest. No way to know for sure.

Halfway down the hall, Marty said, "How was your weekend?"

Miriam thought about it for a moment. Overall, it had been awful. She had learned the Tribunal screwed Derrick, altering his sentence, realized her clandestine operation might not be as secret as she had hoped, discovered she and Derrick were Test Subjects, and that Father and Mother were not who they pretended to be.

Her weekend sucked, but she said, "My weekend was fine. How about you?"

Brad jumped in first. "Took my son fishing in the mountains. Camped right next to the stream. Didn't catch many fish but had a wonderful time."

Marty said, "The wife and I drove down the coast. Walked on the beach and ate dinner at our favorite restaurant. My parents watched the kids. We needed a little alone time, if you know what I mean."

He nudged Miriam with his elbow. She speculated on his meaning and felt uncomfortable at the revelation.

"What did you do, Maranda?" Brad asked.

"Well," Miriam paused. "Nothing as exciting as you." Which was true. It was not lost on her that both men, while more privileged than many commoners, were commoners just the same, and both had described better weekends than she had ever experienced. Finally, she said, "Slept a lot. Last week wore me out. Read a lot. Work stuff. Not much fun." She had told the truth. That was easier than making crap up.

"All work and no play," Brad said.

Miriam didn't know the proper response, so she said, "Yep. That's my life." That was also true and a little sad, actually.

Inside the lunchroom, the three friends got drinks and food and sat at their usual table. To prevent the men from further inquiry, Miriam directed the conversation.

"How old is your son?" she asked Brad.

"Fourteen. That age where he'll still do stuff with me if his friends aren't around. But that won't last much longer. Soon, I'll be an embarrassment. In a few years, I won't see much of him until he's in his twenties."

Miriam thought she detected a tear in Brad's right eye.

Fearing what Marty might say about his weekend exploits, she stayed clear of that subject and focused on eating. The men turned to a discussion about the next football season, which suited her fine.

When the break ended, they cleared the table. Marty and Brad stepped into the hall, and Brad said, "See you tomorrow?"

"Absolutely," Miriam said. "But I was wondering if I could walk with you for a while. Get a tour of the building?"

Brad looked at Marty. Marty shrugged.

"It's irregular, but you're from corporate. I guess it would be okay. Unless this is a trap, and you intend to report us."

Miriam considered the irony since she assumed Brad and Marty were both involved in the trap set for her. "You guys are funny. Trust me. If I were setting up a subversion, it wouldn't be to catch two security guys."

Brad chuckled. "I guess that's true. Besides, if you're part of a sting, we're already toast." He paused and then, bowing slightly at the waist. "Brad and Marty, tour guides extraordinaire, at your service, Ma'am."

Miriam couldn't help but like these two, even though they might be helping to set her up. On the other hand, they might be as innocent as they seemed. She would have to consider that in her planning.

They walked back the way they came, through the shared area of many desks separated by low walls. "What do these people do?" Miriam asked.

Brad looked at her with one eyebrow raised. "Tech support people. I thought you knew. You're working in the Technical Service Supervisor's office."

Miriam paused. She needed to be more careful with her questions. "Right. I know Mr. Patel is the supervisor, but I don't work in Technical Service. They just assigned me to his office. Top-notch computer and all that."

"Makes sense," Marty offered. "Patel would have the most powerful computer in the building, other than the servers, but those are not personal computers."

"Exactly," Miriam said, comfortable that the exchange had gone well.

"What department do you work in?" Brad asked.

"Secret stuff. Remember?" Miriam whispered.

"Right. Sorry."

"I have a mental block on my project. You ever have that? I see the problem but don't know how to go at it. Walking helps me think. So, how about this? You guys are the experts. Just tell me what's what. I'll walk and listen."

"I've never had that problem with this job. Have you, Marty?"

"Had what problem?"

"Mental block."

Marty stopped and laughed so hard he bent at the waist. Finally, he said, "Good one, buddy. Nope, just walk around all night for no good reason. No mental blocks, other than, why didn't I stay in Ohio?"

Brad pointed out the server room. "The most secure room in the building," he said. Then he pointed to the door Miriam entered as Maranda Kingston and told her it led to Pacific Edge. They walked to the section of the building closest to the sea, which housed human resources. Marty said human resources was there to support employees but spent most of their time finding ways to fire people. They retraced their steps through Technical Service. Beyond Technical Service, they entered a large dining facility. It was unlike the lunchroom, where vending machines offered a variety of food and drinks. This was a large room with round tables and glossy floors. On one side stood a long counter with a glass cover. Marty said the day workers got free hot meals. He added that the night shift got imitation food, referring to the vending machines. The metaphor was easily understood by anyone who had eaten a meal from the machines. Behind the dining room was an enormous kitchen of glistening stainless steel, walk-in coolers, walk-in freezers, long countertops, ovens, grills, an enormous espresso machine, and a polished concrete floor. However, in the back was something she needed—exit doors.

She needed another thing, which turned out to be in the next section of the building: Pacific Edge Security. This was Brad and Marty's employment home. Despite their snarky comments about their job, both men's postures changed slightly when they walked through the door and announced they had entered Pacific Edge Security. Brad slowed, pointing out each section, who led each team, and each team's responsibilities. It surprised her that security had a technical division of its own.

"The tech guys watch the system for hackers and outside cyber-attack," Marty said.

Miriam was unfamiliar with the term, hacker, but realized she had become one. Cool. But then her stomach twisted when she recognized that Pacific Edge Security might have been monitoring her computer activity, including e-mails sent to Derrick.

"Are hackers a big problem?" she asked.

"From what they tell us, it's a huge problem. But they don't tell us much. The Tech Security Division pulls a lot of weight, if that's any indication," Marty said.

Brad did most of the talking, but Marty was quicker to give up details, so she looked at Marty when asking questions. Since she impersonated a technical expert high in the hierarchy of headquarters staff, she carefully avoided questions to which she should know the answers. She didn't ask another question until they had moved deeper into the security division.

"Do you know any of the people in Tech Security?" she asked.

Marty said, "My wife is friends with a tech guy's wife. Sue and Chad. I don't pal around with Chad, but he's a nice fella. A nerd, for sure. Doesn't fish or hunt. We have dinner with them occasionally."

Miriam remained silent for a few minutes. "Does he say much about the hackers?"

"He won't talk about work much. Just some general stuff. Occasionally, he'll say something like—you didn't hear this from me, but—I don't press him on it."

"People at headquarters will be pleased to learn that security staff don't share details. Does Chad say anything about what security sees as the principal threat? From headquarters' perspective, it is critical they have identified the right place to focus their resources," Miriam said.

Brad cleared his throat.

Marty said, "Probes from foreign countries. Chad said domestic hackers lack the equipment and skills to be a threat. The only way a domestic hacker could be a threat is if he got inside our network. Portals to the internet are limited and tightly controlled."

Miriam nodded. "Excellent." *Patel's computer seems to have full access to the internet. Probably because he is a technical supervisor,* she thought.

They passed through double doors, entering a cavernous room. The walls gleamed with snow-white paint, and the gray concrete floor glistened. The smell of hovercraft filled the room. In addition, the odors suggested too much metal. As they entered, banks of overhead lights flashed on and lit the room like midday. A row of security transports lined one wall. Most were typical black transports with black windows and Pacific Edge Security written on the doors with florescent green lettering. Much larger transports were covered with heavy metal plates, flat black instead of shiny, like the standard transports. She noted large weapons mounted atop the big machines. She had rarely seen the standard-size transport on the streets of Pacific Edge and had never seen the larger ones. She assumed they mainly patrolled outside the Community.

Hovercraft lined the other wall. At the far end of the building stood a cage constructed of heavy wire-like material, which held flight suits, handheld weapons, thick black vests, helmets, gloves, etc.

Marty pointed. "Outside patrol gear."

Miriam nodded. "Where are custodial staff located?"

"Machines do most of the cleaning in here. Better security." Marty rolled his eyes. "Kitchen staff are responsible for their own area. There are cleaning staff for the rest of the building, but they are gone by the time you come in."

They turned left and walked through a single metal door labeled Building Security and Maintenance.

"Although technically still in the security section, we're lumped in with the maintenance guys," Marty said.

"The maintenance guys are important," Brad offered.

"Yeah, a nice lot too," Marty said. "But shows you where we are in the scheme of things. Stuck in the corner with electricians, plumbers, and grease monkeys. Everyone here is nice folk, except for those jerks." Marty indicated the Pacific Edge Security area with his thumb. "They even have their own maintenance staff. Can't trust the regular guys."

"True," Brad said. "Outside patrol has tried to take this spot over several times. They say it's not good security letting regular staff walk through their area. They would just give us the boot, except maintenance has a lot of stuff back here, transport bays, welding shop, pipe cutting, you name it."

"Word is that they want to cut a doorway in from the other side and close this entrance. Just waiting for funding from headquarters," Marty said. Looking at Miriam, he added, "I suppose you know how hard it is to get headquarters to turn loose of additional funds."

Miriam nodded. "That's for sure." She knew nothing about headquarters, who owned what, organizational structure, nothing. New America Media provided no information. She would learn more about it when she had time in the future. If she had a future. The future was not guaranteed.

They passed a room labeled equipment. Miriam paused and asked, "What's in there?"

"Security equipment for inside patrol. Marty and I check our equipment in and out each night." Brad tapped the heavy leather belt around his waist.

"Could we look inside?" she asked.

Brad and Marty looked at each other. Neither spoke for a moment. Miriam was unsure what to say if they asked why she wanted to see it.

Finally, Marty said, "You're from headquarters, so I don't see why not. Nothing special in there. Just routine stuff."

Brad shrugged.

"Is that part of your assignment? Doing a site inspection?" Marty snickered.

"You guys are sharp," Miriam said with a smile.

"I'm surprised you're not taking notes," Brad said.

"I have an exceptional memory. One reason they send me."

Marty stepped to the supply room door and punched numbers on the keypad.

Miriam put her exceptional memory to work.

32

March 22, Monday, James Carver Academy

THE UNEXPECTED BENEFITS THAT ACCOMPANIED her decision to leave Pacific Edge sooner than expected included not arguing in class. Miriam marveled at the freedom she felt. That's why it rattled her when Mr. Jones asked her to wait in the hall when she tried to enter his class. Her gut, which she knew was not a logical organ to predict the future, told her Jones meant to cause her problems. A likely suspect in a Tribunal scheme to trap her.

Mr. Jones stepped into the hall and pulled the door closed. "I intend to spark a discussion today. I understand why you've withdrawn since the incident with Derrick. But I need the old Miriam today."

"I don't…"

Mr. Jones held up his hand. "Miriam, I'm not taking no for an answer. Please don't force me to drag you into the discussion. It's better if you engage on your own. This will help you. Trust me."

Jones opened the door and stepped to one side. Miriam took the hint and walked to the only seat available near the front. She felt eyes on her back. Mr. Jones started the class with a lame New America Media video describing the fall of the old United States of America. The fall of the U.S. blamed, this time, on science and the rejection of religion in public schools. The narrator added that James Carver, in his wisdom, eliminated public education and replaced it with private education, which he alone or his heirs would own and control. Yada, yada, yada. She had heard it before, to ad nauseam. One thing that was as obvious as a week-old dead whale on the beach, engaging in a discussion on this topic, equated to a death trap. Well, that might be a bit extreme but a trap, nonetheless. *Trust me?* She thought. What made Mr. Jones think that was even possible.

"I know you have all seen this video many times. They show it in the fourth grade, as I recall," Mr. Jones began.

A boy in the front row named Ed raised his hand. Ed often smiled when Miriam debated Mr. Jones but only spoke if spoken to and then gave benign answers.

"Yes, Ed?"

"Third."

"Third, what?" Mr. Jones asked.

"Third grade. They show it in the third grade." Ed glanced over his shoulder and smiled at Miriam.

What was that about?

"Okay. Third grade. Let's discuss science. What makes it evil?"

No hands raised. No sounds made. Miriam scrunched down in her seat, arms folded across her chest. She wondered if those seated next to her could feel the heat rising.

"How about you, Ed? Why is science evil?"

Ed fidgeted in his seat. "I'm not sure."

"You're not sure," Mr. Jones said in a mocking tone. "Doesn't the narrator state the reasons?"

Miriam tightened her arms across her chest. She hated it when Mr. Jones bullied kids. It often proved to be the trigger he used to drag her into a debate. *What's his game? We've been arguing all year, but after they exiled Derrick, he softened, and now he's back to his old self.* Determined to focus on her goals, Miriam said nothing.

"Yes, sir," Ed whispered.

"Humph. Can anyone provide meaningful thoughts on this subject?" Mr. Jones scanned the room and walked between the desks until he stood behind Miriam. Towering over her.

"Marcus. How about you? You're a distant relation to James Carver, aren't you?"

Marcus turned in his seat. His face grew red; his eyes fell on Miriam and then rose to glare at Mr. Jones. "Not all that distant. You should know that. I don't understand why we would discuss this. It's not a debatable topic. Science rejected the Creator and the calling of James Carver as the world's leader. Science told lies about everything from the age of the Earth to its origins. Said man affects the weather instead of the fact that the Creator controls everything. We are much better off without science." Marcus waved his arm, almost hitting the kid behind him in the head. "Look at the commoners! That's where we would be if we still allowed science."

Miriam didn't believe the room could have grown quieter, but it did. As if everyone had stopped breathing and their hearts had stopped beating, well, except for her breathing, which quickened to match her pounding heart. *How can people be so stupid?*

"Thank you, Marcus. Clearly, you're passionate about your beliefs. Anyone like to add to Marcus's observations? Or maybe someone has additional insights?"

"No one?"

The room remained silent. Miriam noticed kids staring at her, but maybe it just seemed that way because they were looking at Mr. Jones, who was still standing behind her.

Mr. Jones said, "How about you, Miriam? You typically have thoughts on such matters."

Miriam pushed up in her seat. "I have nothing to add. Marcus explained it."

Mr. Jones sighed. "Nothing to add. Hard to believe. I know you blame Marcus for Derrick's exile, but it was Derrick's fault, wasn't it?"

"Leave Derrick out of it," Miriam said, twisting in her seat to face Mr. Jones.

"Oh, but we can't do that, can we? Because you are hiding behind his exile, thinking you are no longer required to take part in class."

"What do you want from me?" Miriam snarled.

"A truthful answer. That has never been difficult for you. You used to say what you believed to be true."

Miriam's chest rose and fell. She remained silent. Mr. Jones remained silent as well. Something told her that Jones would remain silent until she answered. She couldn't understand his motive. If the Tribunal was monitoring her breaking and entering behaviors, they didn't need additional charges against her.

"It surrounds us," Miriam said.

Mr. Jones smiled. "What surrounds us, Miriam?"

"Science surrounds us."

Murmurs coursed through the classroom. One would have thought she'd asked for drugs and dead puppies.

"But science is forbidden. How can it surround us?" someone asked.

"She should be exiled for saying that," Marcus cried out. "It's blasphemy."

"Marcus. Did I call on you?" Mr. Jones asked.

"No, sir."

"When I want your opinion, I'll ask for it. Clear enough for you, Mr. Carver?"

"Yes, sir."

"Miriam. When you make a statement like that, you must be prepared to back it up with observable facts. Otherwise, it would be best if you withdrew your claim."

"Fine. How many facts would you like?"

"Let's start with one. One fact."

"Lights."

"You want me to turn them off?"

"No, duh. Electricity. It's science. Lights, electricity, the video we just watched, transports, hovercraft, communication devices, heat, air conditioning, vending machines, espresso machines, roads, houses. None of it would exist without science. Where do you think it all comes from? Magic wands? Fairy dust?"

Miriam stood.

As if on cue, red light bathed the room.

But no one moved.

Finally, Mr. Jones said, "You are dismissed. Go now. Shoo."

Miriam started toward the door, but a hand softly landed on her shoulder. "Not you, Miriam."

When the room had cleared, Mr. Jones stepped to the door and closed it. He leaned against his desk, arms folded, smiling. Finally, he said, "That was quite an outburst. You'll be reported. I assume you know that. You have been reported many times, but I suspect the headmaster will summon you to his office this time."

"Why are you keeping me here?" she asked.

"To let the hall clear. You are free to go." Mr. Jones walked to the door and opened it.

She couldn't read him. Was he pleased with himself? Would he report her? Probably.

Still, obvious as that seemed, she didn't think reporting her was the origin of his smile.

33

IN MRS. SPRINGFIELD'S CLASS, Miriam waited for the fallout from her outburst with Mr. Jones. Any moment, she anticipated a summons to the headmaster's office. Probably a school-wide announcement on the public address system, although he could just as easily call Mrs. Springfield and have her send Miriam to the office. He would lecture her and attempt to diagnose what caused her to be so anti-Chosen. They might call in the Academy psychologist or do some medical testing.

She didn't care but wished they'd get on with it.

Mrs. Springfield gave the class a reading assignment and told them to sit quietly when finished. Miriam flipped through the pages, scanning but not reading. Enjoying the benefits of leaving Pacific Edge soon, study was no longer required. She wouldn't need to know this material. Although, unfortunately, she already knew it. It was a repeat of the same crap that was permanently installed in her brain.

Miriam appreciated the reprieve from having another discussion. She couldn't handle more brainwashed regurgitation of New America talking points. She didn't think she could contain herself. Another blowup would get her suspended, which didn't sound like a bad plan because she could use the time to focus on ending this. She had vowed to lie low, stay out of trouble and out of sight, which she failed to do in Mr. Jones' class. Part of her looked forward to a confrontation with the Academy administration, part of her felt like a total failure, and part of her wished she was an ordinary girl with an ordinary brother.

Mrs. Springfield moved about the students, pausing here and there to ensure they were on task, lingering long enough to make them feel uncomfortable. As she passed Miriam's desk, she slid a folded piece of paper under the book. After a few minutes, Miriam pulled the note from under the book, and the tidy handwriting said:

They will come for you during lunch. Stay calm. This is for the best.

Miriam wasted no time getting to the courtyard. She grabbed a plate and went straight to the table she and Rebekah shared since the incident. Miriam paused when she saw Anna Ford sitting there instead of Rebekah.

"I hope you don't mind," Anna said.

"I don't mind. But your sister might."

"She's not the boss of me."

Miriam smiled.

"What are you doing here?" Rebekah demanded, holding a tray and glaring at Anna.

"Eating lunch, genius."

"Don't get smart with me. Now get. Miriam and I have things to discuss."

"I'm not going anywhere. Whatever you're discussing can be discussed in front of me. Besides, Miriam and I are friends."

Rebekah rolled her eyes and sat. Staring at Miriam, she said, "See what you started?"

"I made Anna brave? Turned her into a smart-ass? Either way, good for me."

"Not what I meant."

Miriam said, "I have news. Do you want to hear it, or not?"

Rebekah looked around, leaned in, and whispered, "Of course I want to hear it."

"The Tribunal changed the sentence. Derrick starts school on Monday."

"Monday?" Rebekah asked louder than she intended. Then, lowering her voice, she said, "Those bastards. He must be terrified."

Miriam nodded.

Anna seized Miriam's hand. "I'm sorry. Are you worried?"

Miriam took a bite of her sandwich.

"What are you going to do?" Rebekah asked.

"Nothing I can do. I'm here. He's there. I assume you've noticed that."

Rebekah said nothing.

Miriam turned to Anna. "I'm not worried. Well, a little worried."

"You don't believe the common world is like what they show us on the news and such, do you?" Anna asked.

Miriam studied her for a moment, glanced at Rebekah, and said, "No. I don't believe it. But I don't know what it is like either. Mostly, I'm worried because Derrick believes New America Media. Like you said, he must be petrified."

They ate silently for a few minutes, and then a tone signifying an announcement came over the loudspeakers.

"Miriam King, report to the vice headmaster immediately."

"What do you think they'll do to you?" Anna asked.

Miriam stared at her.

"I heard about it," Anna said.

"I don't know. Looks like I'm about to find out." Miriam stood, took her tray, and turned away. She looked back and said, "I may not see you for a few days."

"Unlikely," Rebekah said.

Miriam started to walk away.

"Miriam," Rebekah called.

Miriam turned back to face her.

Rebekah said, "You'd better pick up the pace on a plan."

34

MIRIAM WALKED THROUGH EMPTY HALLS to the vice headmaster's office. Vacant halls reminded her of Technical Service, which she realized she liked much better than the Academy. Not because she was alone but because she was learning things there. She felt challenged and useful. She wondered if she would ever experience that in a real job.

A plump lady sat behind a counter inside the outer office, and a nameplate set on top of the counter read Gloria Hirsch. The room smelled of disinfectant. Miriam wondered if something had occurred in the office that required disinfecting, or if Gloria was obsessed with germs or teenagers. A large green, thick-leaved plant filled one corner. Its leaves shone as if polished. Potted plants were uncommon in Pacific Edge. Plants were meticulously maintained but kept in their rightful place, which meant outside. A large plaque next to the door to the inner office read: Senior Vice Headmaster Donald J Harding.

Miriam didn't know they had degrees of vice headmaster.

"I'm Miriam King. Someone paged me on the public address system."

"I know who you are. Sit. Mr. Harding will be with you shortly."

Miriam did not sit but walked around the room, studying the plaques on the walls. She went behind the counter, which she knew was intruding into Ms. Hirsch's space, wondering how uncomfortable she could make Ms. Hirsch before being told to get back on the other side of the counter or sprayed with disinfectant. Ms. Hirsch glanced at Miriam, squinted her eyes, and sighed but otherwise remained silent.

The door to the senior vice headmaster's office opened, and a short man of slight build stood at the door. He looked to a bench where students sat, eventually scanning the room and spotting Miriam by the windows.

"Please step this way, Ms. King."

"Gloria, I am unavailable. Do not disturb me."

"Yes, sir," Ms. Hirsch said, tidying her desk, which looked perfectly organized to Miriam.

Miriam walked into Harding's office. Harding pointed at a seat in front of his desk.

Miriam stood in front of the chair.

Harding stood behind his desk, his fingers fidgeting as if trying to shake bugs from his fingertips.

"Sit," he said, more forcefully than necessary.

Miriam sat.

"I guess you know why you are here."

"Yes, sir. I'm here because there was an announcement on the public address system."

"Well, of course, but I mean the reason."

"Because I'd be in trouble if I ignored the announcement on the public address system."

Harding's face turned red, fading to pink at the top of his balding head, which he had attempted to cover with longer hair brushed up and over one side. "I see the problem already," he said.

"Glad to hear that. Can I go now that you have the problem solved?" Miriam didn't know what came over her. That was not entirely accurate. She was acting like her true self, which she was not supposed to do, but having taken this road, she seemed unable to turn back.

"No, you may not go!"

"Okay," Miriam said slowly. "What can I do for you, Don?" Miriam knew better than to use his first name, and the short, informal version made it worse. She couldn't help herself. Besides, getting suspended would be advantageous. Time spent here was time wasted.

Sweat beaded on the top of Harding's head, and Miriam feared he was having a heart attack or contemplating homicide. A heart attack she could live with—homicide, not so much.

"I've had it with you!" Harding shouted, spit spraying from his mouth. "You and your smart mouth. You're suspended for a week!"

Harding came around the desk, taking giant steps, grabbing her by the arm, and jerking her up from the chair. He dragged her to his door and pushed her out. "Call a transport to take her to her home," he said.

"I can wa…"

"Shut your mouth. You'll do no such thing." He looked at Ms. Hirsch, who cowered in her chair. "She is to be taken straight home. Got it?"

"Yes, sir, Mr. Harding," Ms. Hirsch said.

Harding stepped back into his office, slamming the door behind him. A plaque fell off the wall, and the glass shattered on the floor.

Ms. Hirsch stood and motioned Miriam to come around the counter. "Please sit here, Ms. King," she whispered.

Ms. Hirsch spoke into the monitor on her desk. "Transport from James Carver Academy to Ms. Miriam King's house. No stops, no detours. Ms. King must be delivered to her front door. Administrative override to unlock the front door upon Miriam's arrival home."

Miriam sat as instructed, feeling more disturbed than she wanted to admit. She put her hands between her knees, so Ms. Hirsch couldn't see them tremble.

Ms. Hirsch blushed and looked up from her monitor. "I've never seen him that mad. What did you do?"

Miriam shrugged.

Miriam and Ms. Hirsch were startled when Harding's door flew open.

"Did you call that transport?" He demanded.

"Yes, sir."

"Good. I have entered her suspension in the system." He glared at Miriam. "I'm leaving for the rest of the day."

Ms. Hirsch returned to her monitor and said, "Miriam King record." She studied the screen and gave her head a slight shake.

A few moments later, a tone sounded from her monitor. "Your transport is here. I'll walk you out."

"That's unnecessary. I'll take it home. Don't worry about it."

"I will feel better knowing you got to the transport safely," Ms. Hirsch said as she stood.

Miriam wouldn't have admitted feeling relieved to have Ms. Hirsch as an escort and witness.

Lunch had ended and classes had resumed. Miriam studied the hall, the class doors, the floors, the walls. This might be the last time she saw James Carver Academy. It surprised her when tears trickled down her cheeks. She had not developed an unexpected love for James Carver Academy. Having been a loner and rebel, she didn't have friends. Never thought she needed any, except for Derrick, and she had driven him away and then caused him to be exiled. However, she would miss Anna Ford. A curious girl with a bit of defiance, not unlike herself. She would miss Rebekah too, although she had proven to be a pain in the ass. Her oddest thought, the one that caused her some alarm for her mental health, was she would miss Mr. Jones. Her enemy, or so she had always thought. Miriam was right about most things, but she would later realize how wrong she had been about many, and her plan was not as foolproof as she assumed.

"Stop! Wait right there!"

Miriam turned to see the headmaster, Benny Greerson, trotting down the hall toward them.

"What is going on?" Greerson asked.

"I'm just walking Miriam to the transport," Ms. Hirsch said.

"I can see that," Greerson barked. "I mean this suspension. Did Harding do it? I stopped at his office, but he wasn't there."

"He left for the day. Right after he suspended Miriam."

"What on earth did you do?" He stared at Miriam.

"Uh, I was being kind of a smart-ass with him," she admitted.

"You're a smart-ass with everyone. Did you swear at him?"

"No."

"Try to hit, kick, or bite him?"

"Of course not."

"Ms. Hirsch?"

"I couldn't hear Miriam. I heard Mr. Harding, though."

"Harding was shouting?"

"Yes, sir."

"Well, we can't have this. A week of suspension is irregular. Besides, I have instructions."

"Instructions?" Ms. Hirsch asked.

"Oh, well, never mind that. Not instructions exactly." Greerson looked over his shoulder, but no one was there.

"What would you like me to do, sir?" Ms. Hirsch asked. "You can change the length of the suspension or override it however you would like."

"No, I can't."

"Sure, you can. You're the headmaster. But I saw you had approved the suspension. So, I'm confused."

"That's the thing. I didn't approve it."

"But the computer says…"

"I know what the computer says. That's why I'm here." Greerson took a deep breath. "I didn't authorize the suspension. Someone else did."

"But the authorization has your name on it."

"Exactly. That's the problem. It was not me. Someone else put my name on it. So, it's a done deal. This is not good. Get Harding back in here. I'm not going down for this, but someone is."

35

RIDING IN THE TRANSPORT TOWARD home, Miriam pondered how confusing the past hour had been. She gave Harding a troublesome time, but he nutted up quickly. In hindsight, he was nutting up before the conversation started. Mr. Jones was accustomed to her and, despite her being problematic, he had never reported her. So, who did?

Marcus Carver.

Had to be Marcus.

That Marcus took it upon himself to report me was no surprise. But what did he say that spun Mr. Harding out of control? Harding would have talked to Mr. Jones before acting. What did Mr. Jones say? Had he finally had enough and dumped all his frustration? Must have. Marcus exaggerated, and Mr. Jones released a tidal wave of grief.

Harding overreacted.

But who approved the suspension?

Who could get into the school computer and manipulate it?

Only one name came to mind: AJ Patel.

36

March 23, Tuesday, 12:20 a.m.

THE LECTURE FROM FATHER HAD BEEN more subdued than she expected, and Mother remained silent through dinner. After eating, Mirriam napped before dragging herself out of bed and walking to Technical Service. The night's early mist felt refreshing but failed to revive her spirits. She logged into the computer system and opened the e-mail application. Besides the usual junk, an e-mail from AJ Patel appeared on the list. The coincidence that Patel sent an e-mail after the incident at James Carver Academy wasn't lost on her. Still, she was interested in learning what AJ Patel knew, or at least what he presented. Her spirits and energy surged when she saw an e-mail from Derrick.

She was eager to read Patel's e-mail, but it could wait.

First, Derrick's. She noticed the date. This was written on Friday. Things changed quickly. When this was written, Derrick did not know the Tribunal would change his sentence. She wondered if he saw the message she attempted during their brief communication.

```
Date: Friday, March 19

TO: number1sis@potterville.com

FROM: derrickking0312@potterville.com

Is this really Miriam? I hope it is. It
might be a deception, but it does not
matter. the Tribunal ordered me to start
school next Monday. I am not ready, but
no choice. They will never let me return
to Pacific Edge. It is much different here
from what I expected. But I have been
forbidden to talk about that.

Prove it is you by asking a question that
only I would know the answer to.
```

Miriam read the last sentence twice. Why had Derrick turned this around on her? This would be difficult. He probably felt the same. It would be easy for typical siblings who grew up knowing one another. But typical siblings, they were not. She understood why now, but Derrick didn't. This would take more thought.

It was more important to her to escape, and that is where she planned to focus her energy. She considered not opening AJ Patel's email. However, she decided that not reading it would cause Patel to think she didn't trust him, so she opened it.

```
TO:
marandakingston@techservice/admin.com

FROM: ajpatel@ITservices.com

First, you're welcome. Given Derrick's
situation, you must act quickly. I
thought not attending school would be
helpful.

Second, there are two items on the desk
for you. One is an external hard drive
and connection cord, and the other is a
portable computer called a laptop. The
items are in the black bag. I trust you
can figure out how to use them.

AJ Patel
```

Miriam pulled the items from the bag. It didn't take long for her to discover that the laptop was a computer, except portable, and used the same apps and operating system as the one here. She started it and searched the running applications and saw nothing suspicious. The keystroke logger, not present. The hard drive turned out to be a storage device with more capacity than the flash drive. She needed both to work at home. That AJ Patel had anticipated things she needed bothered her. Regardless, she had to outwit them, including Patel, for her plan to work. She needed a year or two to learn more about computers, networks, and programming. She had a week.

AJ Patel expected her to use the hard drive and laptop. Maybe she should do the opposite and ignore them. She enjoyed doing the opposite, but the fact remained that she needed a storage unit and probably needed the laptop.

On the laptop, she opened the e-mail application. The little spinning wheel spun. Spun for a long time. And then a message appeared that said: You Are Not Connected to the Internet. And below that: This page cannot be displayed because your computer is offline.

Stupid, stupid, stupid. Why am I so stupid?

She didn't know how the system functioned. She didn't understand the Internet. She didn't know what made the computer online or offline. How could she outwit people who understood how to build computers and write applications? They did this for a living, and she only had a few days. A stupid girl who thought being rebellious meant she was smart.

Staring at the laptop, trembling slightly, she thought about how daunting the task was before her. She purposely refused to calculate the difficulty of escaping from Pacific Edge, although that was inaccurate. She had been thinking about how it might be done. Understanding the building layout where she sat, the perimeter thickness, the security measures, defeating 1984, and outwitting AJ Patel had all factored into her calculations. To be truthful, she didn't think her plan would work. She began to consider less desirable alternatives.

The laptop and storage drive must be part of the trap. However, not using them would tell Patel she had discovered their surveillance. She tested several other applications. Some opened as they were supposed to, others failed to open, giving her the same error message stating the computer was not connected to the internet or network. She learned that searching for answers about such things proved useless because the laptop wasn't connected. Reluctantly, she researched internet and network connections on AJ Patel's computer, which had the keylogging software running. After learning how computers connect to networks, she found the wireless application and the LAN port. Critical information because they couldn't track her activity if the laptop were not connected to the network. At least, she believed that's how it worked, but why AJ Patel would give her a device he couldn't track confused her.

Miriam turned off AJ Patel's computer. She unplugged the computer's LAN cord and then restarted it. When the computer booted, she found the active processes and turned off the keystroke application. It was the best she could do, and she hoped it was enough. Then, she located the files she wanted. She had not yet learned how to determine the size of files, folders, and applications. She hoped they would fit on the larger storage device. If not, she was screwed. The files started moving, and a window said the current file would take five minutes. Lunchtime, but Marty and Brad had not knocked.

Derrick's question had been floating in and out of her thoughts, and no good options occurred to her. Then she had an idea. She dismissed it. Too risky. Then, she decided it was worth the risk. If he knew the answer, it would confirm her conclusions.

```
Tuesday, March 23

TO: derrickking0312@potterville.com

FROM: number1sis@potterville.com

It sucks that the Tribunal changed your
sentence. I'm sorry they did that.
Yesterday was your first day of school. I
hope you're okay. Please tell me you are.

I've thought about a question that only
you could answer. I see the difficulty in
asking such a question because we don't
know each other like a brother and sister
should. Do we? There's a reason for that.

Because we never talked about this, it is
risky. Still, I suspect you will know the
answer.

What is my name in your dreams with the
Keepers?

Number1sis
```

She would send the message when back online. She hoped that she and Derrick shared the same dreams that were not dreams. She wanted him to trust her e-mails but decided that it was unimportant for now.

They could talk about the dreams when she saw him. If she ever saw him.

She carefully peered through the small window at the lunchroom and saw Brad, but not Marty. Something wasn't right. Hungry, but she could survive without food.

She turned away from the door and smacked straight into the chest of a man she didn't know.

37

THE MAN CAUGHT HER WITH a powerful hand on each of her arms. Square shoulders concealed under his uniform suggested large muscles.

"Whoa!" the man said.

Miriam almost panicked but managed to say, "Sorry. Silly me, not watching where I'm going."

"No, my fault. I should have announced my presence. Forgive me. Brad was right. You look too young to be a headquarters officer."

He released her and stepped back. Miriam stuck out her hand and said, "Not an officer. Just a geek with an aptitude for specific procedures. Hi, I'm Miriam."

The man looked at her. "Miriam?"

Crap!

"My friends call me that," she offered. "Maranda Kingston."

"Okay," the man drawled, extending his hand. "Strange nickname for Maranda."

Miriam withdrew her hand, hoped he didn't feel her trembling, laughed, which sounded fake even to her, and said, "Not short for Maranda. It's my middle name. I don't use it at work."

The man nodded.

"And you are." Miriam glanced at his name tag but couldn't read the last name because his pocket flap partially obscured the name. "Mike. Glad to meet you, Mike."

He walked to the lunchroom door, opened it, and motioned to Miriam. "Look who I ran into, literally, in the hall," Mike said as they entered the room. "What is the current punishment for running over a headquarters wonk?"

"Straight night shift," Brad said, smiling.

Miriam decided on a cold ham sandwich, chips, and a mocha, all of which she could carry to Patel's office, but she decided that would allow Mike and Brad an opportunity to talk, which might lead to expressing doubts about her employee status. So, she acted like she owned the place.

While standing at the espresso machine, awaiting her mocha, she considered that no matter how well she planned her escape, it would only take one anomaly, like a Mike instead of a Marty, to wreck it. This was a one-shot deal. If she screwed up, there would be no second chance. One and done. Wrecked, nixed, finished, ruined, kaput.

Many things might go wrong. Wrong might not even be a future event but something that had already occurred, drifting along her timeline until the appointed time for a full, dead stop. Mike might be that mistake. She glanced over her shoulder. Mike stared at her.

Or go with the alternative plan—simple and foolproof.

"How's your day going?" Marty asked.

Miriam set her plate on the table. "Boring. Mostly, more reading and such."

"What are you working on?" Mike asked.

"She can't say," Brad inserted. "Secret stuff."

"That's weird," Mike said and bit into his sandwich.

Miriam said nothing.

"How's that?" Brad asked.

Mike swallowed and washed it down with a swig of hot coffee larger than Miriam could have swallowed. "Ever known of something so secret they don't brief Security? At least that someone would be in the building."

Before Brad spoke, Miriam said, "I know, right? I told them they should at least tell security I would be here, but…" Miriam rolled her eyes.

Brad nodded in agreement.

Mike said nothing.

"How was your day, Brad?" Miriam said.

"Fine. Nothing exciting," Brad said.

"What did you do? Must have done something better than I did," Miriam persisted.

"Usual stuff: mowed the lawn, watched baseball, drank beer, came to work. Regular stuff."

"How about you, Mike?" Brad asked.

"Usual stuff." He stared at Miriam. "I can't get over how young you look. I'd guess 13 or 14," Mike said.

"I get that all the time," Miriam said.

"So?" Mike asked.

"So?" Miriam asked.

"So, how old are you?"

Miriam took an oversized bite of her sandwich, held up her hand, pointing to her mouth as she chewed. *Stupid. How old am I?*

"Old enough that you wouldn't go to jail if work grew too boring, and I needed some grownup entertainment." She winked and smiled but felt a shiver race up her spine.

The next bite threatened to choke her.

Brad laughed.

Mike stared.

After several silent minutes, Mike said, "I'm going to check with my supervisor. Doesn't seem right to me. Maybe you guys missed an e-mail or something."

Brad looked at Miriam. Miriam wondered what he was thinking.

"No problem for me," Miriam said. "Except I was not supposed to have contact with anyone. We do that sometimes. People never knew we were at their facility. I screwed up and let Marty and Brad catch me. I convinced them not to report it because it would trigger a ton of paperwork, interviews, and transfers, and what I didn't tell them would probably get me fired. But I understand your position. I've resigned to the fact that this might be my last assignment. I've been too careless for this work, obviously."

The room fell quiet. Miriam heard the vending machines running, a sound she had not previously noticed.

"Transfer?" Mike asked.

Brad nodded. "That's why we didn't report it. We are screwed now. Most likely, Marty and I will be transferred. Probably demoted to food service."

"Transferred," Mike whispered.

"Sorry, guys. I screwed up, and you're caught in the middle."

Miriam gathered her half-eaten sandwich and tossed it in the trash. She had lost her appetite. "I need to get to a quitting place because I likely won't be here tomorrow. No hard feelings." She held out her hand to Mike.

Mike shook her hand. She turned to Brad. Brad stood and hugged her. "Good luck, Maranda."

"You too, Brad."

Miriam sat in front of AJ Patel's monitor, staring at the screen. The file transfer window said it was 60% complete. The half a sandwich she had eaten threatened reappearance all over Patel's desk. She wondered why she was so stupid. She should have known something was wrong when Marty and Brad didn't knock on her door for lunch. But no, she marched right over there without giving it a thought.

She screwed up big time.

38

March 23, Tuesday, 4:40 a.m.

MIRIAM HAD ONE THIN HOPE her quest wouldn't end tonight. Brad might talk Mike out of reporting her because he feared the possibility of a transfer. However, she didn't like thin hopes any more than she liked James Carver's invisible men in the clouds directing everything in everyone's life. Precious time dwindled as she watched the transfer window. Eighty-nine percent remaining to completion. She couldn't get back online until the transfer had finished. By then, it might be too late.

While the transfer progressed, she wrote a second e-mail to Derrick. She delayed the delivery until later in the evening. She would be home, which should cause confusion if she or Derrick were being monitored, which she assumed to be the situation.

```
TO: derrickking0312@potterville.com

FROM: number1sis@potterville.com

Long story. No time to explain. Here's
the thing. They are watching you. They
track every move you make. I can't go into
details. Better that you don't know. Just
keep doing what you've been doing. Not
much else you can do right now. Stay safe
and stay alive. I'm working on a plan.

Things are much worse than I thought.
Marcus Carver's assault wasn't a fluke.
It was staged and planned. Someone, I
don't know who, is angry that you are in
Potterville. But you cannot move. Hear
me? Do not leave Potterville for any
```

reason. They have no authority over you
in the commoner world.

DO NOT LEAVE POTTERVILLE!

When the file transfer was complete, she checked to ensure the key-track logger was not running and reconnected the LAN cord. Would someone be suspicious that the computer had been offline for an hour and a half? There was no way to know, and worrying about it wouldn't change the situation.

She had an idea.

In the HR administration module, she created a duplicate of her headquarters profile, changing the name and division and adding an e-mail address. She found Mike's profile, which proved difficult. She had to search through many Mikes before finding the right one. Fortunately, each profile had a picture, which reminded her to find a photo for the HR profile she had created. She hoped the picture she selected was not someone famous.

She drafted an e-mail that read:

TO:
clarenceparsons@headquarters.com/adminis
tration

cc:
bradhendricks@pacificedge.com/security,
martywashington@pacificedge.com/security
, mikeprate@pacificedge.com/security

From:
marandakingston@techservice/admin.com

Mr. Parsons,

Please be advised that Pacific Edge
security staff have become aware of my
mission here. This was my error. I accept
full responsibility. Please advise what
action I should take.

Respectfully, Maranda Kingston, Special
Investigator

Miriam sent the message and drafted a second e-mail. She waited until the last moment before leaving to send it. She grabbed the laptop and storage device and ran for the door. On three computers, the following e-mail appeared:

```
TO:
bradhendricks@pacificedge.com/security,
martywashington@pacificedge.com/security
, mikeprate@pacificedge.com/security

Cc:
marandakingston@techservice/admin.com

From:
clarenceparsons@headquarters.com/adminis
tration

Please be advised that I have received
Special Investigator Maranda Kingston's
e-mail regarding the breach of security
at the Pacific Edge Technical Service
facility.

I cannot begin to stress to you how much
this concerns me. Special investigations
have been conducted in all Chosen
Communities without a security breach
until now.

I hereby give each of you a direct order
that you are not to discuss any element
of this situation with anyone. This
includes, but is not limited to, your
supervisor, your spouse, coworkers, etc.
I am to be your sole contact regarding
this security breach.

Because of the importance of this
investigation, I authorize Maranda
Kingston to remain in Pacific Edge and to
complete her work with due diligence as
quickly as possible.

I will handle the investigation of the
security breach personally. Each of you
```

is to submit a detailed report regarding Ms. Kingston to me within 24 hours.

Be advised that any disclosure regarding Ms. Kingston's special investigation will be deemed a violation of New America protocols and will result in disciplinary action up to and including termination and will be referred to the proper authorities for criminal prosecution.

Clarence Parsons, special envoy to the premier chair

39

RUSHING HOME, MIRIAM HOPED SHE had met the window for invisibility she had programmed into the surveillance camera network. She scrambled up the drain and tiptoed across the roof, through the window, and into her room. Setting an alarm, she pulled the covers over her head. She didn't expect a knock on her door this morning. She was suspended, and that was that. That the Headmaster disagreed with Harding's decision softened Father's lecture. However, he still pontificated regarding the error of her ways. Most of what he said had little impact. She didn't expect to see Father this morning. He had talked himself out yesterday.

She didn't feel bad about what she'd done or getting suspended. Only when Father said that she wasn't helping Derrick, did she feel a pang of guilt. Father was correct on that count. She was not thinking of Derrick when she vented her pent-up frustration. It didn't matter. She wouldn't be here much longer.

Teenage nature means sleeping half the day is natural or desirable. Difficult to separate the two, but she wouldn't sleep that long. She had work to do and a lot of thinking. However, sleep evaded her because a black cloud named Mike Prate hung over her plans. What if he had alerted a supervisor of her presence before she sent the e-mail pretending to be a high-ranking national official? She should have stopped the file transfer and completed the e-mails first. The file transfer was critical to her plan, but it could have waited. What if Mike Prate didn't fall for her e-mail scheme? Who knows exactly about her presence in Technical Service besides AJ Patel, Marty, Brad, and now Mike? Is AJ Patel the only person tracking her computer usage, or is Patel merely part of a larger trap or test?

Mike Prate might have reported her, but it won't change anything because they have not completed the test or set their ultimate trap. If he reported her, Pacific Edge Security would batter down the front door before her alarm sounded. However, they may not know that she is an unauthorized person. She had hidden her tracks well. Instead, they might be waiting for her when she enters the building tonight. To circumvent arrest, she could avoid Technical Service. But work there was incomplete. Admitting defeat might be her best option, especially if saving herself was the priority. Her odds of successfully escaping Pacific Edge were minimal if she was honest, and she couldn't ignore facts. And that was generous.

The alarm woke her, not the sound of security battering down the front door. So good so far, but not safe. She had downloaded more than she needed: all the folders and files she could find on Test Subjects 6 and 7, current and archived files regarding 1984, and recent documents and e-mails pertaining to Derrick. She had found no current e-mails about herself. She would read through this material if she had time, but she knew that wouldn't happen. Her idea required too much work, and she wasn't sure her plan was possible—such a far-fetched idea.

Being absent from James Carver Academy proved beneficial. She worked steadily and made progress. It was as if time didn't exist, and she begrudgingly admitted that she should thank AJ Patel for hacking the school system and overriding the headmaster's approval. Once the headmaster approves a suspension, it cannot be undone, at least not without going to some higher-ups. The headmaster might be reluctant to bring outsiders into the process or admit that his vice headmaster made a major mistake. Or he might take the issue straight to the bigwigs because of the computer hacking. Greeson might override her suspension. Part of her mind worked on schemes to stay home. She only needed a few days.

She hoped.

Without the clock as an anchor, her heart sank when the security system announced someone at the door. Miriam ignored it. The person or persons might go away. A few minutes later, the system announced that the person remained at the door. After the third announcement, Miriam took a deep breath. She hid the laptop and storage device, but they would find it in a thorough search. Pacific Edge homes were not designed to have secret hiding places. She had never considered whether that was strange, mostly because she had no experience outside her house.

Before she opened the door, she viewed the surveillance camera with a wild thought that she might make a run for it if it were security officers. But it was not security officers. A frustrated-looking Rebekah Ford paced in the driveway with her arms folded tightly across her chest.

Does this girl never give up?

"Hi," Miriam said as she opened the door.

"Took you long enough," Rebekah said as she pushed by Miriam into the house. "Close the door. I don't want anyone to know that I'm here."

Miriam closed the door. "Why not?"

Rebekah studied her for a moment and then said, "Not important."

"Why are you here?"

"Heard about you getting suspended."

"Doesn't answer my question."

"I'm here to check on how you're doing. And to see if you've learned more about Derrick."

"I told you I'd let you know." Rebekah couldn't be told about the e-mails.

"And how would you do that? You're suspended."

"I could come to your house."

"That's a bad idea."

"Why? Doesn't seem like any more of a risk than you coming here."

Rebekah said, "Anna. I can't risk Anna seeing you there."

"Anna?" Miriam puzzled.

"She idolizes you. And she's smart. You might have noticed if you paid attention to anyone other than yourself."

That stung. Mainly because it was true. Miriam didn't have friends. Never thought friends were necessary. In that way, she was like Derrick. Now, that right there was weird, being like Derrick. The truth remained. She had never paid attention to Anna until she copied and used the code Miriam cited in her short fiction. Too late to become friends with Anna, but Miriam vowed she would stop living in her head once she got beyond the current situation.

After a few silent moments, Rebekah said, "Does the suspension mess up your plan?"

"What plan?"

"Your plan to help Derrick. What other plan would I ask about?"

Miriam walked to the espresso machine and pressed the button to grind coffee into the portafilter. Using the handheld tamper, she pushed down, turned the tamper, and then lifted it. She examined the finely ground coffee and then put the portafilter into the machine. The machine would make many beverages automatically, but Miriam preferred doing it by hand. "Coffee? Mocha?"

Rebekah sat at the counter. "A mocha would be great. A little powdered cinnamon on top, if you can."

Miriam retrieved the milk from the refrigerator and steamed it. In a few minutes, she handed Rebekah a mocha with a perfectly formed white leaf on top covered with a light dusting of cinnamon.

"It's beautiful. How did you learn to do that?"

"A little practice. It's surprising what you can do if you stop letting machines do everything for you." Miriam thought about that. Something was important about that statement, but she was not sure what it was.

"Tastes fantastic. I'll be coming here more often." Rebekah winked as she sipped her drink.

Stupid. "Want a coffee?" Stupid girl. The goal is to get rid of her, not encourage her.

"To answer your question, I'm still analyzing that. But to be truthful, I don't see a path forward."

"What does that mean?"

Miriam sipped her espresso. "I give up. I can't help him."

40

March 24, Wednesday, 12:01 a.m.

THE FOG CRAWLED IN EARLY, and the thick night air captured the streetlights, creating a soft gray glow, reducing visibility to a few feet. Miriam didn't put her hood up while walking to Technical Service. She never liked the hood. It was too confining. She preferred freedom. Besides, she was on time, and the cameras ignored her as per her instructions hidden deep in the system's program language. She wondered if she would ever use what she'd learned.

Miriam hesitated at the door, but no armed troops awaited her.

She reached the far end of the shared area when a loud voice called out behind her. "Stop right there, young lady."

Her chest pounded as she slowly turned to see Brad and Marty sporting huge smiles. "You scared me," she said.

The boys came to her side. Brad gave her a one-armed hug. "Your e-mail saved our butts. We'll never be able to repay you."

"I might think of something before I'm done here," Miriam said. "See you at lunch?"

"You bet. We'll knock on your door."

Miriam smiled and proceeded to AJ Patel's office. Her key still worked. Nothing had changed. No messages from Patel. No extra gear. Nothing new. For the first time in a while, she felt optimistic. But the glimmer of hope faded when she opened her e-mail. There were e-mails from Mike, Marty, and Brad addressed to her second fake e-mail account: Clarence Parsons. She would read them later. Her ruse had worked. Clarence would send a succinct response, noting the reception of their reports and indications that he would contact them for interviews.

It was Derrick's e-mail that distressed her. *Did Derrick dream about Number Six?* Asking that question might have been a mistake, but that was not the worst of it. The worst thing was what she had to tell him. After a few moments, she took a breath and opened the message.

```
TO: number1sis@potterville.com
```

FROM: derrickking0312@potterville.com

Miriam, I believe it is you. I saw your gesture in the communication. I assume they had people there watching you closely, but you did well.

Things here are not like they showed us on New America Media. I am nervous, but I am okay. The thing is, I am not sure how you can help me. I do not think they will ever let me come back to Pacific Edge.

You cannot come here. Even if you could, you could not help me. Except it would give me a second chance to be a better brother—still, no reason for you to ruin your life. I want you to be okay.

How did you know about the dreams? I do not recall ever telling you about them. Or Father or Mother. I never told anyone.

To answer your question, in my dream, you are Number Six.

41

March 25, Thursday, 2:45 a.m.

MIRIAM READ THE MESSAGE AGAIN. She touched his name on the screen. She clicked on reply. Tears streamed down her cheeks. It was time, and she needed to get this done before she changed her mind.

```
March 25

TO: derrickking0312@potterville.com

FROM: number1sis@potterville.com

Derrick, I've been thinking about what
happened. I am sorry. It was my fault from
the beginning. I don't understand why I
did the things I did. Someday, I'll figure
it out.

You always wanted the best for me. I was
too rebellious to listen. I'm listening
now. First, I want you to know that I have
tried. I've tried extremely hard. But the
truth is, I cannot help you. If it were
possible, I would come there to be with
you. Even if I couldn't help you there,
we'd be together. Please believe that
I've tried my best.

But I cannot get there. Leaving here is
impossible. I'm sorry. I promised, and I
failed. The one thing I can do for you is
change. I will work hard to become the
person you want me to be.

This will be my last message to you. I
hope you can forgive me.
```

```
Your number1sis (AKA Number Six)

I love you, Number Seven
```

After the e-mail whooshed away, Miriam cried for several minutes. Telling him she wasn't coming was the hardest thing she'd ever done. She had to face facts: she may never see or hear from Derrick again—desperate times called for desperate measures.

She was desperate.

At lunchtime, Brad knocked on the door. Miriam joined them before they had moved more than a few yards down the hall.

"Whoa, you're quick this morning," Brad said.

"Yeah. Kind of wrapping up now," Miriam said.

"That close?" Marty asked.

"I'm afraid so. Plus, with recent developments, management is pushing me. I'd like to spend more time, but they won't allow it."

Miriam decided on a ham and cheese sandwich; she liked ham better than tuna. After sending Derrick's e-mail, she wanted a beer, but beer was not available, and she wasn't old enough. She also didn't know if she would like it. She only knew Father had started having beer at dinner recently because work had become more stressful lately. However, coffee didn't sound right, so she had a soda.

She plopped into a chair and took a bite of her sandwich.

"You look like someone kicked your dog," Marty said.

"I don't have a dog," Miriam said.

"You're a hoot. I mean, you look down in the dumps."

"Yeah, guess I am."

"I hope it's not us," Brad said.

Miriam stared at him for a minute. Here she was, a big-time security violation, sharing lunch with them, and they were worried about how she was doing. It occurred to her that she might ruin their lives when this ended.

"Not you guys. Just that I won't reach my goals on this one."

"It must be nice having goals," Brad said. "In our jobs, we have no goals other than hoping we will live to retirement. Sad when you think about it. The only thing we hope to accomplish is having a few years in retirement before we die."

Miriam nodded, but she had never thought about how people like Brad and Marty lived. That made her feel worse. She didn't know how the next week would go. She didn't need to be here. Although not being here might raise suspicions of those watching her. She told Derrick she wasn't coming, so not going to Technical Service would be another sign she had given up her quest. Part of her wanted to see Brad and Marty for the few days that remained. Then she had an idea. She would bring the laptop, work offline, and do some reading online to avoid suspicion. Having made that decision, she felt better. She wondered if she should work through the weekend. Mike worked weekends. Brad answered her question before she asked.

"Mike wanted me to thank you for taking the bullet on this," Brad said.

Miriam didn't know what taking the bullet meant, but in the sentence's context, assumed it meant taking the blame or something close to that.

"I told him about our first discussion with you and how reporting it would ensure they would transfer us all. He got so worried that he started crying. You see, Mike lives a few miles down the coast. This is a second job he works on weekends. He has a daughter in high school who is a star on the volleyball team. She has scholarships to play in college, but even with the scholarships, Mike is struggling to put together enough money to send her. His wife died two years ago of cancer. His daughter means the world to him. She's all he has left. Transferring now would ruin her volleyball career."

Miriam stared at Brad. She had never heard of anyone dying of cancer. Cancer was cured years ago. At least cured if you were Chosen. A slow burn started deep in Miriam's chest, which she had never felt before.

Brad continued. "Mike said he owes you big time. If you ever need a favor, Mike's your man."

Miriam returned her sandwich to the table. She studied Brad for a moment but detected no insincerity in him. "I'm sorry about Mike's wife. I hope his daughter goes to college."

"Mike is so proud of that girl. She's a great kid too. Wants to be a doctor. An oncologist."

Miriam bid the boys farewell. Lots to do, she told them, but her important work awaited at home. She decided leaving early would be okay. She read a few e-mails written after the Derrick and Marcus incident. Nothing she didn't already know. She checked her e-mail twice, but no response from Derrick, which she didn't expect because Derrick was asleep. She wouldn't hear from him until tomorrow, if at all.

She cried again.

And then she left.

42

March 26, Friday, 12:01 a.m.

ON THE WALK TO TECHNICAL SERVICE, the laptop felt heavier than when she carried it home. The effect of adrenaline when the device was new and forbidden, she assumed. She'd grown accustomed to the walk to and from Technical Service, which was as routine now as walking to school. She still had an eerie sensation along the way. However, it was dark, often foggy, security cameras not watching—nothing to worry about.

Her progress at home moved along, although slower than she had hoped. Putting in some work during the night would help. She had specific goals for tonight. Certain things she needed to see. Yesterday, she had trouble concentrating because of the e-mail she'd sent Derrick. She curtailed her imagination more than once as she coursed through multiple scenarios. *Derrick hates me. Something's happened. He died. He hasn't seen my e-mail. He found another sister.*

While thinking served her well, it was a curse sometimes. She wouldn't know what Derrick thought until he replied. Yet this was one of those times when logic didn't impact her thinking. She opened the e-mail application. No message from Derrick. She had ended it. Told him she had given up. But she hoped he would respond. At least to say goodbye.

Tears flowed. She must face the facts. Facts are cruel. That was all there was to it. She dried her eyes and wiped her nose on her sleeve. No time for tears. Work to do before implementing the desperate course she set for herself.

When Brad rapped on the office door, she was fully engaged in another language, scrolling on the computer monitor.

"You still here, Maranda?"

Miriam didn't bother to hide the computer code. If Brad noticed the black screen filled with white characters, it would reinforce the depth of her work here. Miriam opened the door. "I'm still here."

"Are you joining us for lunch?"

"Not today. I'm in the middle of something I can't walk away from." She motioned to the monitor.

"Wow. Are you in the operating system?"

"Yeah, but you didn't see that." Miriam winked at him.

Brad pinched his thumb and first finger together and pulled them across his lips. "My lips are sealed." Brad paused a moment and then said, "Can I bring you something?"

"That would be great." Miriam smiled.

"What would you like?"

"Surprise me. Plus, a double espresso."

"It will be my pleasure."

Miriam returned to the computer screen. She would miss Brad and Marty. She continued reading the code. The language of computers had become as clear to her as if it were written in English. Continuing was unnecessary, but it drew her. If she were considering a future, developing this language further would rate high on her list. But she wasn't considering a future beyond one last act.

Leaving the operating system, Miriam searched for new documents regarding Derrick but found nothing. She should have gone with Brad to lunch. Her work here almost done. It made sense for her to stay home until the time came. She could tell Brad and Marty that this was her last day.

Say goodbye.

End it.

43

March 27, Saturday

FATHER WAS SITTING AT THE BREAKFAST table when she came down the stairs. He glanced up and smiled but said nothing. A mocha sat in front of him as he read on his tablet. She walked to the espresso machine and made herself a flat-white coffee. She had consumed too much espresso during the night and needed something milder on her stomach. As the shots poured, she buttered a toasted English muffin. It occurred to her that Father and Mother often read stuff on their tablets. She had never wondered what they were reading until now.

"What are you reading?" Miriam asked as she set her plate and cup on the table.

Before she could look at the screen, Father placed the tablet face-down. "Nothing."

"Must have been something?"

Father sipped his mocha. "Some work stuff. Nothing important."

"Working on Saturday? That's unusual, isn't it?"

Father slid the tablet to the side. "You're full of questions this morning. Did you sleep well?"

Miriam took a bite of her English muffin. "Not great. I'll nap later."

"Sorry, you're not sleeping. Should we get you something? The physician can send it over. You don't need to go in for that."

"I'll be okay. Can I go for a walk this morning?"

"I suppose you can. The Academy can't prevent you from going outside on a weekend. I should have confined you to the house for getting suspended, but I didn't. Don't be gone long."

"I won't. I'm too tired for that. Probably nap after I walk."

Miriam finished her English muffin, grabbed a jacket, and started for the door. Father walked alongside her toward his bedroom. Miriam paused at the information station to check the air quality, temperature, and weather forecast, which was unusual for her. Father's brow wrinkled slightly as he reached for the door handle to his and Mother's bedroom. That's when Miriam heard it. The soft click of a lock releasing. She smiled at him and pulled the front door open. Father stepped into his bedroom, and the door closed behind him. When the door closed, she heard the door lock engage.

Why is the door locked?

A Derrick King Novel: Book 2

44

March 29, Monday, 12:20 a.m.

SUNDAY PROVED TO BE a lazy day compared to the past two weeks. Miriam slept most of the day. She needed the sleep, and she didn't want to be around Father or Mother, worried she couldn't conceal her uncertainties about them. She had finished what was possible at home. Now, it was building her courage and picking the day. It would be best to test her plan, but there was no way to accomplish that. It would work, or it wouldn't. If it failed, she had no Plan B.

It would soon be over, one way or another.

She had decided there would be no return trip to Technical Service on Monday. In making her decision, she regretted not saying goodbye to Brad and Marty, which was one of the weirdest things about this strange undertaking. A few weeks ago, had someone told her security officers would catch her inside of Technical Service and they'd become great friends, she would have thought the person was completely and irreversibly wacko.

But she changed her mind about Monday when she heard the lock click on Father's door. She must see what was in their room. The fact that she had never been inside Father and Mother's area had not occurred to her, and that seemed strange. If she were still communicating with Derrick, she would ask him if he'd ever seen it. If yes, then she could let it go. But she wasn't communicating with Derrick and couldn't let it go.

That night in Patel's office, she went straight to work. On the walk there, other things occurred to her that she needed to understand before implementing her plan. But first, the locked door to Father and Mother's area required her attention. In researching door security systems, she found four levels used in Pacific Edge and the building surrounding the Community. The lowest level of security was a metal key, like she used to enter AJ Patel's office. She had never seen a key until AJ directed her to the one hidden under his desk. The next level was a keypad like the one used to enter the Technical Service Building. She had never seen a keypad in Pacific Edge either until she came to Technical Service to retrieve the keyboard and mouse Patel gave her. The next level of security locks was facial recognition. Intuitively, she knew facial recognition was how the entrance to her home functioned. The fourth and highest level of security was facial recognition plus iris scan. The face of a dead person could open a facial recognition scan, at least until the dead face started to rot. But a live body was needed for the iris scan—just an eyeball wouldn't work. She found pictures illustrating several types of facial recognition plus an iris scan system. They were easy to identify. She had never seen such a system before and wondered what required the highest level of security.

The facial scan system was virtually invisible to the naked eye. The camera was often embedded in a nameplate or house number. Now that she saw how they installed the camera, she would recognize one when she saw it.

Because there was no key, keypad, or iris scan device at Father and Mother's door, it must be a facial recognition system. It took her two hours to find the security management system for their home. Once found, setting up access was easy. The security system offered several options. Her picture was already in their home's system, and she only needed to add it to the authorized persons for the room. The system also allowed her to lock herself out if either Father or Mother were in the room, which was a great safety feature for her purposes.

Learning about the security door management system triggered a cascade of ideas. One door here that she passed every day but previously paid little attention to, now required closer inspection. As a precaution, she closed the security door management program and left AJ Patel's office a few minutes early for lunch.

Down the hall toward the exit to Pacific Edge, she studied the door labeled Server Room. She spotted the camera lens of the facial recognition system embedded in the placard that labeled the room. She smiled and wondered if her smile had been captured and recorded somewhere.

The lunchroom was empty. She fixed herself a roast beef sandwich, chips, and a soda. The boys would be in soon. She started to sit and then had an idea. Having eaten lunch with Brad and Marty every weekday, she remembered their favorites. She scurried about the room, preparing each man a tray, which sat waiting for them to arrive.

"You're still here!" Brad said with a grin.

"Yep. But not much longer. I hope you don't mind. I fixed you both a tray."

Brad and Marty stood by the table, staring at the food. Both positioned themselves before the food choices, as Miriam envisioned.

"Thoughtful of you," Brad said.

She heard his voice crack a little.

"I don't like it," Marty said. A tear was visible in his eye. "This feels like goodbye. You said it was coming, but I hoped it wouldn't be so soon."

Miriam smiled. "Sit and eat. I'm not gone yet. Let's enjoy what little time I have left."

It proved to be one of the best meals Miriam could remember.

* * *

Back in Patel's office, Miriam checked the e-mail application. Several e-mails were of no interest, including the reports from Marty, Brad, and Mike. She deleted each until she came to an e-mail from AJ Patel. For several seconds, she debated the wisdom of opening it.

What trap do you have for me now, Mr. Patel?

Finally, because not opening it would be suspicious, she clicked on the message and read:

```
TO:
marandakingston@techservice/admin.com

FROM: ajpatel@ITservices.com

Your time is short. I'm hoping you have a
plan you can implement soon. The box on
the desk is for you. You have never seen
this device called a cellular telephone
or, more commonly, a smartphone. I assume
you can figure it out. Virtually everyone
in the commoner world has one. It is a
small  computer  that  can  also  make
telephone calls. A telephone is like your
communicator, only you can call anyone in
the  world  if  you  know  that  person's
number.

There are two phones in the box. They are
what we call burner phones. Short story
is that each phone has 90 minutes of talk
time  and  200  text  messages  paid  in
```

advance. Cell phones are easily tracked. Because these phones are not registered in anyone's name, they cannot be tracked unless you tell officials it's your phone. These can be life savers if you need them. But because the people you might call are monitored, toss the phone once you use it. Don't toss it away at home because it will lead security right to your door. Do not turn it on until you are ready to use it.

I, too, have been checking on Derrick. Derrick has spent time with two girls. One you may know: Akira Nakamura. The other girl is Nyx Belos. I trust you are smart enough to find their contact information.

Good luck. Your window of opportunity is rapidly closing.

AJ Patel

She opened the packaging and examined the cellular phones. Thin black rectangular devices. She didn't know how to turn it on or make a call. She checked the internet and found instructional videos specific to the make and model. Now, the only challenge was deciding if they were safe to use or if she should toss them into the sea.

After disabling the keystroke logger on Patel's computer, she found several messages about Derrick in the e-mail archive folder, which she moved to the large storage device. She would open them later after getting a few hours' sleep. If her password didn't work, she would convert them to code where she would find the passwords or just read the e-mail in code. Neither was difficult for her now.

As the files and folders were copied to the storage device, she thought about her time at Technical Service. Beyond the danger, brutal hours, frustrations, fears, and necessity, she recognized something unexpected. The past few weeks were the best of her life. She wondered if commoners used computers. If she were to survive, this was the work she wanted to do. Not the breaking and entering part, the computer part. She believed computers were powerful tools for good or evil. From what she saw, evil was their primary purpose here.

After studying the use of cellular telephones, she took the ones AJ Patel gave her, tossing one charger and its packaging into the trash receptacle outside Technical Service. One charger seemed sufficient.

Back in her bedroom, she hid the laptop computer, storage device, and phones under clothing in her closet and then slept a few hours.

* * *

Miriam sat drinking coffee and eating toast when Father and Mother exited their room. She realized they were coming because she heard the locking mechanism on their door.

"I didn't expect you to be up," Father said.

Mother walked to the kitchen and ordered a coffee from the machine with cream for herself and a mocha for Father.

"I woke up early. Can I go out today?"

Father accepted the mocha from Mother and said, "You cannot go out during school hours when you are suspended."

"I hoped you would approve it. I'm getting depressed shut in all day."

"You got out over the weekend," Father said.

"That's true. I should have gotten out more." Miriam took a bite of toast. "So, is that a no?"

"That's a no. Maybe tomorrow. I'll think about it."

Father and Mother ate breakfast sandwiches provided by the home food dispenser, drank two more coffees, and studied things on their tablets. Miriam made more espresso and waited. On weekdays, Father and Mother typically left for work before Derrick and Miriam awoke. At least, that's what she always assumed.

"Aren't you going to be late for work?" Miriam asked.

Father looked to Mother and then said, "We have a late start because of a meeting. We'll be home later than usual, but we'll be here in time for dinner."

"Okay." Miriam sauntered to the espresso machine for another coffee. "I'm going to hang out down here for a while. It's a change of scenery from my bedroom."

"Are you sure, dear?" Mother asked.

"Yes." Miriam sat on the couch and requested the windows switch to transparency. "At least I can look out."

"We must go," Father said. "I've sent for a transport."

Neither Father nor Mother returned to their room to get a jacket or a briefcase or a purse. Miriam watched them get into the transport and leave. She watched until the transport was out of sight. The color of the transport was black.

Walking toward Father and Mother's door, she heard the lock click open. She glanced out the window to ensure the transport had not returned and wondered if cameras were capturing her actions. For a moment, she hesitated, feeling slightly guilty but not guilty enough to change her mind. She pushed the door open.

That moment changed many assumptions.

Father and Mother didn't live here.

They worked here.

45

IT WASN'T A BEDROOM, although there was a small couch in a corner. She eased into the room, studying its contents. Computer monitors lined two walls along with machines that tracked heart rate, respiration, etc. A thick gray mat covered the floor, soft but unlike carpet, an industrial material that cushioned one's steps. The walls consisted of panels covered with fabric. An eerie quiet filled the room. One computer monitor and one machine were active, others were not. A ribbon labeled TS-#7 ran along the bottom of the monitor, providing summaries of the data tracked.

Miriam studied the active computer monitor, which displayed a black screen with white lines and a green glowing dot: 1984. She memorized the street names.

On the desk, she saw a notepad with a list of names:

Akira Nakamura (former JC student)

Nix Belos

Malcolm Cross

Henry Clark

Rudy Badowski

Antonio Morales

Jim Priest

??? Larry

??? Browning (teacher)

Backing out of the room, she headed upstairs and locked her door. She sat on her bed, her back to the headboard, studying details, estimating where they had hidden the surveillance devices. She found them now that she understood where to look. In Father and Mother's room, no active monitors displayed her bedroom. Maybe they weren't watching because she was home. Maybe she was spending so much time at Technical Service that someone else had been assigned to watch her. Or perhaps they were so focused on Derrick that she was of little importance. She hoped it was the latter but recognized that hope didn't mean much in the real world.

She spotted two cameras in her bedroom but none in the bath. They might have allowed privacy in the bathroom, but more likely, they used a camera that provided better concealment, like embedding it in a mirror. After studying the bath, she returned to her bed, where she stared at the ceiling, thinking about how she could block the cameras' view of her work. Such concealment was several weeks too late, but it still seemed important to make the effort. Yet, if they were watching her, and if she covered the cameras, they would know that she'd discovered their observation room.

There it is. Father and Mother are not our parents. They are Keepers. Miriam recognized this already because she understood her nightmares were not mere dreams but a leakage of memories. But she refused to accept the truth in a tangible manner. Now, she could no longer block it from her mind. And with this came a flood of conclusions about Derrick. She would study this further if she ever got the opportunity. All the information was on the storage device, onto which she had downloaded thousands of files. She knew the basics without further research, the conclusions obvious. She and Derrick were not anyone's children. They were test subjects, engineered in a laboratory.

Her conclusion answered one question. She and Derrick were unalike because they weren't brother and sister.

After an hour of deliberation, she left the cameras unmolested. If they were watching her, and they must be watching her, covering the cameras would signal that she was on to them. Her only chance of success depended on letting them think they knew everything and then doing something unexpected.

Something desperate.

Something unpredictable.

She retrieved the laptop and opened the last e-mails concerning Derrick. She read an exchange between someone who oversaw the test subject research program and the person who supervised the Number Seven experiment. Miriam marveled at how much the oversight person knew about Derrick, but she couldn't determine the person's identity. The e-mail address didn't contain a name, it was number.sevenoversight@pacificedge.com/tsprogram/admin. The other party was more mysterious. Instead of an email address, it was a series of numbers: 192.169.52.1.

The number person wanted Derrick back in Pacific Edge. This person was unaware of the recent TS-#7 experiment and didn't approve. Now, the testing had gone wrong. How it went wrong was known to the people communicating and, therefore, was not further explained. It required backtracking to learn details, but she knew all she needed to know for now.

They had lost control of Derrick.

In the final e-mail exchange, the world closed around her, making it difficult to breathe. The number person ordered Derrick to be returned as soon as possible. Lured, if luring was necessary, with the promise of a complete exoneration on all charges. Tell him that Marcus Carver had accepted responsibility for starting the fight. Promise Derrick he will receive a homecoming ceremony to ensure all Pacific Edge knows he is innocence.

If that were the end, as much as she hated Pacific Edge, she would acknowledge that letting Derrick come home was best for him. He loved everything about Pacific Edge. She accepted that he wouldn't change and would never see things as she did. But it didn't end there, and the additional instructions were crucial to her decision. The mysterious number clarified that Derrick would receive no reprieve.

There would be no welcoming ceremony.

Use of force was authorized if Derrick refused to return.

Bringing Derrick back alive was preferred but not required.

This forced her to implement her plan before being fully prepared.

46

March 30, Tuesday, 2:20 a.m.

MIRIAM LEFT THE HOUSE LATER than usual on Tuesday morning. One task remained, and she assumed it wouldn't take long. She eased into the entry, listening before moving forward. There would be no lunch with Brad and Marty today, and she didn't want to see them. She didn't trust that she could eat lunch with them without crying openly.

The task proved more difficult than she had expected. At lunchtime, they rapped on the door, and she remained silent until they left. With only 15 minutes remaining before she had to go, the information she needed still eluded her. She considered sending Derrick an e-mail but didn't because someone must be monitoring their communications. With only three minutes remaining until she had to leave to meet the window of invisibility, she found what she needed. It was only ten numbers. She didn't need to write them down.

When she reached the work cubicles, she heard familiar voices: Marty and Brad. She ducked under a workstation as they approached.

As they passed where she hid, Brad said, "You think she's gone?"

"I don't know. Maybe. Probably," Marty replied.

"I thought she would have said goodbye."

"Maybe they didn't let her."

"Possibly. Still …"

"I'm going to miss her too."

When the voices faded, Miriam eased from the cubicle. She could see them walking down the hall away from her. She was already one minute late leaving. She backed down the hall, keeping them in sight until she reached the exit. Miriam eased the door open and then eased it shut. And then she ran.

While running, she pulled a cellular phone from her sweatshirt pocket and turned it on. The device took longer to activate than she expected. She had slowed to a fast walk, tracking the time intervals between cameras in her head. She punched the ten numbers on the keypad. A buzz sounded every few seconds. It was 4:30 a.m.

Answer the phone. Answer the damn phone!

47

March 31, Wednesday, 4:30 a.m.

MIRIAM DIDN'T LEAVE THE HOUSE on her regular schedule on Wednesday. She didn't need to go to Technical Service, but she needed darkness. Her decision was desperate. She understood that. So many things could go wrong. Her odds of success were not good. Derrick might never know that she had tried to keep her promise.

During the past few days, she analyzed data related to her plan, ocean currents, maps to Potterville, and information on test subjects. She didn't have the correct clothing, and she didn't have the skills either. A week before they suspended her from the Academy, she had been swimming for an hour each day at the Community Center after school. She improved rapidly, which surprised her, but she had no illusion she could swim well enough for the task at hand. Her original plan didn't include swimming.

But then things changed.

Derrick had no time left.

She raised her window for the last time. She left it open. She wouldn't use the escape route again. She walked down the street, the eastern horizon glowing. Wearing a bright red and white shirt, no hood. Being seen was no concern today.

At the wall, she turned toward the sea.

She kicked off her shoes and paused at the water's edge. The Pacific Ocean lapped at her ankles. The water was much colder than she had imagined. She could swim in the community pool for an hour. But the pool was heated and had no current. She didn't know how long she would last in the sea.

She looked back as she waded deeper into the icy water.

She didn't notice a person standing on the bluff watching her.

She didn't know the person was crying.

She couldn't hear the person say, "Good luck."

PART THREE

1

MIRIAM ALMOST DROWNED ON WEDNESDAY, March 31, before Pacific Edge Security plucked her from the sea. She started the day determined and then thought it would end in the frigid Pacific Ocean. When she saw a Pacific Edge security hovercraft approach, she waved to be sure they were coming to rescue, or more accurately put, capture her.

Miriam no longer had a keyboard, mouse, or laptop. She left them in AJ Patel's office. She left no trace of her explorations. Even her black hoodie went into the trash at Technical Services. She had returned the security cameras to working condition.

Security officers searched her room and found the open window. They removed the device she had crafted to defeat the lock and sensor and then went a step further and secured the window so it couldn't open. When the security team left, they changed the lock on the door so it could be controlled from the outside.

That afternoon, Father came to her room, home early.

"How are you doing?" Father asked.

"I'm okay," she said. She didn't say, sorry. She wasn't.

Father said, "So, this might cheer you up. We have a communication with Derrick. We don't get to talk to him, but we get to watch."

"When?"

"Right now. They are here to set it up."

"That's nice. I would like to see him."

"Then even better news," Father said.

Miriam said nothing. She knew what was coming.

"Derrick is coming home," Father said with a smile.

Miriam didn't like his smile. It didn't feel genuine. Nothing did anymore.

"I thought you'd be happy."

"Just a lot to process," Miriam lied.

"We need to hurry. They are just about in position for the communication."

"What do you mean, just about in position?"

"Derrick is not at his condominium. They are going to where he is."

"How would they know where he is?" Miriam asked unnecessarily.

"Oh, well, I don't know for sure."

"Right."

When Miriam came down, a scene was already playing on the monitor—handheld because it had a bit of shaking. The image appeared to be from a craft descending onto a football field. Miriam spotted Derrick standing with some other kids at the far end of the field. When the transport landed, the image blurred as the person moved inside the transport and then exited. The camera followed a man across the grass toward Derrick and the others.

The camera panned, and a man identified himself as James Bolden. Then the camera turned to face Derrick. Three men stood with Derrick. One she recognized was Paul Jorgensen, the man who took Derrick to Potterville. One man wore a polo-type shirt, and the third man wore a uniform, some sort of security person. She paused the image in her mind and focused on Derrick. He looked well. But different. He didn't look perfect: perfect hair, perfect skin, perfect teeth. His hair was longer than he usually wore it. The color had started to change too, as if it were fading, but then maybe it just looked faded because his skin was darker, as if he had been in the sun a lot. A tear traced down her cheek.

Then Miriam saw two girls standing behind Derrick. One was Akira Nakamura. Miriam remembered her and was surprised when she saw the name on the list in Father's work area. Akira probably remembered Derrick. Akira had a bit of a crush on him, but Derrick was oblivious. Miriam wondered if Akira had kept Derrick's secret. She wondered if Derrick recognized Akira was once a Chosen in Pacific Edge.

Then there was the other girl.

A girl with pink-striped hair.

2

IT BECAME CLEAR NEITHER DERRICK nor the others knew they were on camera. Then something unexpected. Derrick demanded to see his sister. Father knew they would get to watch Derrick receive the offer to return home. Two-way communication wasn't the plan. Father made that clear earlier.

The man named Bolden, who had been talking to Derrick, returned to the transport. The sound ended, but it was clear that he was having a heated discussion on a communication device. When the communication ended, a man named Jackson, who appeared to be the head guy of the team that set up the monitors in the King family's living room, pulled a communication device from his pocket. After a brief conversation, during which Jackson spoke little, he pocketed his phone and said, "They are going to let Derrick see Miriam. You know the rules. No tricks, or the offer is off the table."

Derrick said, "Mr. Bolden says I can come home."

Miriam tried to send him hints, but Derrick wasn't the brightest star in the night when it came to such things. She had told him in her e-mail not to return to Pacific Edge. She had tried her best and hoped it was enough.

To be honest, she had little confidence.

Derrick wouldn't pass up the chance to come home.

After their brief conversation, the communication ended, and Miriam ran to her room, tears streaming down her face. Although crying was not her thing, the tears were real. And sometimes tears work to a girl's advantage. Father and Mother said nothing. They just let her go.

Miriam would have locked the door, but that was neither possible nor necessary. The door locked behind her. Only Father or Mother could unlock the door to let her out. House arrest, but that's not what they called it. They called it mental health protection only until a psychiatrist had evaluated and treated her, they said. Not over 30 days, they said. Nothing to worry about, they said.

She wiped her tears and nose on her sleeve and then went into her bathroom, the only room that didn't have a camera. Instead of a camera, they installed a motion detector. Should she stop moving, it would alert her Father and Mother so one of them could check on her. Father said he had been given a leave of absence from work so he could stay home as long as it took to get her well. Leave of absence. Right?

Once inside the bathroom, with the door tightly closed behind her, Miriam threw her arms over her head and danced a happy dance. She was finally warm inside.

She was certain Derrick had refused Borden's offer.

3

MIRIAM REQUESTED HOT CHOCOLATE AND toast, which Father brought to her room on a tray. She didn't want to talk, and Father didn't press her. Miriam felt exhausted despite all the excitement—almost drowning turned out to have been exciting but not in a good way, and Derrick refusing to return to Pacific Edge, which was over-the-top exciting and in a good way, not to mention unexpected. She had a brief time in the emergency room, where they worked to bring her body temperature up to normal. The nurse said years ago her condition would have been serious, likely fatal, but they were better at treating such things now, but the Tribunal didn't allow them to complete the treatment. Miriam suspected her survival was unimportant.

Notwithstanding the exhilaration, Miriam slept after eating her toast and drinking her hot chocolate.

She needed rest.

She wasn't finished.

4

April 1, Thursday, 2:00 a.m.

HER ALARM, SET ON VIBRATE, required a full minute to awaken Miriam. She wanted a hot shower but couldn't risk alerting Father or Mother that she was awake. Or perhaps she could. They were, after all, locked in their room or soon would be, but enough risk existed in the next few hours without adding to it. Best if they didn't know she was gone until morning. Expecting she would sleep in, it might be midday before Father came to check on her.

In the darkness, she stuffed pillows under her covers, eased off her bed, and crawled to the door to listen for the click of the lock.

At 2:09 a.m., the computer program she had written activated. It checked that Father and Mother were in their quarters and then locked their door, sealed their windows, and blocked their communication. If the house caught on fire, they were screwed. The program also unlocked her door and the front door and shut off the alarms. She wouldn't be using the window or the chain that drained water from the gutters. Tonight, she would walk out the front door.

Miriam dressed quietly, then eased down the stairs. Outside Father and Mother's door, she heard no sounds, but the room's soundproofing might prevent her from hearing normal conversation. How they would get out, she did not know. That was not her problem.

She drank a hot chocolate, then started toward Technical Service for her last shift, albeit a brief one. She didn't need her hoodie because she was invisible to the security cameras that were playing a loop of empty streets. The fog had not yet pushed in from the sea, and for that, she was thankful. She didn't want to think of the sea or its cloak of gray. Yesterday she had almost drowned in the ocean, so it would be some time before its fascination returned.

Miriam couldn't be sure she'd covered every element or that her computer program would work as intended. It was a complex plan that she had no way to test. This was it. Escape rested on tonight.

When she nearly drowned, the need for improvising became clear. She planned to float around for a few minutes before being rescued/captured. That didn't happen. The tide pulled her out farther than she had predicted. So, she swam south. If they were not going to come after her, perhaps she could swim to freedom and find her way to Potterville when she was beyond the Pacific Edge boundary. She still didn't know how she would get to Potterville.

One bite at a time.

But the water was too cold, the distance too great, and the current too powerful. She wasn't going to make it. She saw a buoy that marked the boundary of Pacific Edge. With her last bit of strength, she got to the buoy and wrapped her arm around a tether that held it in place. She couldn't hang on long, as the cold drained her body heat.

She reached a peaceful state, ready to let go, let go of the chain, let go of her pain, let go of Derrick.

It was over.

She had tried

Before she let go and floated away, she saw a hovercraft approaching. *About damn time.*

* * *

Medical staff said two things saved her life that day. One, the closeness of the hospital. It took less than five minutes from when they plucked her from the sea until they wheeled her into the emergency room, and two, someone saw her and alerted security.

Things didn't work the way she planned, yet here she was. Trusting that security would spot her was a mistake. She should have predicted that, having already learned that they were not as effective as one might think. But she could not explain how someone had seen her.

How that happened made little sense.

It didn't matter. She survived, and the computers were doing their job.

Everything was back on track.

Until a figure stepped out of the shadows.

5

THE PERSON WALKED TOWARD MIRIAM. A blue hoodie covered her head and obscured her face, but Miriam recognized her.

"You scared the crap out of me. What are you doing out?" Miriam asked.

"Escaping with you. I have been watching you for weeks. I suspected the swim in the ocean was a ruse. Looks like I was right," Rebekah Ford said, and added, "I thought something dark was what one wore to an escape."

"I'm escaping. Me. Not you. Watching me for weeks?"

"Yes. I'll tell you more when we are out of here. Shouldn't we be going?"

"How did you get out of your house?"

"Taped over the window latch and alarm."

"They will know you're gone. That's not a failsafe way to defeat the alarm."

"Right, you are. But my dad will reset the alarm and forget about it until he finds I'm gone later."

"How do you know your dad will reset the alarm?"

"I've been setting it off for the past few days. I removed the tape before he could investigate. He thinks it's a bad switch. He's a procrastinator, so he hasn't called a service technician."

Miriam nodded. "Clever. But it doesn't change the fact that you're not going. This is a one-person operation."

"There wouldn't have been an operation if I hadn't called security when you went swimming," Rebekah said, pulling down her hood. She stared at Miriam for a moment and then added, "Thank you for saving me, Rebekah. I wouldn't be alive if it weren't for you. So, I'll take you with me."

"That was you?"

"Yes."

"How did you know I was out there?"

"I've been watching you. Did your time at sea affect your memory, or are you not listening?"

Rebekah was stubborn. That much was certain. Another unforeseen glitch in her plans. "You'll never see your parents or your sister again."

"I know." Rebecka wiped her cheek. "I've thought it through. I'm going."

Miriam did not need this complication, but she also didn't have all night to argue with Rebekah, and from experience, she doubted anyone could win an argument with the girl. "Let's go then," Miriam said, turning toward Technical Service.

After walking a block, Miriam asked. "Why have you been watching me?"

"Because I knew you would help Derrick."

"Those days at school when you looked horrible. That's when you started watching?"

"Yep. I stayed up all night. After a few nights, you developed a pattern, and then I watched you go to and from and got some sleep in between. Made life a lot easier."

Miriam grunted. Rebekah was smart. Determined. But that wouldn't be enough.

"How did you know it would be tonight?"

"I didn't. But, like I said, I hoped swimming wasn't your actual plan. That seemed like a good bet because your chances of survival were next to nothing. You're too smart for that. But you overestimated security's competence."

"True. I was lucky." Miriam walked silently for a few yards. "Thanks."

"So, what is the plan?"

"I've disrupted the computer system. We go inside, get some supplies, walk out the other side."

"What's a computer?" Rebekah asked.

"It's a bunch of machines that run stuff," Miriam said.

"Simple as that? You just, like, shut off the machine?"

Miriam glared at Rebekah.

"Right. Defeating the machines must have been difficult," Rebekah said.

Miriam nodded.

"So, what happens to the machines after we are gone?"

"They are going to crash. They might have it running in a few hours, but I hope it takes longer, much longer. Worst-case scenario, they recover all the data, know who we are, and what we did," Miriam said.

"Okay. And at best?" Rebekah asked.

"That system will never run again." Miriam smiled.

Rebekah said nothing for a few moments. "Why did you pick today?"

"I didn't. It picked me."

"What does that mean?"

"I learned stuff."

"What stuff."

"Later. No time for that now."

They arrived at the Technical Services entry. Miriam stopped by the trash container and reached under the large bin, feeling around until she found a small package. She unwrapped the plastic, pulled out the cellular phones, and dropped them into her pocket. At the door, she entered AJ Patel's access code. It didn't work. That told her someone either found her intrusion or knew about it but allowed it as part of their plan, or AJ Patel blocked her.

Now came the test.

Were they smart enough to anticipate her computer hijacking?

She entered a new number.

The door lock rolled.

Miriam opened the door a few inches and paused. "There's a problem I'm not sure how to handle."

"What problem is that?"

"I've gotten to know the security guys on the night shift."

"You what? How did you…"

Miriam held her finger to her lips and whispered, "No time to explain. We could probably sneak by them."

"Let's do that then."

"But if they can recover the computer system, they might discover the security guys knew about me. It wouldn't be good for them."

"But that is not our problem."

"They have families."

"So, what are we going to do?"

"Not sure yet."

"You're scaring me, Miriam. Doesn't sound as if you've thought this entire plan through."

"Good catch."

6

MIRIAM EASED DOWN THE HALL, past the server room, through the shared area. Rebekah glided along behind her, which pleased Miriam. Rebekah must have a thousand questions but asked none. Rebekah would ask questions all day if Miriam allowed Rebekah to escape, which she did not intend to let happen, but she was not sure what to do with her either.

Miriam stopped at AJ Patel's office. She tried the key, and it still worked. Inside, she walked straight to the computer and logged on, or more accurately, tried to login. Her username and password no longer worked. That narrowed her suspect list or at least confirmed that AJ Patel was on the list. She tried the new username and password she had created as part of the computer hijacking.

The screen lit up. First, Miriam checked her e-mail, hoping she might have something from Derrick, but knowing she wouldn't because she and Derrick had exchanged their last e-mails days ago.

In the Maranda Kingston account, were several e-mails that meant nothing to her and one that did—an e-mail from AJ Patel.

The subject line read:

`Open before you leave`

A trap? Trigger an alarm?

The black bag that held the laptop and storage device sat where she had left it. She pulled out both devices. She connected the storage device to Patel's computer and dragged the e-mail to it. She didn't know if the e-mail would open if the computer were not connected to the network. It was too risky opening the e-mail any other way. She started the laptop, ensured the wireless systems were disabled, connected the storage device, and opened the e-mail.

A window said the message was cached at 4:55 PM.

The e-mail read:

```
TO: Maranda Kingston

FROM: AJ Patel
```

```
Miriam, if you are reading this, you have
exceeded my hopes. You are one smart and
determined girl. Take the laptop and
external drive when you go. It's yours.
Don't worry, they are not mine, and I will
suffer no problems because of you taking
them.

I'm certain you understand they will find
you with 1984 unless you defeat it. That
is the biggest problem because I don't
think defeating 1984 is possible. I was
invested in the system when I worked on
it. My mistake. But if anyone can do this,
it's you.

Until we meet again, AJ Patel
```

"Who is AJ Patel?" Rebekah whispered.

"Long story."

Miriam didn't trust Patel. She would take the laptop but wouldn't turn it on until she felt confident it couldn't be tracked. Or it might wind up in a river.

Miriam navigated to 1984. She needed Derrick's location before they left. The screen lit up with green dots.

"What are those?" Rebekah asked.

"People. Every person in Pacific Edge, to be exact."

"Holy crap," Rebekah whispered.

Miriam quickly expanded the map, hoping Rebekah wouldn't notice the two dots that represented them in Technical Services.

She located Potterville and zoomed in closer.

No green dot.

No Derrick.

7

TEARS FILLED MIRIAM'S EYES. She moved out but found no green dot near Potterville. She zoomed out farther. Nothing. She zoomed out farther still. Nothing. She typed Derrick King into the search window. A message appeared on the screen: Derrick King not found.

Miriam clinched her hair on either side of her head. "No, no, no," she cried.

"What? What's wrong?" Rebekah asked.

Miriam wiped her face with her sleeve. "Derrick has a tracking device. Now, the system says he is not out there. Something bad has happened."

"Could it have stopped working?"

"I don't think so. Maybe. Probably not, because the failure rate is extremely low. If they had stopped tracking him, the message would have said something different."

"How do you know all this?"

Miriam turned and glared at Rebekah.

"Now what?" Rebekah asked, tears trickling down her cheeks.

On the computer, Miriam turned the clock back 24 hours. Now Derrick's green dot showed up on the screen. Miriam memorized the address. Derrick was not moving. Sleeping.

She forwarded ahead to 8:00 a.m. Derrick had moved. School. She went ahead to when Bolden offered Derrick a safe return to Pacific Edge. Still at the school. Next, she moved ahead hour by hour. The dot that represented Derrick kept moving, but still near Potterville. At 9:00 p.m., Derrick was gone. She reversed the clock until his beacon reappeared, then moved forward in time until 8:12 p.m., which was when Derrick's signal disappeared. She checked the GPS coordinates. She put the system on a time-lapse forward mode, and the clock moved ten times faster than real-time.

Rebekah peered over Miriam's back, her hand squeezing gently on Miriam's shoulder.

A flash of green, off to one side of the screen. "There," Rebekah pointed. "Go back."

Miriam moved the time back a few minutes at a time. The green light appeared, then disappeared. Miriam moved the time back ten minutes and let it run in real time. The dot was moving. Then, after ten minutes, it flickered and disappeared. Then reappeared. Then disappeared. It was moving, flickering here and there. Then the screen turned black, and the green light didn't reappear.

Miriam turned back to the last time the dot glowed on the screen. She checked the GPS coordinates.

"What does that mean?" Rebekah asked.

"Something happened there." Miriam tapped the screen. "I don't know what."

"Where is he?"

"Somewhere outside of town. Several miles, actually."

"What was he doing out there at night? Derrick didn't go outside when he was here."

"True. He's changed. A lot, apparently," Miriam said.

"What are we going to do?" Rebekah asked.

"Go find him," Miriam said.

8

MIRIAM NAVIGATED TO RUNNING APPLICATIONS and disabled the keystroke logger, which might be unnecessary if her computer code worked as intended. She did a search and found recent e-mails and other documents regarding Derrick. She didn't have time to investigate them but saved them to the storage device. She also looked at the storage device to see if anything had been recently added. Nothing changed that she could see. She had deleted everything before she left it and moved all the files she'd collected and programs she'd written to what she hoped was a hidden location inside the ghost file she had created. This file also contained the execution file that had hijacked the computer system, unlocking her door, securing Father and Mother in their quarters, disrupting the security cameras, and allowing her into the Technical Service Building. She moved the hidden folder back to the storage device and then initiated the destruct sequence that would wipe out the system for a while. She knew they archived the system daily, so she embedded a similar program in the archive server, erasing six months of history and any trace she was ever in the system. Going back further would be malicious. She didn't need to be malicious. Not yet. Maybe later.

Miriam transferred the last file she'd written—after discovering the Keeper's observation laboratory that she once thought was Father and Mother's bedroom—to the storage device.

"This will take a few minutes. There are other things we must do. Just follow my lead and be quiet otherwise. Can you do that?" Miriam asked.

"I'll do my best."

"Let's go," Miriam said.

Miriam tiptoed down the hall, listening. Rebekah followed.

Miriam had memorized Brad and Marty's routine, having watched on AJ Patel's monitors as they moved around the building. She hoped they were predictable. They had been thus far. *Just one more night, please.* Miriam and Rebekah reached the security section.

Rebekah stopped and whispered, "This is the security section. We should stay away from here. This seems like the last place we should be."

"We need stuff stored here. In and out, one more stop, and then we're gone," Miriam said.

"What's your plan when we get out?"

"Don't have one. Yet."

"I must be crazy," Rebekah said.

"Agreed."

Miriam moved through the outside security section, noting the transports and hovercraft and wondering if she should have considered stealing something. *Too late now. Stick to the plan. Which keeps changing.*

They passed through to the inside security section. The door to the equipment room was locked. Miriam used the code she had created. She remembered the code Brad used but decided using it would put the guys in jeopardy if the data was recovered. She heard the lock roll and opened the door, giving Rebekah a sly smile. "Right this way."

Inside, Miriam pulled an empty black bag off the wall. She selected several items from the shelves and stuck them in the bag. She knew the purpose of some items, and others she thought looked useful. Plus, she needed to distract Rebekah.

What to do about Rebekah Ford?

Rebekah had been a pain in the butt since they exiled Derrick. She was also the only person worried about him, despite knowing Derrick did not plan to choose her as his bride. Strange girl. Rebekah had no future in Potterville. She had one in Pacific Edge and a little sister who needed her—no reason for her to go to Potterville. If Derrick didn't love her here, he wouldn't love her there.

Rebekah complicated things.

There was no good reason to take her along.

Miriam kept stuffing the bag. Had Miriam only taken one item, Rebekah might have grown suspicious, and Miriam needed a relaxed Rebekah, a not-paying-attention Rebekah.

"Could you grab another bag? This one is almost full," Miriam said.

"Sure."

Rebekah turned and reached for an empty black bag.

Miriam pulled a stun gun, switched it to high, stuck it in Rebekah Ford's back, and pulled the trigger.

9

WHEN MIRIAM AWOKE, HER HEAD was pounding, her ears ringing, and her muscles aching. She struggled to her hands and knees. Rebekah sat with her back to the door, holding a stun gun in her hand.

"That hurt like hell," Miriam said.

"No shit! Why did you do that?" Rebekah demanded.

With a grunt, Miriam sat on her butt. "Had to."

Rebekah pulled the trigger on the stun device, sending a blue arc between two metal poles. "Had to, what? Get rid of me? What happened next? Accidentally zapped yourself? Serves you right."

"No accident. I zapped you first because I didn't know if you'd let me do it. Couldn't take the chance. Sorry."

Rebekah stared at her for a minute. "Answer my first question?"

"First question?"

"You suddenly go fuzzy in the head, genius?"

"Actually, yes."

"Why did you zap me?"

"Zapped us both," Miriam corrected.

"Okay, zapped us both."

"To fry the GPS chips embedded in our backs. Otherwise, they could track our exact location."

"Oh. Like the green dot that represented Derrick?"

"Exactly that."

"Maybe someone zapped him."

Miriam said nothing. She nodded. "You could be on to something."

"Now what?"

Miriam struggled to her feet. "Now, we'd better go talk to Brad and Marty." She stuck out her hand, helping Rebekah to her feet.

On her way down the hall, Miriam explained the plan, which was simple, yet risky. As nice as Brad and Marty seemed, they were grown men and, although lackadaisical, trained to some extent, which meant that two teenage girls would be no match for them in a fair fight. That's why Miriam wouldn't fight fair.

Miriam peeked into the lunchroom. Marty and Brad sat at their favorite table, full plates in front of each of them. She ran the scenarios through her mind again. As much as she hated doing this, it still seemed like the best option.

Miriam eased the door open. "Hi, guys."

Brad waved his arm. "Hey! Look who's here. Join us. We thought you had left."

"This is my last night. I wanted to give you a little warning. A peer is here to check my work. She knows about the security breach and will be here any second."

"This does not sound good."

"It's not good. But I will try to keep you guys out of it."

At that moment, Rebekah came through the other door.

"Guys, this is Ms. Ford. She is here to check my work."

Brad and Marty stood. Each extended a hand, which Rebekah shook.

"This is Brad, and this is Marty. As you read in my report, they are not to blame for the breach. It was all my fault."

Rebekah frowned and nodded. "I trust we can depend on your discretion in this matter?"

"Absolutely," Brad said.

Marty nodded. "Join us?" Marty asked.

"It will be our pleasure," Miriam said.

Miriam and Rebekah filled two trays with food and drink. They set their trays on the table, and Miriam stepped behind Brad. Rebekah stepped behind Marty. Before either man could twist around to see what they were doing, they hit both men with a high-voltage shock.

Brad jerked and slumped in his chair. Miriam eased him to the floor. Marty had fallen forward into his food tray, spilling his drink onto the table. Miriam helped Rebekah ease Marty to the floor. With wide gray tape they had found in the security storage room, they taped the men's hands and feet and put a strip across their mouths. Each grabbing a shoulder, they drug both men to the middle of the room.

Miriam retrieved her plate, leaving the tray in a pool of Marty's spilled soda. She moved to a table near the boys and sat. "We'd better eat. No telling when we'll get our next meal."

Rebekah brought her plate. "What about those two?"

"We need to wait until they wake up."

"What? Wait? Why would we do that?"

"They already know who did this. Well, not exactly who we are, but when they give our description, and it matches the two girls missing from Pacific Edge, I think even this security force can figure out who did it."

"True. But how is talking to them going to change that?"

"Think about it. Two security staff taken out by teenage girls. Their future is bleak."

"So?"

"So, they both have families. Besides, I like them."

"You're a strange girl," Rebekah said.

"Thank you," Miriam said, taking a bite of her ham sandwich. "I was thinking earlier that you're a strange girl, too."

Rebekah nodded. "Touché."

Brad groaned.

"Don't move, Brad," Miriam said. "Hurts like hell for a few minutes. Best thing is to lie still."

Brad struggled against the restraints and moaned again.

"Don't listen to me. Do whatever works for you," Miriam said.

Marty moved, groaning. Miriam offered him the same advice. Marty remained still, his eyes searching the room as best he could. Miriam realized they couldn't see Rebekah or herself.

Miriam moved to Brad's side. Rebekah stood nearby with a stun gun in her hand. She pulled the trigger, and an arc of electricity sizzled. Both men shook their heads.

"Guys, I'm sorry to do this. I really am. It was my fault that you learned I was here. I'm not from headquarters. I'm just a girl from Pacific Edge."

Both men stared at her with wide eyes.

"I'd like to talk to you before I leave. I'll take the tape off if you promise you won't scream. Can you promise me that? It won't do you any good, and my friend will stun you again. Nod if you agree to cooperate."

Both men nodded. Miriam pulled the tape off with a quick yank.

"Sorry," Miriam said with each pull.

"I don't understand," Brad said. "How did you, I mean, how could you get in here? And the e-mails, all of it?"

"No time to explain. Besides, one thing I said was true. The less you know, the better off we all are. Here's the deal. My brother is in trouble, and I need to help him. This was the only way for me to do it."

"You're the girl they pulled from the ocean," Marty said.

"You heard about that?"

"We hear things, but I would deny it if asked," Marty said.

"So, sometimes it's best to not tell the truth?"

"Sometimes," Marty agreed.

"This is one of those times. It's best we make something up. Like men ambushed each of you in different parts of the building. We'll move you. You tell us where."

"That won't help," Brad said.

Miriam saw a tear in his eye.

"Why not?" Miriam asked.

"Because there are security cameras. They'll search the recordings, including the last few months. They'll see Marty and I walking around with you like a couple of numskulls. We're screwed."

"I'm going to crash the entire computer system. Nothing left. No evidence."

Marty shook his head. "Won't work. They archive the system."

"I took care of it as well. No computer data for the last six months. None, nada."

"You guys should listen to her," Rebekah said. "She's in here, and you're taped up on the floor. Think about it."

"She has a point, buddy," Brad said.

"Guys, I never wanted to hurt either of you. If things go bad, can you leave here?"

"Maybe," Marty said. "Depends on if we see it coming."

"Well, if you see it coming, go to Potterville, California. Promise you'll tell no one I told you that."

Both men nodded.

Marty said, "What's your plan from here? I'm not looking for details. Only wondering if you have help, how are you going to get where you're going? Security will search for you. Do you have money? You know, general stuff."

Miriam looked at Rebekah and then at Marty. "We're still working on it."

"You don't have help?" Brad asked.

"No," Miriam said.

"That's crazy," Marty said. "Do you know anything about the world outside Pacific Edge?"

"Only what we see on New America Media," Rebekah said.

Brad chuckled. "Then you know nothing."

"You have no money?" Marty asked again.

"No," Miriam admitted. She was feeling less confident with each question. She had been so busy working on the technical stuff that she had given little thought to what she'd do outside the perimeter of Pacific Edge.

"Take my wallet?" Marty raised to one side as best he could.

Miriam hesitated, then pulled the wallet from Marty's back pocket.

"Take the money and toss the wallet in the trash."

"I can't take your money," Miriam said.

"It looks better for us if you do. Robbery. Right? I mean, bad guys take your money. Right?"

"I suppose," Miriam said.

"Mine too," Brad said. "Marty is right, looks better for us. Besides, there's not much money in my wallet. Maybe enough for a bus ticket away from here."

"Toss the wallets in a trash bin near where you leave us."

"Take the cash," Brad said.

"I'll pay you back," Miriam said.

"How?"

"I'll find a way."

"Forget it. Get out of here before someone shows up. Good luck, girls. You'll need it."

"Where do you want us to put you?" Miriam asked.

Brad said, "Take me to the tech-shared workspace. It's close."

Marty said, "Take me to the security bay. Sorry, it's farther, but it would look better if we were some distance apart."

The girls dragged both men to their respective resting places for the remainder of their shift. The girls took their duty belts and communication devices and checked the tape on their legs and arms, in both cases adding additional wraps. Both men cooperated. Finally, Miriam covered each man's mouth with tape.

"We'll clean up the dining room before we go," Miriam said.

Miriam leaned down and kissed each man on the forehead. "I love you guys."

Before returning to AJ Patel's office, Miriam went to the server room. She stopped several feet away from the door. "Stand here." Miriam pointed to a spot next to the wall. "It may not open if it sees your face. I'll be right back."

"What if someone comes?"

"Run like hell."

Miriam approached the server-room door. She smiled when she heard the lock cycle open. The room was warmer than she had imagined. Banks of computers mounted in racks filled the room. This would take longer than she expected. The program would download automatically upon insertion into a computer port. She tested a nonlethal version on the laptop. The download took 22 seconds. To be safe, she allowed 30 seconds between each machine.

Thirty minutes later, Miriam stepped into the hall.

"I was starting to think you left through a back door."

"The thought had not occurred to me, because no back door exists to that room."

"What's in there?"

"Computers. Lots of them."

"I still don't understand computer."

"A machine. That's all you need to understand for now. I was working on one in AJ Patel's office. Enough chatting. We need to get out of here."

Back in Patel's office, Miriam shut down the computer and packed the storage device and laptop. After finishing their last task, cleaning up the dining room, Miriam and Rebekah walked and sprinted down the hallway.

They did it.

They were free.

10

MIRIAM LED REBEKAH TO THE back of the food service area. This seemed like the best place to exit because the roads would lead to the streets, and the streets would lead to Potterville. Somehow. Miriam thought about leaving through the security bay but then decided against it. Security staff might be outside, probably stationed at every exit.

When they reached the back of the kitchen, Rebekah headed straight to an exit door. Miriam caught her by the arm.

"Slow down. Let's think this through," Miriam said.

"What's there to think about? We need to leave before people show up. Food service people and food deliveries probably come first."

"True, but we need to know what's on the other side of the door, or we might walk straight into security staff."

"You have an idea?"

"No, but let's look around. See if there's information on the doors or something."

Both girls moved quickly around the kitchen, which had grills, ovens, and work surfaces made of gleaming stainless steel.

Then Miriam spotted a map near a door. "Over here."

On the wall was a map of the food service area showing the exits, fire extinguishers, fire alarms, rooms, halls, and outside the building. The area outside looked large and surrounded by a fence. There was one gate, and next to the gate was a security station.

"Now what?" Rebekah asked.

Miriam said nothing.

Rebekah said, "I don't like this. Someone could see us as soon as we walk out of here and then we are sunk. I can't believe we are doing this."

Miriam touched the map. "Here. Looks like a narrow walkway with walls to each side. When we get to here," she pointed at the end of the walkway, "we'll need to hide. Maybe we can sneak aboard a delivery transport or something."

Rebekah nodded. "Might be our only hope."

They found the door to the walkway. Rebekah reached for the doorknob and then looked at Miriam. "What if we get separated?"

"Let's not." Miriam counted the money they had taken from Brad and Marty and gave Rebekah half.

"But if we do. What's our plan?" Rebekah asked.

Miriam said, "We'll meet where Derrick is. He's in Potterville or was. Somewhere outside Potterville. Do you know how to find it?"

"No."

Miriam said, "Me neither. Good plan."

Without saying another word, Rebekah threw her arms around Miriam and hugged her tightly. "Thanks for taking me with you."

"Don't thank me yet."

Rebekah eased the door open. The walkway was clear. Not brightly lit. Barely enough to see. They stepped outside. The door closed and latched behind them. They were committed now. No going back. Not that they could. What would they do? What would they say? *Hey Mom, Dad, funny thing happened tonight.*

They eased down the walkway, 15 yards toward the large open lot. As they neared the opening, a man stepped from the shadows.

AJ Patel.

Miriam froze. "What are you doing here?"

"I'm here because you are here." Patel clapped his hands lightly. "Congratulations. You have met my expectations and more. Excellent job."

"What do you want?" Miriam took a step back. Eyes searching the walkway, not finding an escape route. She reached into her bag and found the stun gun.

"What is your plan? What are you going to do next?" AJ Patel asked.

Miriam glared at him. "As if I would tell you."

Patel held his hand to his chest. "Miriam, that hurt. After what I've done to help? You wouldn't be here if not for me. And at significant risk, I might add. How long before they know you're gone? Have you hacked 1984? I think not. They will find you instantly. And what are you doing here, Rebekah? This is most unexpected." Patel stepped toward Miriam. He extended his hand. "Come with me. We need to get away from here as quickly as we can. I have a plan…"

Miriam glanced at Rebekah. Rebekah had her hand in her bag. Miriam nodded.

Miriam reached out and took Patel's hand. "I don't understand what you want."

With one forceful movement, Miriam pulled herself toward Patel at the same time the stun gun came out of her bag, and when they collided, she pulled the trigger.

The shock sent Miriam to the ground. The stun gun skittered across the pavement. Patel bent at waist, his eyes wide, but he remained standing.

Before he could react, Rebekah held her stun gun to his side. He jerked upright and then fell into a heap on the ground.

Rebekah helped Miriam up. "Is he dead?"

"Maybe. I don't know." Retrieving her stun gun, Miriam said, "Let's get out of here."

At the end of the walkway, Miriam peeked out. Nothing moved. She edged farther until she saw a small building containing the security guard. The building had windows on all sides. A metal bar painted red and white stretched across the drive. The guard appeared to be reading.

A large transport, Miriam figured it must carry food or other supplies, was parked between them and the guard. It would provide some cover, but they would still be exposed at times.

Miriam pulled back. "Guard at the gate. He appears to be reading. There's a big box transport thing that will give us some cover, but if he looks up while we are in the open, he'll see us."

"Plan then?"

"We run, staying low to the transport and then to the back of the building he is in. We'll be coming toward his back, so he should not see us unless he looks around. Next, we crawl along the wall of the building, under the windows, out the gate, and to the back of the building on the other side of the fence."

"Then what?"

"We run like hell."

Rebekah nodded. Miriam looked into her eyes and saw fear. She also saw courage. It occurred to her that you cannot have one without the other.

"Ready?"

Rebekah adjusted the sling of her bag and nodded.

Miriam eased out until she saw the guard, looked back at Rebekah, and sprinted hunched over to the box transport. She eased along the length of the transport and peered around its front. Next, she ducked low and zipped to the rear of the small shack where the security man sat reading. She squatted with her back to the wall, her heart pounding. The reality of what she was doing sank in. Miles away from Derrick but only feet away from freedom.

Rebekah joined her, nodding that she was ready. Miriam eased along the wall of the security shack below the window.

At the corner, she peeked around the edge. The door was closed. Specifically, the bottom was closed, and the top half was open. Miriam saw the fence and, beyond that, the commoner world. In addition, she saw a problem. At the corner of the guard shack, she saw her reflection in a rounded mirror. Looking up, she saw one above them as well. If the guard glanced at either mirror, he would see them. Miriam turned to Rebekah, pointed at the mirrors, and then took her hand, giving it a squeeze. "Here we go." She mouthed.

Miriam glided along the front of the shack. She heard the crunch of each step as if amplified by some mysterious force. She made it to the door, then to the corner of the shack. Her legs burned, and her back hurt. Sweat formed on her brow. Her breathing increased, sure that she was making too much noise. She pulled the stun gun from her bag and flipped it on, ready if the need arose.

Rebekah joined her. Miriam took several deep breaths.

Rebekah nodded and mouthed, "You first."

Miriam stayed low, running as silently as possible. After what seemed like forever, but was about 50 yards, she came to a street running at a 90-degree angle. She turned left, sprinting across the street. Looking back, she saw Rebekah following and the guard still reading. After rounding the corner of the building, the guard could no longer see them. Miriam stopped. Hands planted on her knees, breathing hard. Rebekah did the same.

After a few moments, Miriam looked at Rebekah, who had a huge smile. Rebekah Ford was a strange girl. Miriam was starting to like her.

They walked two blocks. The buildings changed from gray industrial concrete to red brick retail shops. Some store windows displayed items for sale, and others had colorful handwritten signs stating the current deals. Miriam found it all captivating. Validating her rejection of how New America Media portrayed the world outside of Pacific Edge.

"Hello." Rebekah waved her hand in front of Miriam's face.

"What?"

"I've been trying to get your attention. You're in a daze. Did that stun gun affect your brain?"

Miriam thought for a moment. "Yes. I believe it did. But I'm amazed at this place. Aren't you?"

"Fascinating, but we need a plan. How long before they start looking for us?"

"Good question. I hope a few hours before they discover Marty and Brad. Once they know we breached their security, all hell will break loose. It will intensify when their computer system goes dark. I hope that causes panic, confusion, and chaos. Your parents will notice you're missing as well."

Rebekah said, "Your parents will see you're gone too."

"No. They won't, but they'll know something's up."

"What does that mean?" Rebekah asked.

"I'll explain later."

"What about Patel?"

"Right, Patel. He should be stirring by now."

"What will he do? Sound an alarm? Come after us himself?" Rebekah looked over her shoulder.

"I don't know what he will do. Come after us himself, I guess."

"We need to get out of here. Come on, girl, you're the genius. I'm the moral support."

"To be honest, I'd prefer plucky comic relief to moral support."

Rebekah rolled her eyes. "I'll try. But try thinking instead of window shopping."

"Window shopping. I like that phrase. It's catchy."

Lights reflected in the store windows, and beams of light streamed down the street. Miriam heard a transport like the one that took Derrick the night of his exile.

"What do we do?" Rebekah asked.

Miriam glanced around—no place to hide. Whoever was in the transport had probably already noticed them. "Keep walking. Act natural."

The transport crawled along the street behind them. Miriam resisted the urge to peek over her shoulder. She saw the front of the transport come alongside them. It was not as big as the one that took Derrick, not as tall, faded dark-blue or black paint, hard to tell in the dim pre-dawn light—moving a little faster than their pace. It might be Patel. He could be armed.

As the transport came alongside them, Miriam heard a familiar voice say, "Miriam? And Rebekah Ford?"

Mr. Jones.

Miriam spun around. "What are you doing here?"

Jones stopped. "Looking for you. Get in so ..."

Before he finished, Miriam pulled the stun gun from her bag, flipped the switch on, and pulled the trigger, causing a surge of electricity to dance between its poles. "Stay away from us."

"Miriam, put that away. I'm here to …"

Miriam grabbed Rebekah's hand and ran. The transport followed them. Outrunning it wasn't possible. They saw a park full of trees, bushes, and flowers. Jones couldn't drive in there. They sprinted into the trees. When Miriam last looked, Jones remained in his transport, talking on a communication device.

"How would he know?" Rebekah asked.

"I have no clue."

"What now?"

"Keep running."

On the other side of the park, they stopped behind a large tree, hid in the shadows, and tried to catch their breath. There was a small area for parking. A different transport was parked in the lot. The transport was empty.

That's when it happened.

From behind them came another familiar voice.

"Miriam. Do not run. We are trying to help you."

Miriam turned.

Astonished, Miriam said, "Mrs. Springfield?"

11

MR. JONES' FADED BLUE TRANSPORT entered the parking lot. Both transports looked old, not dirty, but Miriam didn't think washing would make them shine. Mr. Jones stepped from his transport and waved them over.

"It's okay, Miriam. Thomas will take you to Potterville," Mrs. Springfield said.

"Thomas?" Miriam asked.

"Yes, child. We have first names."

"But how? Why? I always thought Mr. Jones…"

"Didn't like you? He didn't enjoy that part, but it was necessary to spark the debates, wasn't it?"

Miriam looked at Rebekah.

Rebekah looked at Miriam. "I'm as confused as the look on your face."

"Rebekah Ford? What are you doing here?" Mr. Jones asked as he approached.

"Same thing as Miriam. Escaping, or trying to until now."

"We'd better get moving. Thomas will take you," Mrs. Springfield said.

Miriam looked at Rebekah, shrugged her shoulders.

"How long before they know you're gone?" Mr. Jones asked.

"I don't know," Miriam said.

"Best guess?"

"Anywhere from 30 seconds to 4 hours."

"Thirty seconds? How is that?" Mrs. Springfield asked.

"We had to stun a guy," Miriam said, pointing back toward Pacific Edge.

"What guy?" Mr. Jones asked.

"You wouldn't know him. His name is AJ Patel. He was waiting for us outside the building," Miriam said.

Mr. Jones looked at Mrs. Springfield, then turned back at Miriam and said, "Why would Patel be waiting for you?"

"Long story. Wait, you know him?"

"Yes, we do," Mrs. Springfield said.

Inside Miriam's head, gears spun at a ferocious speed. *What was going on here?* Just a few days ago, she suspected that Mr. Jones and Mrs. Springfield were part of a trap. Now, here they are saying they will help. Add that they know AJ Patel. She reached into her bag and wrapped her fingers around the stun gun. She glanced at Rebekah and saw that she also had her hand in her bag. Rebekah gave a slight nod of her head.

Mrs. Springfield looked from one girl to the other. "I hope you won't hurt us. We're here to help you. Honest."

"How did you find us?" Rebekah asked.

"We've been out driving around the perimeter every night for the past two weeks," Mr. Jones said. "Trust me, it didn't make going to school pleasant."

Miriam looked at Mr. Jones and then at Mrs. Springfield. "Why would you do that?"

"Because we assumed, I should say, we hoped Miriam would escape. We believed if anyone was smart enough, it was Miriam. We had not expected Rebekah, though. I guess that changes nothing if she is sure this is what she wants to do," Mr. Jones said.

"You hoped?" Miriam asked.

"Yes," Mr. Jones said.

"Why would you hope for that?" Miriam asked.

Mr. Jones said, "Because you *are* our hope. You and Derrick."

Miriam said nothing, thoughts churning.

Part of the trap? Maybe.

Crazy? Definitely.

Before Miriam spoke again, a siren sounded. Both girls and both adults covered their ears. They had heard the siren before when security tested the emergency alert system, but they had only heard it during tests. There had never been a genuine emergency.

"No time, girls. Into the car with Thomas. Trust us."

Miriam looked at Rebekah.

Rebekah shrugged. "Your call."

Miriam analyzed the situation. Everything told her this was a trap, a backup plan should they get by AJ Patel. The siren hurt her ears, but her gut told her to get into the car. She hated it when intuition overrode intellect.

Miriam said nothing. She walked to the faded blue transport and waited. Rebekah followed and went to the other side.

Mrs. Springfield followed Mr. Jones to the transport.

As Mr. Jones opened the door, Mrs. Springfield kissed him hard and said, "Good luck, Love. And be careful."

As they pulled out of the parking lot, Mr. Jones said, "There's a blanket back there. Best if you get down and cover up. If we are lucky, they won't have the roads closed yet. But to be safe, I'll take back roads out of town. Still, best for you to be hidden. I'll tell you when it's safe."

The girls did as Mr. Jones instructed. Miriam didn't like it. She couldn't see where they were going. He might drive them right back to Pacific Edge. Miriam focused on the motion of the transport, which was much different from the silent and silky-smooth ride of the transports to which she was accustomed. It made noises—lots of them. A sound came from the front of the transport that she assumed to be the power plant. She didn't understand the source of power used in Pacific Edge transports. Never something that interested her, which she thought odd because she had considered herself curious about everything. This transport was nothing like a Pacific Edge transport, of that much she felt certain. There were other noises, too. Some were associated with bumps and jars from the road surface, and others were from the wind.

She couldn't estimate speed and distance because she had no concept of either. Rarely did she use the transport in Pacific Edge. It only took 20 minutes to walk from one side of Pacific Edge to the other. The weather is never so hot, cold, or wet to make walking impossible. Yet few people walked anywhere. Miriam believed the Chosen felt walking was below their status in life. They were conditioned to think that being outside was dangerous, being inside was safe. Being inside was comfortable. Life didn't get better than being in a building inside the protective Pacific Edge walls.

She could distinguish forward and backward and turns left and right. First, they went backward a short distance. The transport moved forward from that moment on. She kept track of the number of turns and the turn direction. In her mind, she pictured Pacific Edge and their direction of travel. If they turned back, she would stun Mr. Jones and hope the wreck wasn't too severe.

"You guys okay back there?" Mr. Jones asked.

"Not comfortable, but okay," Rebekah answered.

"When we get out of town, you can sit up. But we must watch for hovercraft."

"How far until we are out of town?" Miriam asked.

"Soon, but it's still not safe to sit up. I want to put some distance between us and Pacific Edge," Mr. Jones said. "Besides, you're not missing much."

After several minutes, Mr. Jones said, "You can sit up, but be forewarned. We're in the dead zone."

"Dead zone?" Miriam asked.

"Yeah. They clear everything, creating a dead zone around Chosen Communities. Nature has taken some of it back near the coast. We are in the dead zone now, but we'll just clip the corner of it because of the back road I am taking."

Miriam said, "You didn't answer my question. How far, not how long."

Mr. Jones chuckled. "I should have paid closer attention to your question. You asked how far, not how long. Silly me. About seven miles. Traffic is light this early, but I won't go over the speed limit. Don't want to risk getting stopped."

Miriam smiled. Now, she could estimate speed and distance in her head. However, they didn't make straight or steady progress. Sometimes they stopped, sometimes they turned, and sometimes they did both. Miriam continued to picture their location in relation to Pacific Edge. She removed her hand from her bag. They were traveling away from Pacific Edge.

"Mind if I play some music?" Mr. Jones asked.

Miriam cringed. She hated music—patriotic New America crap or worship of the founding fathers or, worse, worship of James Carver.

"It's your transport," Miriam said.

"Thanks. And we call it a car."

Music, unlike anything Miriam had ever heard, filled the car. She felt the vibration of the low notes, the beat driving, the vocals soulful.

"I hope you don't mind rock and roll. But wait, you don't even know what rock and roll is, do you? Give it some time. You might like it. If not, there are other styles you might enjoy more. Anything but Country is okay with me. I don't do Country." Mr. Jones laughed.

Miriam had never heard Mr. Jones laugh. "I like it already."

The car kept stopping briefly.

"Lots of stop signs on these back roads," Mr. Jones said. "I'll feel better when we've put some distance between us and Pacific Edge."

"See anyone looking for us yet?" Miriam asked.

Mr. Jones said, "Just a minute."

The next time they stopped, Miriam felt the cool morning air. Mr. Jones must have opened his door or window. She felt the transport shift. Mr. Jones must be moving around to see the sky.

"I don't see anything. Wait. Three hovercrafts to the east of us. Crap!"

When the car moved again, the power plant made more noise, and the acceleration pushed Miriam into the seat. Her sense of relief faded. Then the car turned, but differently. The turn felt gradual this time, and the car did not stop. Then the inclination of the transport changed. They were climbing. This bewildered Miriam. The transport—car, Mr. Jones called it—didn't look high-tech or more advanced than the transports she was accustomed to, but this one could fly? Another turn, and they climbed higher. Miriam wanted to look. They would be in Potterville quickly flying, but it did not feel like the car was going fast enough to become airborne.

"May we come out now?" Miriam asked.

"Sorry, yes. Come out. And watch the sky for hovercraft."

Miriam threw the blanket off and sat upright. She looked out the window. She gasped. They were not flying. They were on the side of a mountain. Miriam scooted away from the window. She saw the land far below stretching to the sea. Her stomach leaped into her throat. She had flown before on family vacations, but those machines were windowless. Otherwise, she had never been on anything higher than the roof outside her bedroom. Therefore, she didn't realize she was afraid of heights until now.

Small, drab-green twisted trees and sage-colored bushes battled for space on the mountainside. Large rust-colored rocks forced their way through the soil in chaotic intervals. A trip off the road would be a misadventure with painfully lethal consequences.

"Uh, you trying to rip my leg off?" Rebekah asked.

Miriam looked down. She had dug her fingers into Rebekah's thigh. "Sorry."

"It's okay. It's an amazing view. Isn't it?" Rebekah asked, leaning over Miriam for a better look.

"Uh, yeah, I guess. I've never been this high when I could see out."

"Right. Me either. It's amazing."

Miriam realized something important about Rebekah. Rebekah was brave in ways she was not. That could prove to be important in the future. The car rounded another corner, and now the view outside Miriam's window was the side of the mountain. She liked that better. The view out of Rebekah's side was of the valley below. Rebekah pressed against the window. Miriam looked up the road and saw another turn coming, putting her on the downhill side again.

Miriam realized something. The ocean was on her right. She calculated their relationship to Pacific Edge and understood their direction of travel: They were going southwest, while Potterville was northwest.

It *was* a trap after all.

12

MIRIAM TAPPED REBEKAH ON THE leg. When Rebekah turned to look at her, Miriam mouthed, "We are going in the wrong direction." Rebekah's eyes narrowed, and she looked at Mr. Jones. They rounded another corner, which put Miriam back on the uphill side, and the scrubby pine trees appeared. Miriam slid to the middle of the seat and sat forward, close to Mr. Jones, stun gun in her hand. Too dangerous to zap him on the side of a mountain, but she wanted to be ready when an opportunity occurred. She studied how he operated the transport he called a car so she could drive it.

"Where is Derrick?" Miriam asked.

"In Potterville. I assumed you knew that."

"How do you know he's there?"

"I saw him there."

"Wait. What? How? Why?"

"Now that's a weird thing. My sister teaches in Potterville. We are close and talk or text often. So, one day she tells me about this new boy at their school—sad story. Boy's parents were killed, and he came to live with an uncle. But the kid is kind of weird. Rumors are circulating that he's Chosen. Then she tells me the boy's name is Derrick King. So, I drove to Potterville on the weekend. Sure enough, I saw Derrick at a bakery. In fact, that's when Erica and I decided we could help."

"Erica?" Miriam asked.

"Mrs. Springfield. We're married. They like to keep that from students, so she uses her maiden name at the Academy."

"I thought teachers were Chosen," Rebekah said.

"Heavens no. And a good thing, or we wouldn't be able to help."

The car took another turn. They had reached the top of the mountain. The road was straight for some distance. Miriam adjusted the stun gun in her hand. "How far is the next town?"

"About 40 miles. Why?"

"I may need to stop before then."

"Well, try to hold on if you can. I'd rather not stop out here in the open. And I thought we might get some breakfast there."

"Derrick would have recognized you," Miriam said.

"Well, sure. Under normal circumstances, he would have. If it was Derrick, and he was lying about where he was from, I didn't want to cause him problems. So, I wore a disguise. I'm in theater, and I'm good at makeup. Killed two birds with one stone. Had a nice visit with my sister and confirmed that Derrick was in Potterville. Plus, I had one of the best cinnamon rolls ever. Heck, I killed three birds with one stone." Mr. Jones chuckled. "Do you like cinnamon rolls?"

"Never had one," Miriam said. "How long does it take to get to Potterville?"

"Normally, or today?"

"Normally," Miriam said.

"About three hours."

"And today?"

Mr. Jones glanced over his shoulder. "Good question. Eight hours? Three days?"

Miriam said, "I don't understand."

"I should have said something sooner. My nerves are fried. It's making me a little more brain-dead than usual."

Fried nerves? Brain-dead. Mr. Jones never talked like that in class. Had he talked like that, she might have liked him. Wouldn't have been so hard on him. Right now, she had never felt more confused.

"Rebekah, are you still monitoring the sky?" Mr. Jones asked, looking up in the mirror.

"Sorry, no."

Miriam glanced over her shoulder and saw Rebekah searching the sky.

"Why don't you know how long it will take today?" Miriam asked.

"Because we are going in the opposite direction at the moment, and I'm not sure what route we should take."

"Why are we going in the wrong direction?"

"Miriam, I'm disappointed in you," Mr. Jones said.

"What?"

"You're the smartest person I've ever met. Think."

"Oh," Miriam said.

"Oh, what?" Rebekah asked.

"If they are looking for me, they know I'm going to Derrick. They know where Derrick is. They will have the roads going to Potterville blocked or under surveillance." Miriam sat back in her seat. She put the stun gun in the bag.

Mr. Jones looked in the mirror. "That's the Miriam I recognize."

They drove on for an hour and a half. Now, the road weaved through the forest, sometimes into a green meadow and then back into the forest. Mr. Jones pointed to three deer along the road. Both girls sat up to watch them.

"There's more I should tell you," Mr. Jones said. "I talked to my sister a few days ago. Derrick is drawing a lot of attention to himself. He told people he was from Denver, and his parents had died in a house fire, and Paul is his uncle."

"Doesn't surprise me," Miriam said. "Derrick was terrified of commoners. He was convinced they'd kill him within hours."

"I understand that, given what New America Media tells you and what we have to teach you."

What we have to teach, was not wasted on Miriam.

"But then he lied about other things that are not helping."

"Like what?" Miriam asked.

"Said he wasn't a runner. Told the coach he had never played sports, run, etc. Then he tries out for the track team, and within a week, he's on varsity, one of the top runners in several events. People saw right through that lie."

"But he didn't lie. Derrick never exercised. He hardly went outside for any reason," Rebekah said.

Mr. Jones glanced up at the mirror again. Miriam saw his eyes studying her, and then he said, "That makes no sense. He can't go from couch potato to track star in a week."

Miriam said, "That's not entirely true."

"What's not true?" Rebekah asked.

"That Derrick didn't exercise. It's a long story. I don't completely understand, and I'm not ready to discuss it."

"Not ready to discuss …"

"Rebekah, let it go," Mr. Jones said. "Miriam said she's not ready."

The three fell silent. Miriam and Rebekah sat as far away from each other as possible and did not look at one another. Forty minutes passed, and the car slowed.

"What's wrong?" Miriam asked, sitting up.

"Nothing. We are coming into the town I mentioned. It's still early. I hope something is open."

"Open for what?" Miriam asked.

"Food and a restroom break. You said you needed to stop."

"Right," Miriam said.

Mr. Jones looked in the mirror. "Sorry, I snapped at you, Rebekah. I'm feeling a lot of pressure here to protect Miriam. Truth is, I need to protect you both."

"I'll live," Rebekah said.

Mr. Jones slowed. What he called a town was unlike anything Miriam had ever seen. Small wooden structures covered with faded paint, and in some cases, the paint had disappeared long ago. Transports, some like the one they were in, some like the one that took Derrick away, sat in front of the buildings. Smoke rose from small round pipes that protruded through the slanted roofs. A few transports moved along the streets. Mr. Jones waved as he passed, and the other drivers waved back. Miriam assumed Mr. Jones didn't know these people.

Mr. Jones turned right, and the buildings changed. Two-story brick buildings lined this street for two blocks. The lower half of the buildings had glass windows displaying goods like the ones she saw after leaving Pacific Edge. Some had a plant or other decoration in the front. One sign read real estate, another insurance, and one taxes. The newest and nicest building on the corner read Bank.

"Ah, this looks promising." Mr. Jones angled into a parking place in front of a sign that read *Main Street Café*.

Mr. Jones turned around in his seat. "We need a strategy before going in."

"Strategy?" Rebekah asked.

Miriam said, "He means, who are we, where are we going? Things like that. We should be in school. Such a small place, people will know we are strangers."

"Exactly," Mr. Jones said. "How about we are going to a school activity?"

"Sounds weird to me," Miriam said. "One male teacher, two young girls in a private car?"

"Good point."

"How about a funeral?" Rebekah asked.

"Whose funeral?" Mr. Jones asked.

"Ours, if they catch us," Miriam said.

Rebekah giggled.

Miriam giggled.

"Glad to see you haven't lost your sense of humor. If we are going to a funeral, you might want to act a little sadder."

"Uncle Bob," Miriam said.

"Right," Rebekah said. "I never liked Uncle Bob. But he was good enough to have his funeral on a school day, which is why I'm in a good mood."

Miriam laughed.

Rebekah laughed.

When they finally composed themselves, Miriam said, "We'll behave."

Then Miriam started laughing again.

Rebekah laughed and laid her head on Miriam's leg.

"When you two get yourselves under control, we'll go in," Mr. Jones said, trying to frown but unable to suppress a grin.

Rebekah sat up and wiped her eyes.

Miriam took a deep breath. "I'm sorry too, Rebekah. I'll tell you about Derrick when I understand it better. I have the information here." She patted the bag that was sitting at her feet. Then she looked at Mr. Jones and said, "Okay, we're ready."

"Uncle Bob is your mother's brother. Your mother is already there. I went to school with Bob and agreed to take you both to the funeral. Your mother is divorced, and your father lives in Nevada. Can you remember all that?"

"Was," Miriam said.

"Was what?" Mr. Jones asked.

"Uncle Bob was my mother's brother. He's dead now." Miriam laughed.

Rebekah laughed.

"Smart aleck. Are you done?"

Both girls shook their heads, giggling.

"Where is the funeral?" Miriam asked.

"Kerns," Mr. Jones said.

"Where is that?" Miriam asked.

"It's on the way to Potterville, sort of. This is not the fastest way there. We are taking a scenic route. The funeral isn't until tomorrow. Let me do the talking."

"I'm hungry," Rebekah said, opening her door.

"One more thing," Mr. Jones said. "Don't talk much. We might say something that would raise suspicion. Fits our story too. We are going to a funeral, so we are not cheerful people. Instead of talking, listen. Someone may say something that will be helpful."

They walked into the café.

"Sit wherever you'd like," a lady called out from behind the counter.

Mr. Jones picked a booth that allowed them to watch the car. One man sat at the counter. Otherwise, the place was empty.

The lady brought menus. "Coffee?"

"Yes, please," Mr. Jones said.

"A double espresso," Miriam said.

The lady wrinkled her brow. "You look a little young for a double espresso. Besides, we don't have espresso. Just coffee. I could make you a hot chocolate."

"Coffee is fine," Miriam said, studying her menu.

"I'll take a hot chocolate," Rebekah said.

"I'll be right back to take your order."

The lady returned with two coffees and a hot chocolate. Miriam ordered eggs, bacon, hash browns, and toast. Rebekah ordered oatmeal. Mr. Jones ordered a pancake with one egg over easy. From her bag, Miriam pulled the money Brad and Marty had made her take and tapped Mr. Jones on the leg.

Mr. Jones glanced down and whispered, "Where did you get that? They don't allow cash in Pacific Edge."

"Friends wanting to help gave it to us," Miriam said.

"What friends. Patel?"

"Not Patel. Just friends."

"Put it away. I'm buying breakfast. Besides, you may need it later," Mr. Jones said.

The chime on the front door sounded. Two men wearing plaid shirts and faded blue pants entered the café and took a table nearby. Both ordered the usual, which the lady understood without further explanation.

"You hear about the commotion on the coast?" one man asked.

"I heard something on the radio but wasn't paying attention. Something about lots of hovercraft and Chosen patrols out early?"

"Yep. I heard someone attacked Pacific Edge. No word on how many dead. Must have been a hell of a thing: no power, no water, no communications. Everything is out. Hovercraft forced to land outside the compound. Can't operate without their computer system." Coffee arrived. The man took a sip and then added, "Came from the sea, I suspect."

"Who would want to attack Pacific Edge? Unless someone wanted to break them poor folks out."

"Right. Well, most of them wouldn't leave if they could. Pretty fancy prison, from what I hear."

The man turned to the three new arrivals. "Where you headed?"

"My uncle's funeral," Miriam said.

"Sorry for your loss. Around here?"

"Over in Kerns," Mr. Jones said.

"Where did you start from?"

Mr. Jones hesitated. "Los Alamos."

"You're headed the wrong way."

"True. The funeral is tomorrow, so I wanted to take a scenic route."

"Humph. If you say so. Have you heard about the problems over at Pacific Edge? See anything on the way here?"

"I haven't had the radio on. We haven't seen anything unusual. Pacific Edge, you say? That's the Chosen community near what used to be Carpinteria, isn't it?"

"That's the place. Most folks don't know it used to be Carpinteria."

The lady walked up carrying a big plate in each hand and balancing a third on her forearm. "Here you go. Warmups on the coffee?"

"That would be great," Mr. Jones said.

When she had left, Mr. Jones said to the two men, "I'll turn on the radio when we get back on the road. Thanks for the heads up. I hope you two have a wonderful day."

"So, how did you know?" the man asked.

"Know what?" Mr. Jones asked.

"That Pacific Edge was built in Carpinteria?"

"Oh, that." Mr. Jones paused. "An old friend of mine is an instructor at the Pacific Edge Academy."

The man studied him for a moment. "What's your friend's name?"

"Thomas Jones. Why do you ask?"

"I'm curious by nature, I guess. That and I saw your car coming from that direction. Not from Los Alamos."

Miriam looked at Rebekah. Rebekah sprinkled some sugar on her oatmeal.

Mr. Jones chuckled. "No wonder. I got lost. Had to backtrack."

The man studied Mr. Jones for a moment. "And what's your name?"

"Dirk Springfield."

"Well, pleased to meet you, Mr. Springfield. You drive safe and look after those young'uns. And you won't get much radio until you get on the other side of the mountains."

Mr. Jones nodded and turned back to his breakfast, signaling to the locals that the conversation was over. He gave the girls a quick wink. Miriam didn't make eye contact with the men for the rest of the meal. Mr. Jones poured maple syrup on his pancake and placed the egg on top. *Strange meal,* Miriam thought as she grabbed the pepper. The two locals didn't discuss the incident at Pacific Edge further. Instead, they discussed the weather and the local high school baseball team. Miriam wondered if high school was the commoner equivalent to the Academy.

After breakfast, Mr. Jones pulled into another business at the edge of town. "I need to fill up here. You can use the bathroom if needed. The next opportunity will be a few hours."

Both girls had used the washroom at the café and stayed in the car. Miriam assumed Mr. Jones was filling the car with fuel. He put a metal thing on the end of a black hose into the car. Miriam could smell the fuel but didn't know what it was called. It occurred to her how little she understood the commoner world despite thinking she knew a lot. It must have overwhelmed Derrick. In all the excitement, Derrick had not been on her mind. More precisely, she had refused to think about his disappearance.

"Are you thinking about what I'm thinking about?" Rebekah asked.

"Maybe," Miriam said.

"What are you thinking about?" Rebekah asked.

"That stuff Mr. Jones is putting in the transport," Miriam lied.

"You mean the car?"

"Yeah, I'll start calling it that," Miriam agreed.

"That's it?"

"That's what?"

"That's all you're thinking about?" Rebekah asked.

Mr. Jones put the black hose back in its receptacle, and Miriam said, "Also, how can we find where we saw Derrick's 1984 beacon go dark? What are you thinking about?"

"Wondering if Derrick is alive."

13

IN KERNS, THEY PARKED THE car and walked across a park with a small playground where young children played. Their mothers sat on a nearby bench, watching. The bushes and trees, still mostly bare, stood motionless against a clear blue sky. A few early flowers braved the cold. Mr. Jones pulled a folded paper from a compartment under the windshield and put it in his back pocket. Kerns was different from the town where they ate breakfast. It was different from that town, as it was from Pacific Edge. Where the first town looked old and worn, Kerns looked old, but as if they worked hard to make it look that way. It was old in a polished, new sort of way. Miriam liked it.

Mr. Jones avoided towns on the way. When a town approached, he took back roads leading through farms, forests, or dry barren places. In the mountains, sometimes the roads went nowhere, and they had to backtrack and find another way. His efforts were successful because they were here. It was 2 p.m., and the sun felt warm, but the air felt brisk, unlike any weather Miriam had ever experienced. Mountains rose on all sides. A clear river tumbled over polished rocks through the center of the town.

"What sounds good?" Mr. Jones asked.

"Not sure what you mean by that," Rebekah said.

"To eat. What sounds good to eat?"

"Oh, I'm not hungry," Rebekah said.

"It's at least two hours to Potterville. We should eat here. Besides, I needed to stretch my legs. How about pizza?"

"What's a pizza?" Miriam asked.

Mr. Jones said, "I forgot. It's a commoner food, but never say that out here."

"Don't say commoner food or pizza?" Miriam asked.

"Don't say, commoner. People don't see themselves as that. Commoner is a New America term used to degrade us."

"Oh, I didn't know. Sorry," Miriam said, adding, "There's so much we have to learn here."

"Don't worry about that now. When we get to Potterville, Derrick will teach you. You'll learn fast enough."

"You don't know about Derrick?" Miriam asked.

"Know what about Derrick?"

"Something happened. He has disappeared," Miriam said.

"What do you mean he disappeared? How do you know that?" Mr. Jones asked.

Miriam wondered how much she should say and then decided it didn't matter. Mr. Jones had brought them this far. If he had been part of a trap to take them back to Pacific Edge, he would have done so already unless he had been using them to find Derrick. Her gut told her that was not the case. She hated it when her gut talked to her.

"We have trackers," Miriam said.

"Trackers?" Mr. Jones asked.

"You were not aware of that?" Miriam asked.

"No. Do I have a tracker?"

"I don't think so. Only the Chosen."

"So, what's this about Derrick." Mr. Jones stopped in the middle of the small park. His face grew white.

"I checked the tracking system before we left, so I could find Derrick when we got to Potterville, but his tracker gave no signal. I went back in time and found him, and then the signal disappeared. I moved forward in time, and it flickered and then disappeared again. It didn't return."

Mr. Jones wobbled a little and then sat on a nearby bench. "Why didn't you tell me?"

Miriam sat on one side of him, and Rebekah sat on the other.

Miriam shrugged her shoulders. "Worried that you'd change your mind about taking us, I guess. Maybe because I've tried to not think about it. Now that we are so close, I can't stop thinking about it."

Mr. Jones pulled a device from his pocket, like the two AJ Patel had given her. Its screen lit up. "I'll call my sister. She might know something. Maybe Derrick is okay, just a malfunction."

Speaking into the device, Mr. Jones said, "Hi sis. Everything is okay.

—

"I'm on my way to Potterville. —

"About three hours. —

"Yes, she's with me. —

"Damn. I hoped you'd have better news. —

"Yes, she knows. —

"Long story. I'll tell you when I get there. —

"Love you too."

Mr. Jones shook his head. "No one knows where Derrick is. They've been out looking for him, but no sign of him."

"I'm not hungry," Miriam said.

"Me either, but we need to eat. No telling when we'll get our next meal. Plus, we need to do some intelligence work," Mr. Jones said.

"Intelligence work?" Rebekah asked.

"Eavesdrop," Miriam said.

They walked down the street to a place that brewed beer and made pizza. Mr. Jones ordered because the girls didn't understand pizza. He asked if they liked the ingredients used in making the pizza. He lamented he couldn't have a beer and got three sodas instead. The girls didn't recognize the names of the sodas, so they tasted each before deciding. Mr. Jones picked a table close to other people. They listened and waited.

When the pizza came, Mr. Jones served a slice to each girl before serving himself. "Careful, it's hot."

Miriam took a bite, waved her hand in front of her mouth, and said, "It's hot, but it's wonderful."

Rebekah, her mouth full, nodded in agreement.

Then a man joined the table next to them. "Just confirmed it with Howard. The state trooper set up a roadblock around a blind corner on the pass. Damn dangerous, but he doesn't care about that. He's got the sheriff's deputies ferrying people to jail for any minor infraction. Course, he's hoping to find them escapees from Pacific Edge. As if Kerns is on the way to Potterville from Pacific Edge. What an idiot."

"Crap. Not that I have anything to worry about, but I assume he's got traffic backed up for miles," another man said.

"Yep. That's what I heard."

"Stupid. If those escapees went that way, they'd turn around when they saw the roadblock."

The first man nodded. "Yep. But that guy worships the thought of the Chosen. Buys into the idea that you can go there if you're good enough. A crock if I ever heard one. But he'd be the happiest guy in the world if he could just be a Pacific Edge security guard. He applies every year. Must figure capturing those escapees would be his ticket."

Mr. Jones looked at Miriam and shook his head.

Outside, they walked back to the small park and sat at a table.

"Now what?" Rebekah asked.

"I don't know," Mr. Jones said, adding, "Do you guys have these trackers?"

"Yes. Sort of. We killed them," Miriam said.

"But how …"

Miriam cut him off. "There must be another way to Potterville."

Mr. Jones pulled the folded paper from his back pocket and spread it on the table. "We're right here." He put his finger on the map.

"Looks like we can go straight north and then turn east through the mountains," Miriam said, pointing at a line on the map.

Mr. Jones said, "That road goes into Sequoia National Park. It's mountainous. The roads may not be open yet. The park is probably still closed."

"How could we find out?" Rebekah asked.

"I noticed a sporting goods store on the corner. Because of the national park, this is a tourist town. Someone in there might know."

Miriam had seen the store Mr. Jones referred to. She was ten yards across the park when she turned. "What are you waiting for?"

"Try to look like tourists," Mr. Jones said just before they entered the store.

"I thought we were going to a funeral," Miriam said.

"Not anymore," Mr. Jones said.

The girls looked at clothes. They would need more clothes. But they wouldn't buy much at these prices. Mr. Jones was at the counter waiting for an employee to finish with a customer. The girls moved close enough to hear the conversation.

"Hi," Mr. Jones said. "We're hoping to see the park. Is it open?"

"Nope. Not open yet."

"Dang. We are on our way home from vacation and hoped to see it. You know, just drive through."

"Where's home?"

"Idaho," Mr. Jones lied. "Can we get to Johnsondale?"

"I'm supposed to say no, but they keep the road open to Johnsondale, but there are no park employees yet, so they don't like to have tourists."

Mr. Jones nodded. "How about from Johnsondale to Potterville? Could we get out of the park that way?"

"Nope. The pass still has snow on it. There'll be washouts that need to be repaired too before it's open. They lock the gate across the road, so people don't get stranded up there."

"Thanks for the help."

Mr. Jones motioned for the girls to join him in the back of the store. "You heard?"

"Yes," Miriam said.

"I don't know what to do now. We can't go the route we had planned. It will be a long detour going east around the park. Probably take us an extra day. Maybe waiting a day or two isn't a bad idea."

"Derrick might not have a day or two," Miriam said.

"We can't go back south and take main roads to Potterville. Too risky now that we know they are looking for escapees."

"We go to Johnsondale, and I walk from there," Miriam said.

"Over the mountains? You can't do that. You heard the man. The road's still snowed in."

"Correction. We walk from there," Rebekah said.

Miriam looked at Rebekah and was about to say something until she saw that look on Rebekah's face. Then, she decided to save her arguments for Mr. Jones. At least arguing with Jones felt normal, which made her smile despite the situation.

"It's too far. I can't let you do it. Too dangerous. Besides, you're not dressed for it."

"It's 21 miles to the next small town, which reduces the distance. You drive around and get us on the other side of the mountain."

"How do you know it's 21 miles?"

"I looked at the map."

"Did the map show mileage? I doubt it on a forest service road."

"No, but it had squares and a mileage legend."

"As amazing as it sounds—that you could read the map upside down and for only seeing it a few moments—I believe you," Mr. Jones said. "But it doesn't change anything. Still too far, still too dangerous. It will be cold on the mountain at night."

"True. We need coats," Miriam said.

Rebekah said, "And some snacks and water. I think we have enough money if we are careful. I noticed closeout coats. If we're lucky, we can find sizes that fit."

"Look. We are not doing this. You still must get to Johnsondale, and I'm not taking you. I won't do it."

"Fine, we'll start walking and hope someone will give us a ride to Johnsondale. If they try anything funny," Miriam opened her bag so Mr. Jones could see the stun gun.

"Were you thinking about using that on me?" Mr. Jones asked.

"Yep," Miriam said.

14

MIRIAM AND REBEKAH FOUND COATS ON the closeout rack, but they paid the full price for gloves and knitted caps. Boots were too expensive. Rebekah grabbed a handful of power bars. She didn't know what they were, but they said high protein, which sounded like something they would need. Mr. Jones stood with his arms folded, watching them from the other side of the store. He saw them calculating their purchases and counting their money.

"You still need better shoes. Something warm, something sturdy. Boots." Mr. Jones had joined them at the back of the store.

"We don't have enough money for boots. These shoes will do." Miriam looked down at her lightweight sneakers designed for warm temperatures.

"Seriously, guys. This is a bad idea. We can drive around. I'll drive all night. We'll be there by morning."

"No, we won't," Miriam said.

"What does that mean?" Mr. Jones asked.

"It means they will catch us."

"You can't know that."

"Think about it. There will be more guys like the one on the highway fantasizing about the reward."

Mr. Jones said, "If that's true, they'll arrest you when you get to Potterville. So, what's the point in going there, let alone die trying?"

"We won't die."

"Maybe he has a point," Rebekah said. "I'm getting a bad feeling about this."

"I didn't invite you in the first place," Miriam said.

The muscles in Rebekah's jaw rippled.

"Miriam, you're just being stubborn. Listen to reason," Mr. Jones said.

"I've listened. I can't help that you're wrong and I'm right."

"You don't always have to win, Miriam," Mr. Jones said.

"You're not listening to me. It's not about winning. It's about getting to Derrick. He does not have time for us to go around or risk being caught."

"I think Mr. Jones is right this time," Rebekah said.

"Fine. Go with him. I didn't invite you."

"Fine."

"Fine."

"Stop it, both of you!" Mr. Jones looked around to see if he had drawn anyone's attention.

"Miriam, are you sure this is the only way?" Mr. Jones asked.

"Yes. Do you think I want to walk across those mountains? I'm not stupid. I know it's a huge risk, but it's the only way we'll find Derrick."

"What about getting arrested when we get there?" Rebekah asked.

"There was a lawman there when they tried to take Derrick. He stood up for Derrick. Ran the Pacific Edge guys off. Potterville might be the only place we *won't* get arrested."

"Find boots. I'll get flashlights. Meet me at the front of the store." Mr. Jones took their coats and a basket they had filled.

"We don't have money for boots," Rebekah said.

"I'm buying everything. Get good boots. They will last you a long time."

"But…"

Mr. Jones held up his hand. "No more arguing. We need to go. You'll be up there in the dark as it is."

The drive to Johnsondale was silent. Miriam studied the river, which was often visible from the road. It was beautiful, wild, and free. Mountains rose on both sides of the canyon. Often, she couldn't see the tops of them, only the steep slopes and rocky outcroppings. Sometimes, the rocks jutted up as if lifted by a giant hand, exposing colorful layers of unique rock formations eons in the making, not a few thousand years, as Mr. Jones had argued in class the day Derrick clobbered Marcus Carver. Miriam recalled the argument. *Was Mr. Jones saying the Earth was only a few thousand years old, or did he ask questions in a way that drew her into the argument? Was it still part of a plot? That seemed unlikely. Too many variables to predict the outcome. Still…*

She wanted to ask him about that day but decided it could wait. She would ask him tomorrow if they were still alive. Halfway to Johnsondale, she saw snow on the tops of the western mountains, the ones they had to cross. She had never seen snow in real life. Part of her was excited to see it up close, part of her scared as hell. It was no accident that she picked a fight with Rebekah back at the store. She didn't want Rebekah to go with her across the mountain, but she needed Rebekah to go. Rebekah had invited herself on this quest for reasons Miriam still couldn't understand. Okay, so she had a crush on Derrick but also knew that Derrick had rejected her. So, why? Hoping that without Jana Somersworth as competition, Derrick would pick her? Rebekah does not know about the girl with the pink-striped hair.

Miriam didn't want Rebekah to cross the mountain because it was too dangerous. Mr. Jones was right. As they drew closer to Johnsondale, fear rose in Miriam, causing her stomach to churn like an angry sea. Yesterday, Miriam almost died in the ocean. Now, she might die on a mountain. She didn't want Rebekah to die with her.

Yet Miriam wanted Rebekah with her. She wasn't sure why. Maybe it just seemed safer with two. Maybe she didn't want to die alone. Miriam wasn't sure. Rebekah had a strength Miriam didn't understand. Hell, Miriam didn't even understand why Rebekah was here. The more that Miriam thought about that, the less sense it made. Rebekah Ford must be crazy.

Miriam needed crazy. She looked at Rebekah and smiled.

A small town appeared as they rounded the corner. Not much, really. A few weird-looking dwellings and a shabby vacation spot with a pool, which was closed. The town, if you wanted to call it that, was mostly deserted. The few people outside stared as if the newcomers didn't belong there.

"I hope I can get you past town a few miles before I have to turn around," Mr. Jones said.

Without thinking, Miriam asked, "Mr. Jones, did you notice the rocks with all the layers?"

"I did. They are beautiful, aren't they?"

"They are. How old do you suppose they are?"

"Hundreds of thousands of years," Mr. Jones said.

"Thanks," Miriam said. *Well, that explains a few things,* Miriam thought.

Just outside Johnsondale, a closed gate prevented further travel on the road.

Miriam grabbed her stuff and opened the door. "See you on the other side. We should be there around midnight."

"Midnight?" Rebekah asked.

"Fifteen miles, three miles per hour, five hours, add in some rest stops," Miriam said, adding, "You don't have to come."

"Right," Rebekah said as she grabbed her bag from the floor.

Mr. Jones pulled a black canister from the front seat. "This is called bear spray. I don't think there are bears up there this time of year, but there could be other animals. Just pull this pin and pull the trigger. The spray burns like hell, making it hard to breathe, so don't get it on you. Should work on any animal, including a human."

Miriam took the canister and put it in her bag.

"Put in on your belt," Mr. Jones said. "In case you have to get to it quickly."

Miriam fished it out of the bag and threaded her belt through the loops on the canvas case that held the canister. "Like that?"

"Yep."

Miriam noticed Mr. Jones's chin quiver.

"I'll meet you on the other side around midnight. I'll be parked at the gate like this one, wherever that is. If we are lucky, it will be near the top, and you won't have to walk the full distance. Be careful. And good luck."

Rebekah hugged Mr. Jones. Miriam hesitated and then hugged him as well.

Then Miriam and Rebekah ducked under the barrier. They walked up the road. Neither of them looked back.

Miriam wondered if she would ever see Mr. Jones again. What if he was not waiting on the other side? He might get arrested on the way there. He might abandon them and go home, where he could carry on with his life. She and Rebekah might not make it to the other side. If they made it, and Mr. Jones was waiting for them, they still might not find Derrick.

Derrick might not be alive to be found.

And what if he was alive? What future did they have?

Perhaps no future worth living.

15

HALF-A MILE PAST JOHNSONDALE, a bridge crossed the Kerns River. Underneath, the snow-fed waters tumbled over polished stones. To say that Miriam didn't fit into the entire Chosen culture in Pacific Edge was an understatement of grand proportion. She loved the sea, except yesterday when she clung to that buoy, nearing fatal hypothermia. And she loved this river. Odd as it seemed, she felt this river somehow connected her to Derrick.

"It's nothing like they showed us on the media," Rebekah said, pausing on the bridge, watching the water cascade over the rocks below.

"No, it is not," Miriam said.

"It's beautiful. If we don't make it, I can think of no better place to die," Rebekah said.

"Don't talk like that. We'll make it. We have to."

"Because of Derrick?"

"Yes." Miriam thought for a few moments. "And more than Derrick."

"What does that mean?" Rebekah asked.

Miriam said, "I don't know."

"We should go. It will be dark soon." Rebekah turned and walked away from the river into the mountains.

The road turned and changed from a solid black surface to dirt, and it started climbing the mountain. Going uphill proved more difficult than Miriam had expected. She recalculated time and distance. It would be closer to three o'clock when they reached the other side. The road followed the river up a canyon for three miles, then turned left, and the river turned right. At the turn, a large bank of dirt and stone lined one side of the road, and it was covered with brush and young trees. Miriam was no expert regarding nature, but she recognized that a man or machine made this.

Miriam stopped. "What do you make of this?"

"Make of what?"

"This mound of dirt?"

"Uh, it's a mound of dirt. Some rocks too. How would I know why there's a mound of dirt? We can't stop to discuss mounds of dirt."

Miriam said, "It doesn't look right."

"Okay. I agree. Wrong-looking mound of dirt. Now, can we go? I wonder how far we've come. My feet hurt," Rebekah said.

"Three miles."

"How would you know that?"

"Counted the steps."

"Seriously?"

Miriam looked over her shoulder at Rebekah. "How else will we know how far we've gone?"

"You can do that? In your head and not lose track?"

Miriam didn't answer. Instead, she walked toward the dirt mound. It was too steep to climb. Someone intended to keep people out. Miriam wanted to know why.

"What in the hell are you doing?" Rebekah shouted.

"Finding out what is behind this mound of dirt." Miriam started around the side of the mound.

"Get back here. That's dangerous," Rebekah shouted.

"Right. So, you stay, and I'll tell you what I find."

"Miriam King, you get back here!"

Miriam disappeared into the brush.

A few steps into the thicket, Miriam was reconsidering her options. The mound was steep and the brush thick. Some brush had long thorns, and some had purple berries that smelled wonderful. She wondered if the berries were edible. Something told her they were, and something told her bears ate berries. But she couldn't turn around. Physically, she could turn around, but some force drew her forward. She wanted to think she didn't understand what compelled her, but that would be a lie. It was intuition.

She hated intuition.

Miriam learned to pull herself through the brush and weave between the trees. One thing for sure, she would give Mr. Jones a big hug for the boots and gloves. The flimsy shoes she was wearing would have been in tatters, and her hands torn and bleeding. She sensed the mound of dirt turning inward, and suddenly, she burst into the open. Now she could see why the mound of dirt was there. It hid a wide road made of the same black substance as the major roads. But a deep pit separated the mound of dirt on which she stood and the road. In addition, there was a heavy steel barrier erected across the road. Beside the road stood a large, weathered sign with only a few letters visible. The large letters read:

U F AD N LEA   SE
　ORIZ PER L Y
　　S   ES PA NT F D F E

Miriam worked her way back to the other side. She considered trying the uphill side but ended up going back the same way she had come. Getting back was easier because she had made a small trail.

"Miriam, never pull that crap again. You scared me," Rebekah said, pulling leaves and twigs from Miriam's hair.

"There's a road on the other side. A big sign, too old to read. A big pit too and a heavy steel barrier across the road."

"Okay, great. Now, can we please go?"

Rebekah started up the road.

Miriam didn't move.

Rebekah turned around. "What?"

"I have to follow that road."

"That's crazy? You don't know where it goes?"

"It follows the river."

"There was no road that followed the river north of here on the map."

"Exactly," Miriam said.

"Exactly what?"

Miriam said, "It's a secret road."

"Great. It's a secret road. If we survive tonight, if we aren't arrested when we get on the other side of the mountain, and after we find Derrick, we'll come back here one day, and I'll explore that road with you."

Miriam said nothing.

"Say something."

Miriam said, "I'm thinking."

"Great."

Finally, Miriam said, "You go ahead. Just stay on the road, and you'll be okay. You take the bear spray stuff, extra food bar things, and extra water." Miriam held out a handful of food bars.

"Put that stuff away. We are not separating."

"But you can't go with me," Miriam said.

Rebekah rolled her eyes. "Go where? You don't know where that road goes, but I can tell you where it doesn't go. It does not go to the other side where Mr. Jones is waiting for us."

Miriam said, "I understand that. But I must follow that road."

"Why? Why do you have to follow that road?"

"Because it will lead me to Derrick."

Rebekah said, "That is crazy. Did you hit your head on the way over there? How could you possibly know that? There's no reason to believe that it would."

"I agree. That's why you shouldn't go with me."

"Miriam, please. Let's just stay on this road," Rebekah whimpered.

"I can't. I must take the other road. You don't. Too dangerous. If I don't find Derrick, I'll find Potterville. Tell Mr. Jones thanks for everything, especially the boots."

Miriam turned and disappeared into the brush.

16

THE THIRD TRIP THROUGH THE brush proved even easier. Miriam emerged on the other side and studied the pit that separated her from the road. The uphill side looked too steep, and the pit they dug steeper still. She was sure she'd slide to the bottom and then be unable to climb out. Something began thrashing around behind her. Fumbling with the bear spray, she almost lost her footing. She unholstered the spray, pulled the safety pin, and held it at arm's length.

An animal burst from the brush.

Miriam screamed.

Rebekah Ford stood inches from the bear spray.

Miriam lowered the canister. "Damn it, Rebekah, you scared me. What are you doing?"

Rebekah adjusted her bag. "What's it look like I'm doing? Going with you. For a smart girl, you sure are dense sometimes."

"That makes no sense. You need to meet Mr. Jones. That way, at least someone will know where to search for Derrick and me."

"True. But maybe not knowing where to look is better. What if they arrest Mr. Jones? They might force him to talk, or they might follow him to our meeting spot. Besides, you're not sure about Mr. Jones, are you?"

Miriam thought for a moment. "Points well taken. It's still too dangerous for you to come with me. As for Mr. Jones, I'm feeling better about him." She paused. "Have you noticed something I've missed?"

"No. I'm feeling pretty confident about Mr. Jones as well. As for dangerous, everything we've done so far has been dangerous. Maybe I like danger. It's kind of fun, isn't it?"

Miriam gave Rebekah a crooked smile. "Well, Ms. Dangerous, how do we get to the other side?"

Rebekah studied the pit in the fading light. "I see what you mean. This is really something. Someone didn't want people on that road."

"Agreed. I don't think we can go that way?" Miriam pointed to the uphill side.

"Agreed. Or that way." Rebekah pointed into the pit.

"That only leaves going down the mountain and climbing back up," Miriam said.

"Yep. At least it's a natural slope. Not like this monster." Rebekah pointed. "What does that sign say?"

"I don't know, but I intend to find out." Miriam eased by Rebekah. "I'll go first. Be careful."

Miriam situated her bag over her shoulder and started down the mountain. She skidded and grabbed limbs and slid. Dirt and small rocks Rebekah dislodged skittered beside her. After they reached the bottom, near the river, they worked their way beyond the pit. So far, so good. Now, the challenging work began. This time, Rebekah went first. The bigger of the two, Rebekah reasoned she could reach back and help Miriam. Miriam couldn't argue with Rebekah's logic. Miriam liked logic. Twice, Rebekah lost her footing but stopped her descent by grabbing a limb. Miriam avoided the loose rocks that caused Rebekah problems.

Near the top, the incline increased to near vertical. Using both hands, Rebekah tossed her bag to the road and used small trees to pull herself to the next large rock. At the first landing, she motioned Miriam to hand up her bag, which Rebekah also tossed to the road, and then she reached back to help Miriam onto the rock. Two more landings, and they were standing on the forbidden road.

No one had traveled the road in many years. Weeds pushed through cracks, where sections of the black surface had been thrust upward from unknown forces, and other sections had sunk.

Daylight turned to dusk. They walked to the sign. Up close, some letters were partially visible. Rebekah used her coat sleeve to rub a letter, and it became legible. Miriam joined Rebekah, and they scrubbed at the weathered paint. Finally, enough letters were visible to read the sign.

USAF NORAD NUCLEAR DEFENSE
AUTHORIZED PERSONNEL ONLY
UNITED STATES DEPARTMENT OF DEFENSE

Miriam looked at the sign. Then she looked at Rebekah.

Rebekah said, "What does that mean?"

"It's an old United States of America nuclear defense site."

"Duh, I can read that. What does nuclear mean?"

"Hard to explain. I know a little. Read about it in AJ Patel's files regarding 1984."

"1984?"

"The tracking device in your back."

Rebekah nodded.

Then Miriam saw something else. Small numbers in the bottom right-hand corner of the sign. She kneeled and rubbed with the heel of her gloved hand.

"What?" Rebekah asked.

Miriam said nothing. She rubbed harder. She dug into her bag and found a water bottle, pouring it on the small numbers and rubbing them with her fingers.

"Hey, don't waste that," Rebekah said, raising her voice.

When the letters were visible, Miriam stood. "Oh, my."

35°58'14.7"N 118°32'18.2"W

"What is it?" Rebekah asked.

"GPS coordinates," Miriam said.

"Say what?"

"Global Positioning System," Miriam said.

"It's a way of telling where we are, I take it. So, what? We know where we are. I mean, we are here. I mean, we saw Johnsondale on the map, so we know where we are, basically," Rebekah said.

Miriam said, "It's not that."

"You mean it's not a location? I'm confused," Rebekah said.

Miriam said, "It is a location."

"You're killing me here. What's the big deal?"

"Remember when we saw Derrick's last signal?"

Rebekah sighed, "Of course, I remember. I can't get it out of my head."

"I checked the GPS coordinates."

"I saw you do that. A little window flashed on the screen for a couple of seconds. Don't tell me you memorized that. I mean, how could you?"

Miriam said, "I can, and I did. Derrick's last location is a few miles from here."

"Amazing. On several levels, amazing. To be honest, your insisting we follow this road is a little scary now. You are scary."

"Thanks." Miriam turned away from the sign. The color had drained from her face.

"But we don't have a GPS thingy, so how will we find him?"

"I can kind of track our time, distance, and direction in my head, and I'll know when we are getting close."

"Now you really *are* scaring me."

"I'll know when we find the right location," Miriam said.

"How will we know?"

Miriam said, "I'll just know, and to be honest, that part scares me."

They picked up their bags and walked. The road turned away from the river, up a steep incline. The sun dipped below the mountains. They walked in silence for a mile. Then, they began to descend on a snake-like road chiseled into the rock walls. The turns were tight, yet extra wide. Miriam wondered what kind of machines created such a road. As the canyon came into view, they saw a waterfall cascading over the edge of the canyon wall, mist drifting in the air and disappearing into darkness. They had followed the Kerns River to Johnsondale, but Miriam was unsure if this was the same river. When the road reached the bottom of the canyon, they could hear the water tumbling over the rocks below. The scent of pine and damp wood filled Miriam's nostrils. Onward they walked, the darkness closing in around them. Every 100 yards or so, signs appeared. They didn't bother cleaning the letters.

The message clear: **Stop. Go no farther.**

In the fading light, Miriam noticed a small, gray concrete building covered with vines next to the road. She assumed it was a fortified structure that once housed sentries. But those guards were long gone. The need for them faded like the words on the signs. Possibly deeper in the forest were structures more lethal. She wondered how something like this could become worthless to the point of abandonment. A question she intended to answer, if she survived to do so. She started to say something to Rebekah about the guard shack but decided against it.

They walked. The air grew still and colder, the scent of fresh pine and berries intoxicating. For another 30 minutes, Miriam said nothing. Not because she had nothing to say, but because she wanted to listen to their footfalls, the rushing river, and soak in the scent of the mountains.

After another mile, Miriam said, "I'm glad you came."

"Me too," Rebekah said, then added, "No matter what happens, I'm glad I saw this for myself. I thought what New America Media showed us was a lie. Now, I know I was right."

"You noticed they cycled the same videos?" Miriam asked.

"You saw it too?" Rebekah asked.

"Yes."

"You probably saw it before I did," Rebekah said.

"Probably."

Rebekah pushed Miriam on the shoulder.

Miriam exaggerated a wobble and giggled.

"Rebekah, can I ask you a serious question?"

"Sure. I might not give you an answer, though. Depends on the question," Rebekah said.

"Why are you here?"

"We've been through that."

Miriam said, "Not why did you follow me to this road? Why did you watch me? Why did you leave Pacific Edge?"

"Why do you think?" Rebekah asked.

"Well, I guess, I mean, I assume…"

"You think it's because I love Derrick, and without Jana Somersworth, he'll throw his arms around me, and we'll live happily ever after in a beautiful little commoner cottage in a beautiful little commoner town and have wonderful little commoner children? Is that what you think?"

"That's over-dramatized but sort of."

"You could be right to a point. I liked Derrick. I didn't like being a prize in a contest. When I was placed on Derrick's list, at first, I was happy. But then I realized I was not a real person, not in Pacific Edge. Then things clicked. I recognized they recycled images to scare us and used propaganda to convince us we were special." Rebekah held both palms up toward the sky. "So fortunate to be Chosen. So blessed to live in Pacific Edge. That's when I saw Pacific Edge for what it really is."

"And what do you think it is?" Miriam asked.

"A prison."

17

AS THE LIGHT FADED, SO DID THE COLORS. The road remained easy to see, but the bushes, rocks, and trees blended in a mosaic of black and gray, making it impossible to distinguish what was there. The western sky above the mountains turned dark purple. Stars appeared. Just a few at first, then thousands, like a giant had thrown diamonds across the sky. Sounds Miriam had not noticed before suggested things moving in the forest. Miriam pulled out the bear spray. She refused to admit that fear had clawed its way into her brain, grabbed her by the throat, and refused to let go.

"This is getting spooky," Rebekah said.

"I hadn't thought about it much," Miriam lied.

"Right. Is that why you have that bear spray in your hand?"

"Best to be ready. Probably no bears here, though," Miriam said.

Rebekah chuckled. "How would you know?"

"Mr. Jones said, probably no bears."

"Mr. Jones bought us bear spray."

"Good point. Everything looks different now," Miriam said.

"Sounds different, too. Do animals tend to come out at night?" Rebekah asked.

"I don't know. I don't know everything."

Rebekah said, "Sorry. I didn't mean anything by it. Just a question."

Miriam said nothing for a while. Truth was that she was more scared than she wanted to admit, which surprised her. She had never feared the night in Pacific Edge. She thought of darkness as a friend, not an enemy. But that was there. This was different. Rebekah had a point about Pacific Edge being like a prison, but it was a safe and comfortable prison. There must be a reason for that.

Rebekah shone her flashlight on the road and then clicked it off. "Better not use these until we have to. I don't know how long the batteries last."

"We should have purchased more batteries," Miriam said.

"Good point," Rebekah said.

Miriam said, "Won't need them much though."

"Because?"

"Full moon tonight," Miriam said.

Rebekah said, "How do you know that? Never mind. Honestly, you're kind of scary smart. I mean that in a good way."

"It's nothing I've done," Miriam said.

"Well, it's a blessing."

"It's a curse."

Rebekah said nothing.

They walked on.

"How did you do it?" Rebekah asked.

"Do what? Get smart?" Miriam asked. "I told you, it's just how I am."

"Well, how did you get into Technical Service?"

"Long story," Miriam said.

Rebekah said, "We have a long walk. Give me the highlights."

"AJ Patel."

"What did he have to do with it?" Rebekah asked, stopping for a moment.

"Everything."

"Everything?" Rebekah asked.

"Back in December, he gave me my first keyboard and mouse and showed me how to access a limited computer system using my home communications monitor. Then, after they exiled Derrick, I used his personal identification number to enter the Technical Services. He had left his office unlocked, and when I logged onto his computer, he'd set up an employee profile for me and left further instructions. He helped me do everything. Or at least, he got me started."

Rebekah said nothing for several minutes. "And he was waiting for you outside the building. Why? Maybe he was trying to help."

"I think it was all a trap or a test. Or both. Probably both," Miriam said.

"But he could have been there to help?"

Miriam sighed. "It's possible."

"But you stunned him."

Miriam nodded. "Right. If he planned to help, he has probably changed his mind."

"You learned to use this computer system you mentioned?"

"Some of it. It's complicated. I learned what I needed to," Miriam said.

They walked without talking for a few minutes. Miriam thought she saw movement by the side of the road ahead. Rebekah must have also seen it because she turned on her flashlight.

Two eyes reflected in the light and then dove into the brush.

"What was that?" Rebekah asked.

"I don't know."

"A bear?"

"Not a bear. Maybe a cat."

"Cat? That's a big cat."

"Mountain lion," Miriam said.

They stood searching the forest for eyes.

"You think it will attack us?" Rebekah asked.

Miriam said, "I don't know. Probably not. I think it was more frightened than we were."

"I hope you are right." Rebekah kept her flashlight on, searching the road ahead and then searching the road behind. Miriam appreciated the light, but Rebekah was also frightening her. Miriam, as was her nature, ran calculations in her head, estimated the dangers, analyzed scenarios, and explored their best response. She decided the animals didn't pose much risk. But that didn't reduce her fear.

That she could not reason her way out of fear terrified her.

The moon rose above the mountains. When it was high in the sky, it lit the road, and Rebekah turned off her light.

They walked and listened to the sounds—a chorus of animals large, small, and unknown—pressing in from the forest. Miriam noticed a dark gash across the road, like a shadow. But not a shadow.

Miriam grabbed Rebekah's arm just before she stepped into the gash. "Turn on your light."

Rebekah turned on her flashlight. "Crap. What the hell?"

"Trap."

"For what?"

"Big transports."

The road had opened from one side to the other, ten yards across, ten feet deep, with huge metal spikes at the bottom.

Miriam got her flashlight too. "See the metal plates? They can move and cover the pit, so they could drive over this if they came back."

"You think they opened the trap when they left?" Rebekah asked.

"Probably," Miriam said.

"Must have," Rebekah said.

"Unless…" Miriam said.

"Unless what?" Rebekah asked.

"Unless we triggered it."

18

WALKING AROUND THE PIT WASN'T difficult. It was built to stop large transports, not teenage girls. They walked to the uphill side and eased through the trees and rocks to the other side, then back to the road.

"We should probably use a flashlight now," Rebekah said.

Miriam found hers. "I'll use mine. You can hold the bear spray."

Miriam swept the light from side to side as they walked, scanning the sides of the road more than the road itself. She thought about the trap in the road and decided it wouldn't be the lone defense. There would be more. The question circulating in her head: was the trap left open or did something trigger it? She decided they must have left the pit open. They had not heard it open, and from the thickness of the steel plates, it wouldn't open quietly. Besides, what would power it? They had abandoned this place a long time ago.

"How far do you think we are from where Derrick's tracker disappeared?" Rebekah asked.

"Another hour if nothing slows us down."

"What could slow us down? The road is easy walking."

"Too easy," Miriam said.

"Whatever," Rebekah said.

The road made a sharp turn. A massive mound of rocks stood in their path. The flashlight's beam didn't reach the top of the pile. Miriam searched the area with the light. The river flowed below in a narrow canyon. A steel rail on the river prevented transports from plunging into the chasm. The uphill side was a vertical wall of stone.

"What happened here?" Rebekah asked.

"They blocked the road," Miriam said.

"Wow. How did they get all this rock in here?"

"They used something big," Miriam said.

"Now what? We can't go around it." Rebekah walked to the side, shining her flashlight into the canyon. "It's a straight drop to the river."

"We go over it," Miriam said.

"You're not serious."

"You have another idea?"

Rebekah shook her head.

Miriam walked up to the smallest rock. "Come, give me a boost."

Rebekah did as Miriam requested. After two attempts at lifting her, Rebekah put both hands together, providing Miriam a step.

From the top of the stone, Miriam said, "Toss up your bag."

Rebekah tossed her bag, and Miriam caught a strap. "What are you doing up there?" Rebekah called.

"Just a minute." Miriam appeared at the stone's edge on her stomach. She lowered Rebekah's empty bag over the edge. "Grab this and I'll help you up."

Rebekah grabbed the bag with one hand, and then wedged herself between two stones, and using her other hand, her feet, and her back, she inched upward, cursing as her back scraped the stone. Finally, she pulled herself alongside Miriam. Both rested on their backs, breathing deeply.

"This will slow us down," Miriam said.

"Agreed. They seriously didn't want people in here."

"They didn't." Miriam agreed.

"Wonder why, though? I mean, it's not like this place can still be important. For sure, nothing works after all these years. Right?"

Miriam stood, gathered her things, put them back in the bag, and tossed the bag up the mound of stones. "Let's go."

Stone by stone, they worked their way to the top. Most stones were smaller than the first layer, which meant the girls could climb from one to the next with little help from one another. Slow, challenging work. When they reached the top, both shed their coats, their shirts damp from sweat. Miriam shone her light down the other side. Going down would be a little easier but perhaps more dangerous.

"I wonder how long that took?" Rebekah asked as they walked along the road again.

"Forty-seven minutes," Miriam said.

"I'll take your word for it," Rebekah said.

The river descended deeper into the canyon, and the road descended toward it. Darkness expanded on either side of them, the road making 90-degree turns as it worked its way to the river. Once they were alongside the river, the road again made gentle turns, following the stream's natural path. Miriam liked the sound of the tumbling water. It lulled her with a feeling of safety. Her mind drifted.

Suddenly, Rebekah grabbed her arm. "What's that?"

Miriam saw something but wasn't sure what. Not alive, that was for sure. Something on the side of the road. A disheveled brown lump. They inched closer, both flashlights blazing. Miriam cast her light off the side of the road.

"More of them." Miriam pointed into the forest.

Rebekah eased toward the river. "Over here too."

Both girls swung their lights into the forest and down the pavement. They saw debris scattered across the entire road.

"Smell that?" Miriam asked.

"Yes. Smells terrible. What are those?"

"Dead animals," Miriam said.

"But not recent?"

Miriam said, "No, they've been dead a while. There's so many of them."

"What killed them?" Rebekah asked.

"I think we are about to find out."

They eased farther through the bones.

"Stop," Miriam said. "See that?"

"I see something. I can't make it out."

"There's another one on the other side." Miriam pointed her light to the right.

"White buildings of some sort. Tall, covered with vines and brush," Rebekah said.

"I don't know what it is, but it's not natural. I think it killed these animals. See how between the two white things is where most of the bones are scattered?"

"Yeah. I see that. Hard to miss."

"What are we going to do?" Rebekah asked.

Miriam took a step forward, reached down, grabbed a large leg bone, the flesh had rotted from long ago, and tossed it down the road.

"Yuck," Rebekah said.

The bone hit the road, tumbling end over end, scattering smaller bones.

Instantly, the girls were bathed in brilliant white light. A rattling sound came from the white towers.

"What the...," Rebekah stammered.

"Weapons," Miriam said.

"Shouldn't we be running away?"

"Out of ammunitions. Used them all killing animals."

"That's crazy!"

Miriam said, "It is, but thank these dead animals. They are the reason the weapons are empty. Otherwise, we'd have joined these scattered bones."

"Now what?" Rebekah asked.

"We keep going."

"Are you crazy? I'm not going through there." Rebekah pointed down the road. "What if those machines find a few rounds to fire?"

"We'll die. I'll go first. If I get blown apart, turn around. If you find Derrick, tell him I tried."

Rebekah said, "You're an asshole sometimes, Miriam King. You know that?"

"Thank you." Miriam turned and walked into the bones.

"Not without me, you don't," Rebekah said as she came alongside.

"You're a crazy bitch. You know that, Rebekah Ford?"

Rebekah nudged Miriam with her shoulder. "No wonder I like you."

The machines rattled and hummed and clicked.

Miriam and Rebekah walked between the twin towers, hand in hand.

19

THEY WALKED ONWARD SHINING both flashlights from side to side, looking for white towers and black, open traps. They saw many eyes, but they all disappeared into the forest. Miriam was correct. The locals were afraid of girls. Then they saw them. Up ahead in the road. A large animal. It looked at them and froze.

"What is it?" Rebekah asked.

"I think it's called a deer or an elk. Maybe a moose, but I don't think it's big enough for a moose," Miriam said.

"How would you know?" Rebekah asked.

Miriam said, "A video of Carver's Yellowstone Park. Our family went there. We didn't see a real moose on the tour."

"How old were you?" Rebekah asked.

"Eight."

"And you remember that?" Rebekah asked.

"Yes."

Rebekah swept her light to the sides of the road. "Are they dangerous?"

Two more of the animals stepped out of the darkness.

Miriam said, "Not unless we get too close. They eat plants. This would be a suitable time to rest. They'll move on soon enough."

They found a rock at the side of the road they could climb onto, which put them out of harm's way from their uninvited four-legged guests. Miriam dug out two of the bars and water for each, handing a water and bar to Rebekah and then turning off her light. Rebekah turned off her light, too.

For a moment, Miriam couldn't see anything. In the darkness, she took a bite of the bar. "This is pretty good," Miriam said.

Rebekah made an agreeable humming sound.

Miriam's eyes adjusted to the darkness. The moon cast long, dark shadows. Fear of the night had lost its edge, and she would be okay walking in the moonlight, but they still needed light to see the traps. But there were no monsters out here. Just animals. Animals that wanted nothing to do with them. No wonder, given the carnage she witnessed earlier at the twin white towers. The towers and the pit conjured images of what New America Media portrayed as the commoner world. People had gone to great expense and effort to protect what they had hidden in these mountains. Yet, they abandoned it. Were the elaborate protections unwarranted?

"We must be close," Rebekah said.

"Not far."

"You'll know when we get close?"

"Within a few yards, yes. But I don't think it will matter. We'll know when we get there," Miriam said.

"I don't understand how you can assume that."

Miriam said, "I don't understand either."

"That's scary."

"Yes, it is."

They ate their bars and drank their water. The deer or elk or moose had wandered into the forest. Finally, Rebekah said, "Mr. Jones will be looking for us. I wish we could let him know we are all right."

"I agree," Miriam said.

"You're a talkative one."

Miriam said, "Sorry. Just thinking a lot."

"Care to share any of it?"

Miriam remained quiet for a few moments. "Derrick has changed. You need to be prepared for that. I need to be prepared as well."

"What do you mean? He can't have changed that much. It's been less than a month."

"You heard what Mr. Jones said about the track thing."

"Yeah, I have to admit that does not sound like the Derrick I know," Rebekah said.

Miriam said, "The amount of time is not the issue."

"Huh?"

"He's made friends. At least, I assume they are friends," Miriam said.

Rebekah took a drink. "Okay. That's good, right? How do you know this?"

Miriam said, "They let us have a video call with Derrick."

"When was that?"

"Wednesday."

"As in yesterday?" Rebekah asked.

"That was when Derrick refused the offer to return to Pacific Edge. So, he must like it there. But that can't be all of it," Miriam said.

"That's a good thing," Rebekah said.

"One of his friends is Akira Nakamura."

"As in our Akira? Pacific Edge, Akira?"

"Yes," Miriam said.

"What is she doing there? And why didn't you tell me this before?" Rebekah stopped.

"Living there, I suppose." Miriam shrugged. "I haven't told you a lot of things. Too much to tell, plus so many things I'm not ready to discuss."

"When will you be ready?" Rebekah asked.

"Depends on which things. Some, I need to understand before I talk to anyone. Other things I need to tell Derrick first. Regarding Akira, it didn't seem important," Miriam said.

"That's a weird coincidence, don't you think?" Rebekah asked.

"Which part?" Miriam asked.

"Akira being there," Rebekah clarified.

"True, but I think it is a coincidence. Nothing more. There's another too."

"What do you mean, there's another?" Rebekah asked.

"Another girl. A girl with pink-striped hair," Miriam said.

"I don't understand."

"Neither do I, but she is important somehow. I keep running the conversation through my head. Studying each of them." Miriam decided not to tell Rebekah about the phone call she made to Nyx Belos. There would be time for that someday when she understood more.

Rebekah said, "You can do that? Watch it over in your head. Doesn't it change, fade over time?"

"It does not."

"You freak me out," Rebekah said.

"There's a lot going on that I don't understand. I found information about Derrick when I was working in Patel's office. The more I read, the less I understood."

Rebekah put her empty water bottle and the wrapper from her bar into her bag. "First things first. First, we find Derrick. Then we'll start figuring things out."

"One bite at a time," Miriam said, then stood, stepped off the rock, and walked on.

20

MIRIAM WALKED ON THE RIVER SIDE of the road, stopping every 20 yards, shining her light into the stream. Then she walked to the other side and shone her light into the forest. Then she turned the light off and stared into the sky. After a few minutes, she'd continue, repeating the ritual every 50 yards. The air felt crisp.

After 30 minutes of the stop and go, Rebekah said, "I give up. What are you doing?"

"My ability to estimate our GPS coordinates may not be as accurate as I had hoped."

Rebekah said, "But you said we would know the place when we got there."

"I did say that."

"You think you were wrong about that too?"

"I'm likely right about that."

"I'm glad," Rebekah said.

"It does not make me happy," Miriam said.

"Are you doing that on purpose?"

"Doing what on purpose?" Miriam asked.

"Saying strange things."

"They are not strange to me."

"Give us mortals a break and explain," Rebekah said, stepping in front, grabbing Miriam's shoulders.

Miriam said, "Now is not the time."

"It's as good as any. Just the high points will be fine."

Miriam took a deep breath. "I'm looking at the stream and its orientation to the stars. I know the stream runs in a northern direction, but it's not always true north. So, I'm trying to get a more accurate location."

Rebekah stared at her. "By looking at the stars?"

"Yes, they used to navigate the seas by using the stars before modern technology."

"Where did you learn to do it?"

"I saw a star chart once."

Rebekah sighed. "You saw a star chart once?"

"Yes."

"And how did you learn to do the navigation part?"

"I figured it out when we started walking."

"You didn't."

"I did."

"That's some scary crap right there," Rebekah said.

"Promise you won't tell anyone."

"No one would believe me if I did. Besides, you have not proven that you know what you're talking about. Maybe you're a little crazy."

Miriam nodded. "If I understood it, I'd tell you. My mind has changed since we left Pacific Edge. It's scaring me. Here's what I think. We'll find the spot in 115 yards. Based on your height, that's 135 steps. Count them off. Then we'll see if I'm crazy."

"You're on. If you're wrong, you owe me breakfast. What about being sure we'll know the place when we see it?"

"That part bothers me the most. The stars are based on facts. Things that can be measured, tested, proven. That I will know it when I see it is a hunch. Intuition, perhaps. I don't like it. But it's there, and there's nothing I can do about it. Like Derrick can't change the fact that he is an athlete."

"You didn't seem surprised when Mr. Jones told you about Derrick being on the track team."

"It made sense."

"How does that make sense?" Rebekah asked.

"I don't want to talk about it," Miriam said.

"Miriam, you really piss me off sometimes."

"Sorry. I don't mean to. There's a lot I need to tell Derrick, but first, I have to have a better understanding."

Rebekah released Miriam and started walking. She did her best to count her steps without losing track, which was more difficult if she was talking. "Are you afraid Derrick won't want to see you? Or will he be angry with you?"

"A little," Miriam said.

"What happened wasn't your fault. And Derrick did the right thing. He will be thrilled to see you."

"Maybe. But that's not the only reason he might not want to see me."

"There you go again. What brother wouldn't want to see his sister?"

Miriam said nothing for a few minutes. "I'm not his sister. He may have figured that out by now."

Rebekah said nothing.

Miriam wiped tears from her cheeks. She knew the flashlight beam would soon reflect off the location where Derrick's transmitter went dark—the end of their quest.

"Miriam?"

"Yeah?"

Rebekah whispered, "What if, what if Derrick didn't make it?"

"Didn't make it here?" Miriam asked.

Rebekah stopped. "What if—what if—he's dead?"

Miriam turned to face Rebekah. "Then I failed him."

"You think he might be dead?" Rebekah whispered.

"It's possible. But I don't think so."

"What do you think happened to his tracker signal?" Rebekah asked.

Miriam said, "I think they came to get him and used a stun gun. Like you said, he probably refused to go."

"That makes sense. But why did we see a flicker of the signal here? And what was he doing out here? We must be a long way from Potterville."

Miriam said, "They were probably trying to reactivate the beacon. We happened to see it. Why he was out here, I don't know."

"Then they might have found him already," Rebekah said.

"That's true."

They walked for a few minutes, and then Miriam drifted to the guardrail along the river, and then back to the forest side, and then turned off her light, and searched the sky.

Rebekah stood silently for several minutes and then said, "I get the river and the sky. Why are you looking into the forest?"

"Looking for stuff."

"What kind of stuff?" Rebekah asked.

"Manmade stuff. The place Derrick disappeared."

"I haven't seen anything," Rebekah said.

"Me either. That can only mean one of two things. We are not on the military base yet, or it's not out here," Miriam said.

"What do you mean, it's not out here? You mean we are not there yet."

"No. I mean, it's in there." Miriam pointed to the mountain.

"What would make you think it's in the mountain?" Rebekah asked.

"I don't know," Miriam said, then continued. "We are almost there. Are you ready for this? I cannot predict Derrick's reaction to you. It makes little sense that you're here."

"I'm ready. One hundred steps so far. I've been rehearsing my speech. He may not like me when I'm done. But that's okay. I'm not here for him. I'm here for me."

Miriam turned and walked.

Rebekah followed, counting in her head: one hundred and one, one hundred and two.

Their lights reflected off a change in the road. The road disappeared into something large and irregular—another enormous pile of rock.

As they stepped to the base of the mound of stones, Miriam said, "We are here."

"One hundred and eighteen steps. " Rebekah said.

"The beacon didn't disappear right here." Miriam pointed up the mound of stones toward the canyon wall. "It disappeared up there."

"We still haven't found him. Just because we found a pile of rocks doesn't prove you're right," Rebekah said.

"To be honest, I hope I'm wrong," Miriam said.

"Climbing this will be difficult in the dark. But we have experience," Rebekah said, placing her hand on the black stone in front of her.

"You stay here, and I'll go," Miriam said, taking her bag off her shoulder. She fished around in the bag until she found the stun gun, which she stuck in her pocket.

Rebekah didn't ask about the stun gun.

Miriam hoisted herself up onto the first rock and then the second. She shone her flashlight, shut it off, put it in her pocket, and clawed her way up the next stone. Miriam heard a sound behind her. She turned on the flashlight and pointed it at the noise.

Rebekah shielded her eyes and said, "Turn that damn thing off. You trying to blind me?"

"I said you could wait."

Rebekah stood on the rock below Miriam. "Yeah, like that's going to happen. Maybe something supercharged your brain, but you're still pretty dense."

Miriam looked down at her and said, "I never understood why people wanted friends. They are such a pain."

"Well, get used to it."

"I'm starting to." Miriam offered her hand and helped Rebekah up.

In the darkness, they scaled the rocks by feel because it took both hands to climb. After much grunting and cursing, the two reached the top. The crest was easier to transverse than expected. Over the years, wind and rain had filled the crevasses between the stones with soil. Tufts of grass and even small trees had taken root. Eventually, in many decades, the mound would look like the rest of the mountain.

Miriam shivered as the cold mountain air pierced her jacket and cooled her sweat. With flashlights blazing, they made their way carefully toward the sheer rock wall of the canyon.

"This is the place," Miriam said.

"You're sure?" Rebekah turned slowly, searching the rocks with her flashlight beam, not wanting to admit Miriam's estimate of 135 steps was accurate.

"I'm sure," Miriam whispered.

"Look at this." Rebekah stepped to a rock next to the canyon wall.

Miriam stepped to her side. "How far down does it go?"

"I can't tell. Quite a ways, I think," Rebekah said, kneeling to peer into the opening.

"We need to go down there," Miriam said.

"You're kidding, right? I'm not going down there."

Miriam said, "Derrick's last signal from 1984 was right here. I must go down there."

"You can't be sure of that," Rebekah said. "Besides, there might be snakes."

Miriam searched the opening with her flashlight. "Looks easier to get down over there." Miriam held her light toward one side of the opening. "You stay here. I'll go look."

"Do you think there might be snakes?" Rebekah asked.

"Possible. I don't know much about snakes. You stay here," Miriam said, working her way toward the far end of the opening.

"Yeah, that's not going to happen. I hate snakes, by the way," Rebekah said, trailing Miriam.

"I'll go first," Miriam said.

"Right behind you," Rebekah said.

"I'm serious. It's okay. You don't have to come. Maybe it's best for you to stay here and keep watch."

Stepping down to the first landing, Rebekah said, "Watch for what?"

Miriam said, "Pacific Edge hovercraft, Derrick, wolves."

"Wolves?"

Miriam giggled. "Maybe. Or bears. Perhaps lions."

"Very funny."

Miriam stopped. Leaning down, she shone her flashlight into a dark hole.

"What?" Rebekah asked.

"Looks like a cave." Miriam eased down another landing, this one farther down than the previous stones. "It's not a cave. It's a tunnel."

"What's the difference?" Rebekah asked.

"A cave is natural."

"And a tunnel is unnatural?" Rebekah asked.

"A tunnel is manmade."

"Don't bats live in caves? I hate bats more than snakes. And I hate snakes a lot," Rebekah said.

"Not a cave," Miriam corrected.

"Do you have to correct everything I say?"

"Unfortunate, isn't it?" Miriam giggled.

"What would it take to make you get serious for once?" Rebekah asked.

"Bats," Miriam said.

"Do you think there are bats?" Rebekah asked.

"No."

"Because bats don't live in tunnels?" Rebekah was now one stone's height above the floor of the tunnel. Both girls pointed their lights into the tunnel, but they could not see the other end.

"No, because Derrick would have scared them away already."

"Derrick might not be here. He might not have ever been here," Rebekah said.

"He was here."

"You can't know that," Rebekah insisted.

Miriam moved into the tunnel.

Rebekah joined her. "What is this place?"

"Nuclear Defense Site or an entrance to it."

"You can't ..."

Miriam sighed, "The sign, remember?"

"Oh, right. But this could be something else, right?"

"It's not something else. This is the place. The road ends here," Miriam said.

"Good point. What about the dead places?" Rebekah asked.

"Dead places?"

"Where all the bones were on the road. The empty guns or whatever they called them."

"What about them?" Miriam asked.

"What if they put them in here too? Nothing to shoot. The gun would still have bullets."

"Another good point. Look at you. Using your head for something besides being pretty."

"Har, har."

Miriam said, "I don't think they would put guns down here."

"What makes you think that?" Rebekah asked.

Miriam said, "Doesn't make sense."

"Doesn't make sense?" Rebekah asked.

"Exactly."

"Damn, you drive me crazy sometimes."

"So, that's what caused it." Miriam muffled a laugh.

Rebekah paused. Ran her fingers through her hair in frustration, but Miriam continued into the tunnel. Rebekah took a deep breath, then trotted to catch up. "So, do you think I'm pretty?"

"Duh."

Rebekah smiled. Miriam didn't see that either.

After several minutes of walking, Miriam said, "Something ahead."

"I see it. Looks like a huge door and a little shack off to the side."

"The entrance into the nuclear site," Miriam said.

Rebekah said nothing. Derrick wasn't there. She wasn't surprised. Miriam thinks she knows everything, and that's not possible. But Rebekah didn't want to say the obvious. She did not even want to say, I told you so.

Miriam remained silent. When they reached the end, she went into the small room. Touched the old chair and the man-size door, made of metal. Then she went to the massive metal door in the tunnel. "Derrick was right here," she whispered.

"For the last time, you can't know that."

"But I do. He was here."

Rebekah folded her arms across her chest. Her breathing deep and ragged. Miriam was beyond infuriating, but then another thought came to her. *Perhaps this has become too much for Miriam. Maybe she's having a breakdown. Now, what am I going to do? Lost in the wilderness, my guide gone bonkers.*

Fear replaced her anger as Rebekah eased to the large metal door. She paused near the center, kneeled, and touched the door with her fingertips.

Then it happened. Then Rebekah said, "You're right. Derrick was right here."

The End

Discovery

A New Beginning

On March 12, The Tribunal exiled Derrick King.

Derrick gave up on ever going home or seeing Miriam King again.

Then, The Tribunal sent an envoy to welcome Derrick back to Pacific Edge.

Derrick refused to go.

Then, The Tribunal sent armed security officers to capture him.

Derrick escaped.

Miriam King tried to escape and nearly drowned.

The Tribunal locked her up.

Miriam escaped.

She is free.

Or did she complete part of a test?

Author's Note:

Thank you for reading my books. If they gave you a bit of an escape, I'm pleased. Please consider **writing a review.** To sign up for my newsletter, visit my website daniellcopeland.com.

Acknowledgements:

Thanks to the love and support of the love of my life and partner, Liz. She is also a writer and illustrator. Check out her books on Amazon Libby K. I couldn't do any of this without her. She is also my best editor and critic.

Special thanks to my first readers: Rod Leonard and Vicky Southwick for providing feedback, guidance, and editing.

More books from Daniel L. Copeland:

Available at Amazon.com in paperback, eBooks for Kindle, and audiobooks.

The Derrick King Series

About the Author:

Daniel is a lifelong Idahoan and grew up on a small farm in Southern Idaho. He worked in the criminal justice system for 35 years and is now retired. Daniel has published nine novels. In addition to writing, he and his wife, Liz love to travel on their BMW motorcycle. They have ridden in most of the US, including Alaska, the Great Lakes, and Florida. They have also ridden in Canada, New Zealand, and Australia. Daniel is an award-winning home brewer and a certified beer judge.

9 781970 773033